A Pigeon Lake Novel

Fine Too Soon

Kayla Dawhn

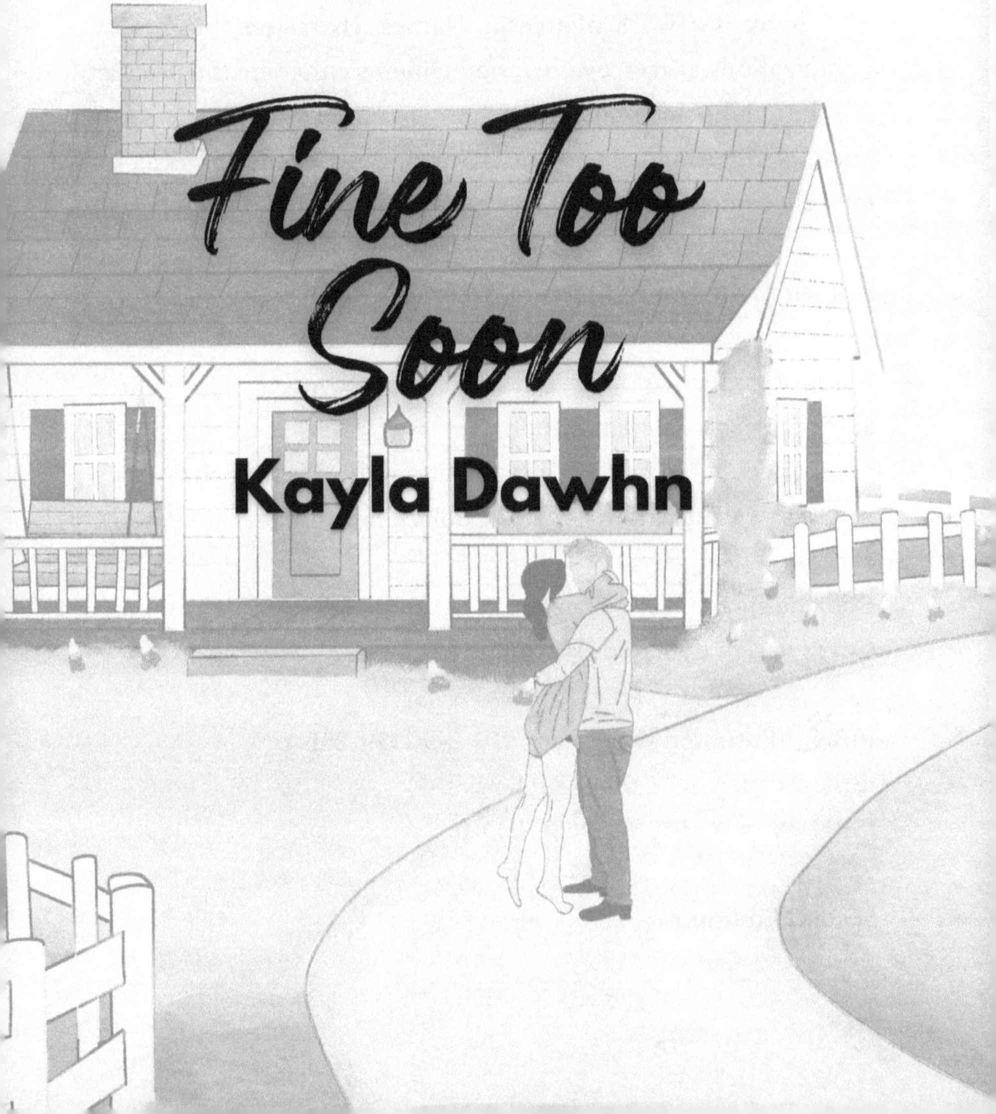

Printed in the United States of America.

For more information or to book an event, contact :
authorkayladawhn@gmail.com,
https://thebookishkayla.my.canva.site/authorkayladawhn
https://www.instagram.com/thebookishkayla

Book design by Kayla Dawhn
Cover design by Kayla Dawhn

ISBN - Illustrated Paperback: 979-8-90329-341-4
ISBN - Paperback: 979-8-89686-252-9
ISBN - Ebook : 979-8-89686-255-0

Second Edition

PLAYLIST
Fine Too Soon

▶	**OVER FOR YOU** Morgan Evans	3:05
⏸	**I HOPE YOU'RE HAPPY NOW** Carly Pearce, Lee Brice	3:18
▶	**SOS** ABBA	3:21
▶	**I HAD SOME HELP** Post Malone, Morgan Wallen	2:58
▶	**BREAK UP IN A SMALL TOWN** Sam Hunt	3:49
▶	**YOU PROOF** Morgan Wallen	2:37
▶	**LIKE I LOVED YOU** Brett Young	3:27
▶	**CHASIN' YOU** Morgan Wallen	3:25
▶	**MERCY** Brett Young	3:37
▶	**MAKE YOU MISS ME** Sam Hunt	3:45
▶	**INTENTIONS** Justin Bieber, Quavo	3:32
▶	**BE ALRIGHT** Dean Lewis	3:16
▶	**BEAUTIFUL THINGS** Benson Boone	3:00
▶	**THE GOOD ONES** Gabby Barrett	3:35
▶	**ALWAYS BEEN YOU** Jessie Murph	2:11

Content Warnings

This book contains mature themes and language that may not be suitable for all readers. It includes explicit language and sexual content. Reader discretion is advised.

All pages that include explicit sexual content will include the 🌶 **symbol in the bottom right corner,** giving all readers the ability to read this book without the mature content if they choose.

Dedication

To the man who held me on a pedestal, and I
hold on a higher one.

Chapter One

PROLOGUE
LUCAS, SEVEN YEARS AGO

The bright morning light ricochets around the room, casting a warm glow across the empty bed. Grumbling and groaning, I roll over to reach for my wife, hoping her warm body would be within reach. All I feel are the cold cotton sheets she left behind before I woke up this morning. She is usually the night owl, causing me to constantly wake up before she does. Not having her next to me is not the norm nor something I want to get used to. I have spent my entire adult life having her body snuggled up against mine, her long black hair splayed over my chest, and our legs tangled together. The initial feeling of her not being next to me feels odd, but after our fight last night, she probably didn't sleep well and needed additional space. Because of this, I choose not to overthink it, stretching in place and releasing a loud groan as my body wakes up.

Lately, I have been spending most of my time working extra hours around her dad's ranch or picking up side jobs around town. Over the last few months, I have focused on banking as much money as possible to help create a savings we can fall to if needed later on. I acknowledge these extra hours have been frustrating for Macy, even causing passive-aggressive remarks when I crawl in next to her after she has already gone to bed. Do we need this extra money immediately? No, but my father always struggled to support me and my mom, causing me to be determined to do the opposite of him. Macy has asked several times whether I am putting in these extra hours because I am either unhappy or need time away from her, but these accusations are furthest from the truth. My mind, body, and soul crave her every moment of the day. My world revolves around her, as it has since we were teens, and giving her a life less than perfection doesn't feel acceptable.

"Macy!" I call out before pausing to see if I can hear the shower running. My voice is hoarse from my deep slumber and our heated disagreement from last night. I hate we fought last night, again, since it feels as if we are doing more of this lately, making me question if putting in these extra work hours is the right thing. I want the loveable, free feeling love we used to have. I want the burning passion back, but as a man, I struggle to determine if providing for my family is more important than being present.

Not hearing a response from Macy after calling out for her, I release a deep breath, attempting to expel any building concern. As I pull myself out of bed, I find myself stumbling towards the bathroom in hopes of finding my wife. While I still don't hear the shower running, I wonder if I have caught her right before she starts the water. "Mace, baby, what are you doing?"

I round the corner to the master bathroom, but as I look around, I see no sign of Macy. At that moment, I realize her shampoo, conditioner, and razor no longer litter the sides of our shower. I'm not always wise, but warning bells ring throughout my mind. My breathing starts to pick up, my heart is racing, and my hands become sweaty as the panic begins to envelop me. I realize there are no other sounds from the rest of the house. What is going on? "Mace!"

My steps quicken as I walk down the long hallway towards the kitchen, continuing to glance through each doorway I pass, praying I catch sight of my wife. The open doors I pass give me quick clarity before continuing my steps down the hall. Not having an open-concept home prolongs my search, Macy's words ringing in my ears as I recall how she wanted an open-concept house, but I pushed us towards the one where we currently reside. I am desperately trying to stay calm, not allowing my apprehension to take over. "Mace, where are you?" I repeat, a sense of urgency filling my voice. The moment I step into the kitchen, taking inventory over the tiled kitchen counters, a small note with Macy's handwriting on it next to the empty coffee machine and cups catches my attention.

Luke,

I'm really sorry. I can't do this anymore. Good luck with everything. I will find a lawyer to draft divorce papers.

-Mace

This note only fuels the terror rising in my gut, my hands sliding through my hair and down my face. In denial, I continue to turn circles in our small kitchen, hoping she is hiding and this is all a joke. I think back to last night, remembering how she was acting strange last night at dinner, avoiding eye contact with me, refusing to commit to plans for next weekend, and even acting with a greater degree of defeat during our argument after dinner. As much as I asked, I could never get her to tell me what was bothering her or if there was something more to it than me working late. No matter how upset I knew she was last night, I never expected to wake up to a silent house this morning.

A piece of me wants to believe this is a joke, but I know Macy would never make this type of joke. I feel lost and confused as I start preparing myself a coffee, if anything, coffee fixes everything. This simple task helps soothe my racing thoughts, allowing me to develop a plan to find her and get the answers to the questions I can't stop thinking about. As I walk through the house, the stunning reality hits me. I realize her computer, clothes, and favorite necklace are all missing - all things she wouldn't take unless she was gone for a while.

My heart drops to my stomach as I realize the truth: Macy has left me. Up until this moment, I fought the idea she may be gone, but there is no way I can continue to fight it. How did I let this happen? Where is my wife? My Macy. The house instantly feels empty, her usual wit and charm disassembled from the house as I swear her sweet perfume scent has left with her. I attempt to steady myself on the kitchen counter when the room starts to feel like it is spinning around me.

I attempt to call her, but it goes straight to voicemail, telling me she has either blocked me or her phone is off. Impulsivities take over as I hang up and try again, continuing to do so for the rest of the day. After a while, I text Abigail, Macy's best friend, to see if she knows anything, but it only accomplishes making Abi as worried as I am. Panic fills her voice as she directs me to meet at Macy's parents, Tessa and Loch, house and see if they have heard from her. Just like any other day, Loch is up early, already working out in the fields as we pull in. He has no idea I am about to halt all of his work for the day, but as I wave for him to follow Abi and me into their house, I am positive he can see the fear written on my face.

As I continue to try to reach Macy, Abi and Macy's parents do the same. Unfortunately, we all get the same results. We all share confusion about where she would have gone, already reaching out to anyone we know she is close to, but none can provide us with valuable information. The sense of despair and uneasiness continues to increase each moment we can't find her. I continue to pace back and forth in Tessa and Loch's living room, unable to give up.

Chapter Two

MACY
NOW

They say a person has no way but up when you have hit the bottom, right? Well, I speculate I am finding myself there in real time. The ground beneath my feet feels solid and unmoving as if it was trying to prevent me from sinking into an even greater low. The air around me reeks of defeat and loss, but it could be all the trash everywhere in these New York City streets. Either way, my failure feels like dead weight on my shoulders, causing my new reality to hurt even more.

Why are we never taught how to prevent causing our own demise and hitting rock bottom in life? I have never felt more passionate about the importance of these lessons than I do at this moment. How to succeed should be ingrained in our minds from a young age. Much more valuable than watching Dazed and Confused daily in history class rather than learning anything of substance for your future self. We all have our rock-bottom definition, and this is mine. I find myself standing outside of my high-rise book publishing building with a broken heart and daunting burdens in my hands.

On one hand, I clutch onto my laptop containing my barely written novels, the current books I was reviewing for the publisher, and my personal emails sent to me as lifelines from my past life. All of which feel meaningless now, considering I no longer have a job. In my other hand, I hold a small box filled with two pictures - one of my family and one of my ex-boyfriend - and a fake plant I have kept on my desk, a sad reminder of what it used to be. I'm such a mess, I can't even manage keeping a plant alive at the spot I spent most of my time at.

Our work lunch started in tension, the argument between my now-ex and myself from last night causing uncertainty since we didn't finish our quarrel. After a slight disagreement with my boss at our lunch meeting, I found myself without a job and, unless I was dreaming, no boyfriend either. To be clear, my boss is — was— my boyfriend. My boyfriend was my boss. I am not sure if it was my boss or my boyfriend who ended it all over lunch, but either way, I find myself single and homeless. I attempt to stop my intrusive thoughts when I look back on how everyone in our office treated us, specifically me, for dating my boss. We both tried to keep those two pieces of our lives separate, never bringing tension or drama from the other part of our lives into the other. That is, until today.

The ironic part of this is how the world keeps moving, spinning around me without a care in the world. As I am standing on this dirty sidewalk at the lowest point of my life, businessmen and women run past me, talking on their phones while tourists snap photos of the towering buildings above us. All while I frantically plan how to pack all of my belongings in just one trip to our apartment. Among my belongings, I make sure to box my vibrator collection, the same collection that caused worry in my now-ex, James, since he did not understand how to emotionally cope with his inability to fulfill those needs. James was fine in bed, but did he rock my world? Not even close, and when he caught me finishing myself after he climaxed, it became an awkward conversation I always dreaded. This should have been my first sign this relationship was not going to work out.

I met my now-ex-boyfriend, James Von Lemont, when we were both interns at the top publishing house in New York City, Bringham

Publishing. He spent the last six years working himself up the ladder while I worked on finding the next up-and-coming American author and writing my manuscripts on the side. We fell into a comfortable rhythm over the years. Everyone knew we had been dating and now everyone knew he broke up with me in the French restaurant around the corner.

The conclusion of our relationship started last night when he came home at 2:00 am, reeking of alcohol and someone else's perfume. As he crawled into bed beside me, I couldn't ignore the trace of another woman along with a hickey blooming on his neck. Needless to say, I am not okay with my boyfriend sharing bodily fluids with anyone but me. How dare I, right? James didn't understand my disgust for him. I am not sure I will ever forget his words to me last night before he fell asleep, "I didn't think you would mind." Well, guess what, I did. I was preparing wedding Pinterest boards, all in hopes we would one day take a step forward.

His words still ring in my ears as another high-pitched ring from inside my purse snaps me back into reality. On my screen, my best friend's photo pops up on my phone, and I quickly answer. There was no hiding the strain in my voice or the inevitable sound of my tear-stained cheeks.

My breath comes out in short, sharp gasps as I try to calm myself. "Hey, Abi," I say, trying to sound nonchalant.

"Hey Macy, what's wrong?" Abigail asks.

"Where do I start? Long story short, I may have officially hit rock bottom." I say as I feel my throat tighten and emotions well in me. I have shed so many tears in the last few hours, and I am shocked I still have much left. When I left Lucas seven years ago, I truly believed I was making the right decision for me. I felt as if I had no choice, but at the same time, I failed myself. I married a man who genuinely adored me and would move mountains anytime I asked. I felt the same way, but with each argument we had, I felt myself pulling further and further away. Leaving such a great man should have been my rock bottom but knowing I have found myself in an even worse situation, I realize how wrong I was back then.

"Worse than when your dad caught you and Lucas getting it on in his tractor on the side of the road? Then everyone would honk as they would pass y'all's land to 'give you a warning?'" Abi quips, trying to lighten the mood.

The quest to lighten the mood works for a second as I release a huff of a laugh. "Wow, you really know how to make a girl feel better about herself, don't you, Abs?" I respond as the realization of my current situation seeps back into me. I prefer to live in a world where I am just a hot mess, not an utter failure.

"Am I wrong?" she responds with a small, mischievous giggle. Finding friends like Abi is not easy, but once you do, you hold on to them harder than you do anything else. I may feel like a complete mess, but knowing my best friend will always jump in to support me gives me hope I will make it out of this mess alive.

With a deep sigh, all I can manage to get out is, "No, as always, you are not wrong." If I were to allow anyone to humble me at this moment, it would be Abi.

"Speaking of which, you will never guess who I ran into at Meryl's the other day?" Meryl's is what is famously known as the best - and only - restaurant bar in Pigeon Lake, Texas, my quaint hometown. When she tries to get me to guess, we both know no matter whom I guess; she would have to say yes, she did see them there.

"Who?" I ask out of sincere curiosity because thinking about Meryl's feels a lot better than thinking about the awful smells emanating from the drainage pipes currently surrounding me. Did I just see a rat scurrying down the alley? Gross.

"Your one and only Lucas Wright," Abigail says after a long silence. Abi has effortlessly stayed neutral between Luke and me, often not commenting when I say anything good or bad about him. While I put my parents in a bad situation when I left, leaving Abi between the two parties broke my heart. I have never asked her to choose, and I highly doubt Luke has either.

Suddenly, I feel an aggressive shove from behind me as a clan of impatient New Yorkers push past me on the sidewalk. "Move, lady!" one says as I hear a snobby lady mumble "You clearly don't have anywhere important to be." Frustration boils inside me, finally pushing me to my boiling point. Without thinking, I let out a loud, primal scream, causing many to give me the side eye. It doesn't stop anyone from continuing their day, but it makes me feel better.

"Mace! Macy! MACY!" I hear Abigail yell from my phone.

"Hey. Sorry," I wheeze into the receiver, attempting to catch my breath.

"Um... was that you? Did you just scream? Are you okay?" The concern in Abi's voice is palpable through the phone.

Sensing her concern, I quickly reassure her. "Oh yes. It was me. But I do feel better. And the only thing hurting is my heart. And my pride."

"What are you going to do now?" She asks gently.

"I think I need to come home," I express, feeling as defeated as one could sound. Nobody wants to admit this to themselves, but sometimes, your last option is your only option.

A beat of stunned silence passes before it is Abi's turn to yell because all I can understand is, "EEECCKKK!"

I let a moment pass before mumbling, "I will see you in a couple of days, love."

"I can't wait! Are you telling your parents? What about Luke?" Abi pushes, her excitement clear with her hurried voice.

"Yes, I will call my mom when I get off the phone with you. But Abs, under no circumstances are you to tell Luke. This has nothing to do with him. I'm sure he will hear about it soon enough, but please don't do your meddling." I can imagine Abi rolling her eyes at my comment. "I mean it, Abi. Please don't bring him into this." I finally get her to agree before I rush to hang up the phone. I already feel a sense of relief at the thought of returning home to my family and Abi. This isn't what I expected, but there is a sense of comfort in going home. I have never felt like I found my place in New York, and without making any of those deep connections, there has been a sense of loneliness for years. I thought I saw some reprieve of this when I started dating James, but with him now out of my life, I am quick to realize those friends I thought I had were really just James' friends, and I was just the one on his arm.

As disappointed as I am from how this all turned out, the fear of returning back home is far less than the loneliness that carries me around here. If only I can find a way to quietly ease myself back into the small town without making too much of a commotion. Is there an easier way to run into your demons than at Meryl's? Probably not.

Chapter Three

MACY

"**How did it feel climbing** out of your window?" Abigail asks, her eyes vibrant with curiosity as we sit at a table in the back of Meryl's bar.

I take a deep breath while I lean back in my chair, running my fingers through my loose curls. "Like I am too old to be doing that shit. I realized the last time I slept in my old room was the night before me and Lucus..." I glance around the room, paranoid that someone is listening to our conversation.

"Got married? Mace, you can say it, and you won't catch on fire." Abigail says, trying to lighten the mood since she noticed I was starting to feel uncomfortable. I wouldn't say I was uncomfortable talking to Abi about this, it was more on what this small town would think about me coming back home. I catch myself as I feel my leg bouncing underneath the wooden table and feel how sweaty my hands have become.

"Ha ha," I say as I roll my eyes, "but you never know. I'm sure people were pretty mad at me when everything happened." I take a large gulp of my beer, watching as a droplet rolls down the side before finally reaching the table.

Abi reaches across the table, squeezing my hands. "At least half of them have moved on. But quit stalling, tell me what happened. I want every detail. Do not leave anything out!"

I sigh, feeling a mix of emotions swirling inside me. "Yeah, yeah, fine. I guess it is time." I take a moment to observe those sitting around us, noticing how the wooden tables have been replaced with newer ones. "But first, are these new tables? I didn't know Meryl knew he could get new tables. I swear the last ones had been here since the Civil War." My hands rub over each ridge, the wood grains prominently displayed. The warm tone gives a warm, welcoming vibe throughout the grungy bar.

Abigail's eyes go wide like saucers as she quickly says, "They are from a local who makes them, but focus. I need to hear about what is going on!" It is clear Abi does not want to waste our time talking about unnecessary topics and more about the drama that is my life.

With a shaky breath, I begin recounting the events that led me back home to her - starting with that Wednesday night when James came home so late. The pain still stings as I recount everything, causing me to routinely pause to slow my rising heart rate with my anxiety. Each time I catch myself about to start crying, I clasp my hands into fists, moving my attention from my own words to the physical pain I am causing myself.

My throat begins to get choked with emotion while I continue taking deep breaths. My stomach churns as I think back to that night, how he was barely able to stand. He was so drunk, and the spiteful words he spewed my way. I am practically yelling while trying not to cry in the back of this bar. In this small corner of the bar, with Abi next to me, I am finally able to release the emotions I have been keeping buried deep in me. No therapy could make it feel better to get this off my chest.

"Please tell me he gave you the best apology any man has ever given someone," Abigail chimes in concern laced between her words. I feel her warm arms wrap around me as she pulls me closer to her side, giving me the full support I looked for from my mom and dad.

I release a heavy sigh before taking another drink of my beer. "Absolutely not. He said, 'I didn't think you would mind.' HE DIDN'T THINK I WOULD MIND, ABI!" What delusional man would even think that?" Despite knowing I did not deserve this behavior from James, I can't help but be embarrassed by his actions. My cheeks flush as I recount how I was not enough for him, not enough to keep him from seeking affection in other women.

"Someone who doesn't give a shit about you," Abigail responds savagely, her lips forming a scowl and clenching her jaw.

I roll my eyes and continue. "That's for sure. But anyway, we decided to just go to bed and the next day, we would revisit the issue. We never got a chance because the next morning, we went to work as usual. Nothing was said about our argument, but I chalked it up to James not trying to take the drama into the office, which I totally respected and appreciated. I felt this was until we go to meet one of our authors at a place around the corner from the office."

My voice starts to shake from anger and sadness. Will I always look back at this meeting and blame all of this on myself? Would James and I still be together if I had done a better job? Could I have prevented this? "Needless to say, the author saw one vision for the marketing plan while I pitched my own, completely different plan. James took the author's side because, how did he put it?" I pause, attempting to remember the exact phrasing used in our meeting. "'I don't understand a male's perspective.'" I take another drink of my beer, shaking my head in astonishment. When I glance over at Abi, she also shakes her head. "The problem is, I knew James hated the author's plan, and we strategically created this pitch for the author together. I guess I looked at him 'unprofessionally,' so he stood up, dragged me to the restroom, and told me he had no choice but to fire me because I came to this meeting unprepared and was choosing to be unprofessional during this important meeting."

Abi's loud gasp gets the attention of those sitting around us. Nevertheless, I continued reliving the events. "I was completely stunned, but he turned around, about to walk out the restroom door, and told me to 'Make sure to have everything out of our apartment by Friday.' And that was it. I pulled myself together, grabbed my purse at the table, and went to our office to pack my things. I'm not sure how James explained my actions, but I'm sure they didn't put me in a positive light."

You could hear a pen drop as Abi looked at me with wide eyes. Befuddled. I don't know if I have ever made her lose her voice before, but I can see her mind racing, trying to find the words to respond with. Finally, after a deep breath, Abigail states, "What a pig! I knew he was no good! Did you have any idea? What man doesn't have the balls to just break up with you like a man and not do it at work and blame it on your quality of work? Mace, you deserve so much better than him. Fuck James and fuck his demeaning you in front of.... well, whoever else was in the restroom."

This made me laugh, despite what I have put her through, she was still willing to take my side, no matter what. "No, I had no idea he could be so cruel. Luckily, there was only one old lady, and she hid in the stall until he left. She then came out, washed her hands, and patted me on the shoulder as she shook her head and walked out." Thinking back, I wish the old woman had given me encouragement, reiterating I deserved better, but what does someone really say in such a situation? I make a mental note to myself to never let a woman just stand there stunned and not give her reassurances. I may not know them, but I don't have to make them feel even more alone in that moment.

"At least it wasn't a whole auditorium. So, he could have made it worse. Good for you for looking at the bright side of things, babe." She states, trying to lighten the mood.

But my heart still feels heavy with the weight of what happened. I know I deserve better than him, but sometimes, when you are in the middle of it, you lose sight of reality. I feel as if I lost sight of reality in my relationship with James.

Abi and I continue to sit at the cozy corner table, catching up on each other's lives. The low hum of chatter and clinking glasses surrounds us as we continue sipping on our beers. Abi gives me an update on the recent attempts of dating, whether good or bad. All of which led to disappointment in the end. Not to be anti-men here, but I get it. Men kind of suck right now. I will never understand how some guy hasn't locked her down yet. She is so loving and has always been there for those in her life. I have always just chalked it up to not finding the right one yet.

As we continue to chat, the atmosphere around us shifts. Those around us have been drinking for a while now, making our moods change from relaxing to rumbustious. Just as I start feeling my own buzz from the alcohol, a gust of wind hits us as a group of guys swing the door to Meryl's open, walking up to the bar. I turn to ask Abigail who they are since it is a small town and everyone always knows everyone. "Most of them are from the oil rigs outside of town, but a couple moved to town when the new lumber company opened up in Langston," Abi informs me, noticeably keeping her eyes on one of them, but I can't figure out which one it is.

Without hesitation, I stand, grabbing her hand in mine and pulling her to her feet. As I start to suggest we go to the bar and hang out with them, Abi quickly stops me, shaking her head and finishing the rest of her beer. "No, Mace, I don't think it's a good idea. I actually went on a date with Jason a couple of weeks ago. He is the one that works at the lumber company." Abi doesn't drop my hand, but her feet are rooted to where we are standing, denying my ability to drag her with me.

"Another dud, I'm assuming? Most J-named men are." I spit out, thinking of every guy I know with a J-name. "Well, what do we have to lose? We can at least go see what they are up to tonight. One of us needs to get laid tonight." I quickly state with a sly grin, trying to be my friend's wingwoman.

"Oh, Mace, I am not sure this is a goo —" Abi retorts before I cut her off.

"Don't be a wuss, Abigail Kline, let's go." Seeing her deflate from being defeated, I grab my beer and successfully pull her with me towards the bar.

The guys are nice enough, but none really catch my eye. A couple of the oil rig guys are trying to seduce me fairly hard, and while they are attractive enough, they aren't worth my time outside of tonight. Good enough to talk and laugh with while Abi gets her man. Abi's eyes continue to dance through the crowd, never giving me insight on which guy she may be interested in. I meet Jason, the guy Abi went out with, and I can confirm, he is boring as hell.

Suddenly, the front door opens behind me, and the warm Texas air rushes into the bar. Without even looking, I feel it. It feels like all of the air has been sucked out of the room as if a tornado just went by. I don't need to turn to see Lucas is the one who walked into the bar. My heart races as fear washes over me, the air seeming to become thick with tension and unsaid words. Fear is a funny thing. Sometimes, you feel it for a logical reason, like if you are getting chased by an angry animal. Other times you can feel fear simply for having to look your ex in the eyes for the first time in seven years. This type of fear is unique, causing feelings of helplessness, trembling in place, being able to hear your thudding pulse in your ears, and your eyesight going foggy.

I frantically look around Meryl's for the quickest escape route - the back door, a window, a space rocket, even a trap door to a tunnel underneath would suffice. But I'm rooted into the floor like the old tree in my parent's backyard, unable to escape quietly as the guy Abigail is talking to smiles big and welcomes Lucas to join us. I don't move. I don't turn my head. I don't speak. I just pray. I pray quicker than any good Christian Southern woman does in hopes of Lucas not noticing me since my hair is much shorter and darker. As we all know, I would never have this luck. Despite my refusal to acknowledge his new presence, I can still feel him take a step closer to me.

"I heard a rumor you were in town," Lucas states in his gruff, deep voice, sending shivers down my spine. I haven't seen him in years, not since the night I left, only a note behind stating my desire, yet his presence still affects me like it always has. His gruff voice automatically takes me back to those long nights in our house right after we got married, him roaming my body as he spoke the dirtiest words to me. Goosebumps pop all over my skin as his warm body takes another step closer to me, making me fight the urge to turn to him and beg him to snake his words over my body like that again. My heart starts racing, from both his close awareness but also unsure of how he will react to me standing in the middle of his friends on his turf.

Chapter Four

LUCAS

The bell above the hardware store's door jingles moments before I hear an old friend calling out my name as he looks for me down each aisle. Once he reaches me, his eyes are wide, taking deep breaths, and shaking his head. I swear if this man tells me he may have gotten his girlfriend pregnant... again, I may lose my patience with him. Instead, he is claiming something much worse for me, he saw Macy entering the ice cream shop down the street with her dad. I immediately knew this was a lie. When Mace ran, she left no signs of ever coming back. There have been many possible sightings over the years, but it is usually just an out-of-towner stopping in while on their way to somewhere else.

Despite my arguments, my friend continues to convince me he is confident this time. Macy hasn't been home in seven years, why would she be home now? In fact, my first thought was whether either her mom or dad had an accident and whether they were ok. A quick, lighthearted text to my boss, Macy's dad, gave me all the comfort I needed when he mentioned tomorrow's work tasks and nothing about any emergency or Macy being in town. I shake off this rumor and didn't think about it again.

But later, as I step foot into Meryl's, I regret coming out with my friends tonight. Leaning on the bar and talking to Wyatt, Macy stands in front of me. She hasn't changed much. Her hair is shorter and maybe darker, but I kind of like it. Her curves and presence still pull me towards her as if I had no other option than to be at her mercy. When she laughs, a familiar jolt of passion flashes down my spine, causing my cock to twitch. I give my body a pep talk, making sure we are all on the same page - we are not giving in to Macy tonight. I was here to share a beer with my buddies and nothing more.

My internal words are weak as I approach her, heading directly to the source, determined to understand why she is back in town. Tension flies up my spine as she hesitantly turns to face me. She has always been drop-dead gorgeous, but the way she now has subtle wrinkles around her eyes when she laughs rips away any hesitation my dick, or heart, may have had. My brain works overtime to remind me to keep my steel, security-grade walls up.

One beer was not going to be enough tonight. I quickly call over the bartender, Courtney, requesting a drink to slow down my heart rate as quickly as possible.

Her breathy voice fills the space between us as she greets me like we see each other every day. "Oh, hi, Lucas. How are you?"

Her calmness gives me a shot of resentment towards her. My sharp words were said to cause her pain. "Confused as hell as to why you are here. Your dad didn't mention any emergency causing you to blow into town like a tumbleweed." I shove my free hand into my jeans pocket, anxious to keep my hands busy so I don't unconsciously reach out to touch her, pulling her closer to me out of instinct.

"Are we really starting like this, Luke?" She can't even look at me in the eyes as she spews out her words. "I'm just here for a small visit. We don't need to talk or even acknowledge the other exists." As she finally locks eyes with me, I see a hint of goosebumps spread over her chest before a pink blush climbs up her neck and rests on her cheeks. Her stubborn ass will never admit I rattled her night when I walked in. "Comparing me to a tumbleweed, real charming Luke." Her words are laced with venom as she turns away to communicate my dismissal.

"Well, forgive me for being surprised by your sudden appearance. You leave in the dead of night, what am I supposed to think? Should I be comparing you to my guardian angel?" I scowl, attempting to keep my walls up.

Macy scoffs at my terse words. "I don't want you to compare me to anything." She shoots back. "Now, please walk away so I can finish this beer with Bryant —"

"Wyatt. His name is Wyatt." I quickly correct her as Wyatt does the same thing. A pang of jealousy rushes my system as Wyatt takes another step closer to her, gently placing his hand on her hip. I can't help but clench my fists as possessiveness rushes through me.

"Ok, Wyatt, whatever. Either way, I'm leaving. Thank you for ruining another night for me." Macy says as she reaches for Abi's arm and whispers something. Abi looks just as disappointed as my heart feels, and Mace stomps off towards the front door. I quickly glance back to Abi, seeing her apology written all over her face, giving me a shrug and a sad smile.

Like the tether I can't escape, I follow her outside to finish our conversation alone. There is no reason to have the whole town hear what is about to be said. "You have no right to be a bitch about me going to a bar I frequent at least once a week, Mace," I state firmly, my voice quickly rising. "You are the out-of-towner, not me. Or did you forget this small fact?"

"I'm being a bitch, Lucas? I would rather be a bitch than the asshole you love to be. I have been sending you divorce papers for seven years, and your stubborn ass refuses to sign them. If I'm keeping a tally, you are much worse than me. Get over yourself."

I can't help the smile spreading across my face, "keeping a tally, huh?"

With a flop of her hands into the air from her frustration, she yells, "Ugh! Forget it, Luke. I don't expect you to have an adult conversation about anything." Macy crosses her arms while visibly attempting to take deep breaths, dissipating her irritation with me.

My smile deflates while I let her continue walking away. The woman walking away from me is feisty and fierce, but I will forever love her. I may know what buttons to push to get her fired up, but I also know when to stop trying. I have practiced what I would say to her if she ever returned a million times, but all those words escape me tonight. I need them to be perfect when we finally sit down and talk about everything. I need to be able to effectively give her my thoughts and feelings about her and us. Macy continues to stalk away from me, leaving me standing in the middle of the road while she gets into Abi's car and starts the engine.

It isn't until Mrs. Miller honks at me that I realize I am blocking a lane of traffic. Too many people are peering out of their rolled-down car windows, curious to watch this standoff unfolding before them.

I'll never understand why Macy just left me that day. Of course, she was frustrated with her job and with me, but I would have done anything to fight for her. I would have, and still will, fight for her until my last breath. She was my whole world - sun, moon, and stars. Despite knowing this, Macy still snuck out in the middle of the night like a coward I never thought she would be. In those late, quiet nights alone, I often wondered if I ever knew her at all, considering I never pictured her leaving in the way she did.

The night she left, we had a drag-out fight because I got home late... again. My text telling her I would be late never went through - just one of the disadvantages of living in the country with poor cell service. Since she never received my text, she made dinner for both of us. A dinner I didn't attend when she expected. It wasn't like I was out running around at bars with my friends. I picked up an extra shift at my mechanic's job to help buy her the purse she had been eying at the store for Christmas. I was also slowly building my savings to start a family with a daughter or two who looked just like her.

I didn't tell her why I was working extra hours, but I assumed she knew how tight our finances were and wouldn't mind. When she gave me the cold shoulder when I got home, I knew I was in trouble. It wasn't until I attempted to hug her all hell broke loose. After our fight, we both went to bed as usual, never realizing it would be our last.

The next morning, I woke up to a note I still have sitting in the back of my closet. It is just one of the many items she left behind when she left. I couldn't bring myself to throw them out. My heart couldn't handle any more disappointment, while my brain was screaming at me to rid anything of hers. Looking back, I know I should have communicated better with her, I should have explained what I was doing and why it was so important to me. At the time, I couldn't fathom how she would handle me always being gone like I was. I would give up anything I had to go back and tell her about these things before bed that night.

Agonizing flashbacks run through my mind as I stand in the street, still blocking traffic. I think about the time we sat under the stars and talked all night before rushing home to meet curfew. I think about our Senior prom, where she wore the green, strapless dress, which provided a high slit in it, making it easy to access on our way home that night. I think about our first night in our new house and how we slow danced to old country music. Those simple times are the moments that have kept me lying awake for years now. The same memories often distract me while working, causing me to halt my movements, just like I am now in the middle of the road.

The honking brings me back to reality, the knowledge Macy has been drinking and now driving home strikes me. I quickly jump into my truck and follow her back to her parents' house. I keep a safe distance so she doesn't realize I am following her, knowing she will assume I am traffic headed to the new oil rig that went in about two miles down their dirt road a couple of months ago. Knowing I wouldn't be able to sleep without knowing if she made it home safely encourages me to continue following her. Even if she doesn't want my help, I will still keep her safe. Sometimes, those actions have to be from a distance.

Chapter Five

MACY

"You were always good** about sneaking out of the house without letting us know." my father grumbles over breakfast the next morning. I don't have the energy to look at him. I may have only had one and a half beers last night, but I feel like I have been hit with the hangover sledgehammer. The pounding behind my eyes beats in time with my pulse.

"You may be good at staying quiet, sweetheart, but our sweet Lucas kept you safe." My mother chirps happily. I can't help but huff my frustration at hearing his name so early in the morning.

"Excuse me, mother? I wasn't even with him last night. I was with Abi, but I suppose that means nothing." I say exhaustedly. I have been in town for less than 24 hours, but I feel like I have run a marathon. But as a positive, I didn't even cry last night when I crawled into bed. Instead, I read part of my book and fell asleep. One night of not shedding tears? Check!

My parents seem to find something amusing in what I said, both exchanging a chuckle between them. Finally, my mom found the strength to break the news to me. "Mace, Lucas has always let us know when you were not at home and snuck out. Just like when you were a teen, Luke texted us when he saw you at the bar last night. That poor boy never wanted us to find you missing and panic. He has always been protective over those close to him."

"What a traitor." I huff, feeling betrayed by my parents and Luke. "So, you always knew?" I ask.

"We always knew, sweetheart, " my mom says with a giggle, spreading strawberry jam on her homemade biscuit.

A feeling of betrayal plagues me as I try to put the building blocks of my life together, realizing there are many secrets I wasn't privy to. How could my boyfriend, turned husband, turned pain in the ass, which I trusted with my entire being, backstab me in this way? A sense of naivety and foolishness washes over me, making me feel like a doll everyone was protecting without me knowing.

I was always a good girl growing up, never swaying from what the rules were, and kept perfect grades throughout school. When Luke and I started dating, I thought I had finally broken my good girl streak and was breaking the rules. I prided myself so much on never getting caught. All of this time, Luke was the responsible one for me. Resentment threatens to rise, making me curious about all of the other things I missed over the years.

As we sit in silence around the kitchen table, my mother's voice breaks through my dark thoughts. "So, what are your plans now? How long are you staying in town?" my mother asks.

My mind races with uncertainty, trying to keep up with everything going on. "Not sure, honestly. I guess I will start looking for a job either in Dallas or New York. Without a job or apartment in New York, I'm not sure if I should even go back. I will be a laughingstock for everyone in the publishing company, so I'm not sure where that leads me."

My mother nods hesitantly, "Well, you know you can always stay here as long as you need." My mother adds, attempting to provide comfort.

The thought of returning to my hometown and crawling back to my childhood bedroom after leaving with such dramatics makes me want to shrink into oblivion. "I know. But being here brings back reminders I don't want." I state in a carried away voice, almost talking to myself. "I may start working more on the book I have pending for the last couple of years. Not sure what I would do with it once I finished it, but it is at least something to keep my mind busy."

My mom reaches over and squeezes my hand comfortingly. "I know, Mace, I know. I think it sounds like a great idea. Keep your brain busy while you wait it out. If you plan on staying around for a while, your dad and I thought maybe you would want to stay in the back cottage. Giving you your own space." My mother gives me a look of desperation as I look up to see if she is serious. "But if you would rather stay at the house, you could always use the cottage for writing." My mom finishes.

I raise my eyebrows in shock," But what about your she-shed? Where will you run and hide from Dad?"

"Who says I don't follow her down there?" my dad asks while giving me a mischievous smile.

I can't help but laugh at their playful banter. Both have always been the missing pieces to the other. "Okay, that is not something I want to know about. But sure, maybe moving down there is a good idea. Is there WIFI down there?"

With a roll of her eyes, my mom comically says, "Yes, honey. We do have some sense of civilization around here. We are not living in the Stone Age."

"Well, I didn't know if you would have any technology out where y'all live. Figured I should ask." I state while a sense of warmth and comfort spreads over me. Despite everything, my parents will always be my biggest supporters, giving me a motivation I have not felt in a while.

I let out a small giggle as I stand from the table, ready to pack my boxes to move to the cottage. Glancing over at my parents, I ask in a playful tone, "When did y'all decide I should go stay down there?"

Another sly smile spreads across my father's face. "About five minutes after Luke let us know that you were with him." My dad quips.

"For the record, I wasn't with him." I jump to clarify. "He walked into Meryl's where me and Abi already were. I had no intention of seeing him."

"Oh, we heard all about your little tiff in the middle of the road," my dad says with a smirk and shake of his head. "Sounds like you gave them a spectacle to watch. Show and a drink, as the young ones may say." My dad continues, causing me to groan and walk away from both parents.

"Where did you hear this from?" I ask exhaustedly.

"Oh, Mrs. Miller called Betsy when she got home, and then Betsy called her granddaughter to see if she knew anything. Then everyone was talking about it over our coffee this morning at Redbirds." My dad explains, still laughing over his coffee.

"So, everyone knows now?"

"That's putting it lightly, sweetheart." My mom chimes in. "We cleaned out all my stuff last night in the cottage. Let Dad know if you need help moving your luggage." My mom adds as I continue walking away from them.

Me

Does everyone already know about me and Luke last night?

Abi

I know you have been gone for awhile Mace, but you know how this works.

But yes, they all know.

Me

Perfect. 🙄

I finish arranging the last of my belongings in the quaint cottage as all the emotions hit me at once.

Embarrassment and dread hit me as my heart starts racing, my brain running a mile a minute as everything around me reminds me what I am going through. Anger, fear, and sadness then take over me as I remember I have to see the people I ran from again, making it even worse when I have to face them. My heart breaks as I realize I have to admit I am back after being publicly dumped by your boss, moving back to your hometown, and now running into your ex.

I am seething at Luke for betraying my trust by helping my parents keep tabs on me. Has he really always been doing this during our whole friendship? Our marriage? I remind myself we are technically still married, certain he believes it is still his responsibility to keep tabs on me. It isn't, but men. What do you do with them? They are protective when they shouldn't be, yet they fail to meet expectations when they should. I release a sigh as if removing the negativity from my soul.

It's too early in the day to turn to wine for comfort, but the thought of finding a way to fill my day feels overwhelming. Maybe my best form of therapy would be writing my book. With this thought, I grab my laptop and head over to the little desk my mom has set up in the makeshift living room in this small cottage. Writing a romance story is a lot easier when you are currently experiencing romance. But since I am fresh out of inspiration and creativity right now, I know I need to just start the writing process and hope it comes to me later.

Over the years, I have started multiple books, but there's always been one I found myself coming back to, continuously lingering in my mind. It's about loving your first love but not loving you back.

I am about halfway through writing it, but I always get stuck on why the couple would get back together. Even when I have been in romantic relationships in the past, I could never create a good reason these two characters would ever willingly reunite.

As the sun sets and the cool Texas air envelopes me, I have become deeply engrossed in writing. The next time I glance at the clock, it was almost 11:00 pm. It has been months since I have felt so absorbed in writing. The words come alive in my mind as I imagine each scene like a movie. With a fresh glass of wine in hand, I continue writing, lost between each word.

I have always been "different" than others when it comes to my creativity. I can visualize a room and mentally paint the walls, install shelves, and know precisely what the room would look like. I have also been able to "visually" see what I am either reading or writing in a book. I can see these scenes play out in my mind like I am standing there watching it play out. That is why, at first, I believed it was just me being too caught up in my writing when I hear a key insert into the front door. But then the door swings open, and a tall figure stumbles in. The scream reverberating throughout the cottage stops the man in his tracks and throws his hands in the air.

Once my heartbeat slows down and my eyes adjust to the darker lighting, I realize that the intruder standing motionless in the cottage is Luke - my rugged and still desperately handsome husband who is also a rancher on my dad's farm. "What are you doing here, Lucas?" I ask, trying to calm my voice and push away any intrusive thoughts on his looks.

"I, uh, had to stop by and grab a small hammer I let your mom borrow last week." He sheepishly responds. "What are you doing in here?" His eyes bounce around the room, instantly nervous by the situation we have found ourselves in. After Luke moved out of the cottage when we got married, my mom went back to using it for her crafts and projects. Since moving into the cottage, I have noticed that it has also been a storage unit of sorts to hold tools between different projects.

"But why didn't you knock?" Despite my actions to keep my voice low, anger is building and getting out of control. "Did you not see the lamp light on through the window? That would have told you someone was in here." I retort more sharply than needed. I assumed he didn't know that I had moved to the cottage for the time being, but an irrational annoyance rings through me.

"I mean, yeah, I did, but your mom leaves the lights on all the time. I didn't think anything about it." Lucas explains nervously. His deep-veined hands run through his hair while still refusing to look me in the eye. "I'm really sorry, I will make sure to knock next time."

I stare at him with astonishment, unable to believe he thought it was acceptable to barge into this building unannounced. Despite my anger, I can't help but take in how good he looks - his rolled-up plaid shirt showing off his muscular arms, his dirty Wranglers clinging to his toned legs, and his sweaty hair falling as if he just ran a hand through it. One man should never look this drop-dead gorgeous after working all day in the Texas sun. He looks like he just stepped out of a steamy cowboy romance book.

It takes me a few seconds to snap out of it "What if I was sleeping?" I dig, refusing to let go of the boiling argument. I quickly take a big gulp of my wine because no matter what his answer is, my heart is racing. Is that due to being scared like I was or because I can feel my nipples harden under my tank top after looking at him? We will never know.

"But you weren't asleep, Mace." He boldly counters. His body turns as he looks at the mess of my belongings strung us. "Can we please just call a truce while you are back in town? I don't want to fight every time we cross paths. This is a small town, and we are bound to see each other frequently. Can we just be civil to each other?" The desperate plea in his voice pushes me to nod my head in defeat. He isn't wrong, but I am too afraid of dropping the wall too much. The last thing I need is to get sucked back in by his charm and decide not to leave again. "What is all of this? Are you staying down here?" Luke asks after a few awkward beats.

"Lucas, that is none of your business. Give me back your key." I snap back, suddenly feeling defensive about my living situation.

"I'm not giving you my key. This isn't your house." Lucas proclaims matter-of-factly. "Now, tell me why you are down here. Where is your mom's stuff?" Lucas says exhaustively.

I realize there is no point in arguing with him. "Yes, I'm going to stay down here until I can find another job. I am surprised my parents didn't tell you since you both discuss my every move with each other." I cross my arms and glare at him from across the room.

"They were more concerned with interrogating me about our argument in the street than to let me know your new living arrangements," Luke says with a smirk on his face.

I take another slow, deliberate gulp of the sweet red wine wine and reach to refill my glass. "Haha. You're hilarious. At least you didn't lose all of your good qualities." I joke, trying to mask the tension in the room.

Silence comes over the room for a few seconds. We stand at a crossroads, unsure how to move forward without spooking the other. With hesitation, Lucas breaks the uncomfortable silence and asks, "So, how long are you staying Mace?"

With a huff, I respond, "Not really sure. I am going to start looking for jobs in either Dallas or New York, but neither of those options sounds that appealing right now. So, for now, I am focusing on a writing project I have been working on for the last couple of years." I shrug in hopes I look nonchalant. "It will at least keep me busy, I suppose. Mom and Dad sent me down here so I don't feel like I must keep sneaking out of the house." A wry smile spreads on my lips as I think about all the times I snuck out and always thought they had no idea.

That drop-dead smirk and dimple spread across Luke's face as he stares at me with those passionate, deep blue eyes. He reaches to give his neck a nervous scratch before finally tearing his gaze away from me. "You're getting too old to keep running, sweetheart." He jabs. While I could read too much into his comment, I know that he is trying to be straightforward and not to hurt me.

"Yeah." I agree with an exhale. "That's what I keep thinking to myself."

"I guess I will leave you to it." Lucas softly says, looking shy as if he doesn't know if he should continue talking. "Can I stop by another time? Just to see you and catch up?"

I have no good reason to tell him no, as his request aches across my heart. I feel the pull to him even after all these years. The hurt and pain we have shared can't overshadow the amount of love I once had for this man. My mind races with a list of questions I wish I could ask- does he have a girlfriend? Why does he still choose to work with my parents when I know he can do so much better? What has he been up to? If it wasn't for fear of giving mixed messages, I would walk to him and just let him hold me in his strong arms. What I would give to have this man wrap me in his arms and tell me everything will be okay. But instead of giving him any indication of my consideration, I quietly respond. "No. I don't think that's a good idea."

I can see the sadness hit him like a slap. Surely, he knew deep down I wouldn't say yes, but by the way, his face fell, he had just enough hope to ask me the question to begin with. "OK, Mace." He says before turning to leave. "See you around then. I will knock next time I need something in here."

A wave of longing and sadness hits me as he walks away. Before closing the door behind him, he turns around and asks, "Hey, how does your book end?"

I can't help the slight grin to his question. "Can't decide if I want it to be a happily ever after or realistic."

"Who says reality isn't the happily ever after?" With a sad smile, he turns to the door again and taps on it like he wants to add something. In the end, he tells me to have a good night and shuts the door behind him.

I am left alone in the quiet room, wishing our history could be rewritten so we could have our happily ever after. I'm not sure any amount of longing could bring us to a different end.

Chapter Six

LUCAS

Seeing Macy last night took my emotions on a tailspin. I never considered she would have moved down to the cottage and neither of her parents mentioned it. Walking in on her mid-typying is the second time in a row where her presence was not expected and shocked me. I quickly realize I need to find a way to keep my distance from Macy when she wants it but still push her to talk to me. A delegate balance that I need to master immediately. Despite Macy being clear she doesn't want me stopping by the cottage anymore, I have never been a man who did what I was told. As the sun set over the horizon and my farm work was completed, I find myself standing outside the cottage door, cautiously tapping a double knock. The familiar scent of freshly cut grass and a warm Texas wind sweeps around me, making the wildflowers surrounding the house wave. I feel the eyes watching me from the cows I take care of during the day.

"I told you not to come back," Macy says as she swings open the door. Her frustration seeps from her.

"Yeah, maybe. But I need to grab another tool." I reply with a large, charming smile. My only hope is to start knocking down a piece of the walls she has built. I came in with a new game plan today, hoping to be intriguing enough to get her to talk to me.

Macy shakes her head, huffing a sigh, proving her frustration did not decrease because of my charming smile. "I have been rearranging the cottage most of the day, and I have yet to find any tools."

"Oh, they are hidden in the bedroom closet," I say confidently. "May I come in?" I take a meek step towards her.

With a weary expression on her face, Macy slowly opens the door and steps aside, allowing me in. "Go ahead. Go get it. I'll be right here to shut the door on your way out."

Little does Macy know, I wasn't leaving any time soon. I strategically maneuver myself into this cottage and wasn't leaving until I was good and ready.

As soon as I step inside, the familiar floral scent of Macy engulfs me, and I'm taken back to all those nights when we slow danced under the stars in the backfield. Memories flood me of her, letting me pull her close and allowing us to sway back and forth to the 90s country music seeping from my truck radio. Looking back, I know how special and simple those nights were. Just me, her, and 90's country while getting lost in each other's arms. It's astonishing how we don't realize we are in the best days of our lives until it is all gone.

I make my way to the sole bedroom, searching for the only tool I know is in the cottage. Luckily, I have a habit of leaving my tools around when I am in a hurry and don't have time to stop by the barn on my way home. With the screwdriver in hand, I make my way back to the living room, where Macy is waiting for me at the door, just as she promised. I walk right past her, ignoring her angry glances, and sit on the couch next to where her laptop sits.

"Um, Luke, what are you doing? You said you were leaving." Macy questions.

"Oh yeah, I forgot. I did bring you something, though." I reply, holding up the coffee I picked up for her in town. "I assume you still take it the same."

Hesitantly, she takes the coffee from my outstretched hand. "Why would you bring me coffee?"

"I figured you would be up all night writing, and this would be good fuel. I almost brought you dinner, but your dad mentioned y'all were having your mom's lasagna tonight, so I didn't want to hurt your appetite."

Macy collapses down next to me and snatches her computer away so I can't glance at it. She is so close I can feel the warmth radiating from her body, tempting me to reach out and touch her. To have the freedom to run my hands over her soft skin and pull her to me. Her paper-thin top and booty shorts leave little to the imagination despite each curve of her body being ingrained into my mind. I used to have each freckle and scar memorized from hours of tracing my hands all over her. After all these years, I can't help but wonder if she has any additions for me to memorize. I can't help but question if she sounds the same when screaming my name. The last thought I want is her screaming another man's name. The image makes my blood boil, and I have the urge to punish each of them for believing they have the right.

"Can I read it?" I ask as I nod my head towards her laptop.

"Absolutely not!" Macy exclaims.

I can't help but laugh. "Why not? You do know the point of writing a book is to have others read it, right?"

"Yeah, well, maybe not yet. It's still new, and I don't have everything plotted out yet." She pulls her laptop closer to her chest, bringing my eye to her breasts being pushed up over her tank top.

"I'm here whenever you are ready. I will give you my honest opinion."

"That's exactly what I am worried about, Luke," she says, looking at me like she has so many questions running through her mind. The tension makes me squirm in the seat. Is she undressing me like I am undressing her? Does she have the same pull to me as I do her? I promised myself not to come down here tonight, but it was like my body and mind had a different plan. It kept pulling me closer to her, like a bug to a flame. I am not sure what I thought I would accomplish coming down here, but as I lay in my bed last night, only one thought came to my mind: Fight for her. Don't let her leave again without you.

"So why did you come sit on the couch? I thought you just needed to grab something." Macy breaks the silence, refusing to look me in the eyes.

"Oh, I got it," I say, showing her the screwdriver in my hand, "but I thought I would just take a seat and see how you were doing."

"I'm doing fine, Lucas. I unpacked some boxes earlier. I haven't come across our divorce papers yet, but when I do, I am going to ask you to sign them for me. Okay?"

A mischievous smirk spreads across my face. "So, I had an idea last night..." It is clear I am trying to escape this uncomfortable conversation, but I have been successful in not signing those documents for seven years, and momma didn't raise a quitter. There is no way I will surrender now.

"Lucas Wright!" she exclaimed with a look of disgust, gesturing towards my crotch. "You better not have thought those types of thoughts."

"Well, I didn't, but now you mention it, you still look drop-dead gorgeous," I say, taking my opportunities to tease her a little more. "I may be thinking about those," I say while waving my hand over her crotch with a sly smirk on my face, "thoughts later tonight."

With a rolling of her eyes, Macy scolds me. "You're incorrigible. Surely you can find at least one other girl to let you in their bed." Her words sting more than they should have, but I quickly hide the hurt on my face while deflecting with humor. Macy may be using words to attack me, but I know, deep down, that Macy truly isn't okay with the idea of me being with other women. She was always the jealous type, so I know she is just spewing words my way.

Despite my better judgment, this makes me chuckle out loud. "Fine, ok. I will try not to think about it." I concede before refocusing on the fundamental nature of why I was here. "But that isn't what I was going to say." I pause, looking around the cottage she is slowly making her own, the one I lived in for many years of my life. Nostalgia floods me as I think about how we would attempt to make dinner in the small kitchen only to set the fire alarms off. Or the time we had to run and hide inside here while a horrific hailstorm came through and we needed shelter.

"Go on a date with me," I blurt out eagerly. "Three dates, that's all I am asking for. Then, after those three dates, if you still want me to sign those papers, I will do it. No arguments from me." I know my request proves how desperate I am, but I am running out of options with Macy. Each of these dates will be a Hail Mary pass like in the last seconds of a football game- but the last chance to win her heart. I have to keep my mind focused on each Hail Mary pass like my life depends on it. I am not sure my heart will live through another round of Macy walking away from me. Self-preservation kicks in, but I have to make her see what I have always seen.

"Never going to happen, Luke. We are not together, nor should we be together." Macy laughs in disbelief. "I'll find the papers, and you will sign them. Even if I have to tie you up and use your hand to sign them myself."

"So, you still like to be tied up every now and then?" I can't resist teasing her one more time.

"Get out, Luke!" She says through laughter, attempting to shove me off the couch. I stand, but not before I look back down at her. Maybe it is my imagination, but I swear I can see a little wet spot seeping through her booty shorts. There's no doubt she was thinking about me tying her up just as much as I was. We may have only done it a few times, but each time was explosive, like the grand finale of a fireworks show. There is nothing like losing control of your own body and succumbing to pure pleasure.

For now, I relent and make my way to the door. Before closing the door behind me, I turn to face her, making sure she looks at my face as I make my declaration. "Three dates. I will see you tomorrow." She may not believe me, but I know I can prove to her she is wrong.

As soon as her plump lips form the word "no," I cut her off by shutting the door behind me. I wasn't shocked when she shot down my date idea, but I couldn't help the ting of disappointment. I want her to be as excited as I am about our dates, but maybe over time, she will meet me where I am. Either way, I walk to my truck with just enough hope to be dangerous. I remind myself how she was looking at me with a mixture of curiosity and hesitation. There was also the physical attraction radiating between us. It wasn't just the physical attraction that brought me to her, it was wanting her good and bad days and her tears and laughs. Initially, instead of focusing on the sexual tension between us, I am going to concentrate on rebuilding our chemistry. I believe if she can feel a connection again, she will be more likely to lower her walls.

***

Every day, for five days, I continue to take the familiar path to the cozy cottage where Macy resides. While I have made this walk countless times in the past, these last five days have felt like I was walking into war, a journey to redemption. It never fails when my heart starts racing, as if it is going to jump right out of my chest. The worst part is always when I have to raise my hand to knock on the door. Will there be a time when she ignores me? What if she gets tired of me interrupting her and takes a firm stance in shutting me out?

Like the night before, I hold a steaming cup of coffee in one hand and a fresh pastry from Redbirds in the other. Each day, I hand her a different kind of pastry, and she gives me annoyed feedback as if she already knows I will be back the following day. Her words tell me never to show up again, but her actions say another. I will do anything to get through the door each evening.

Over the last few nights, she has slowly opened up to me during our conversations. Not big things, like why she came back home or why she left me, but more about her hopes and dreams, her longing for her family and friends, and her ever-present wit shines bright just as it always has.

I also know while she behaves like she doesn't want me there, she has been leaving her door unlocked for my nightly visits. It isn't an open-door policy, but it is damn close, and I will take any win I can get. Luckily, I was able to stop the ruse. I left something inside the cottage. While my creativity was getting comical, it was getting tiresome.

Many nights, we would sit together, her writing and me reading the book I brought. She never went out of her way to communicate with me, but somehow, these mindless interactions added to my growing hope. My heart dangerously swells when I glance over at her to see her engrossed in her writing, both of us existing in the same room without fighting.

I even ran into her in town one more time since the middle-of-the-road incident from last week. This time, she didn't run away from me, but she didn't necessarily go out of her way to talk or even welcome me into the conversation. I'm sure the town is disappointed we are not giving them any hot gossip to spread. Maybe if we eventually come back together, Macy and I can plan some exaggerated scenes to keep the gossip hens at bay, buying us more time from when they start asking us how our relationship is going.

On this particular day, I find her sitting in her favorite chair with a book in hand. Memories flood me as I recollect the countless nights when we kept each other company as we read together. It was a comfortable pattern I would kill to experience again. In the past, she would spend countless hours sipping tea and getting lost in the pages of whatever novel caught her fancy. Books were always scattered around so effortlessly that I eventually built her a bookcase to leave right next to her.

As always, I offer her the cup of coffee I brought her from town. This time, as we trade mugs, we fumble and end up spilling the hot liquid on her lap and blanket. We both rush to grab napkins from the kitchenette, but as we do, our hands delicately graze each other. At that moment, a spark ignites between us, sending shivers down my spine. When I look into her eyes, they have widened, proving she felt the same spark.

We both freeze, standing chest-to-chest, trying to catch our breath. As soon as I see her eyes flick to my lips, all reservations have left me. Without thinking, I clear off the counter with one swift motion, lift her by the back of her thighs, and sit her on the counter. A small gasp fills the small cottage as I quickly spread her legs wide, taking the space between them. The warmth radiating through her thin fabric shorts only adds to my desires.

Breathly, Macy asks what I'm doing. She is unable to break her eyes from mine as she slides her hands up my arms and around my neck.

My answer is simple, "About to ask you if I can kiss you." Unable to distract my eyes elsewhere, I pull her closer to me. My words seem to never portray just how I feel when it comes to her, so I am hoping she sees my intentions and feelings in my eyes.

"I'm going to say no." Macy holds eye contact, but I can feel her hands gliding into the hair at the base of my neck and giving a slight tug.

"Then I better not ask." Her voice hitches as her lips slightly parted in anticipation. I slip my hand behind her neck and firmly press my lips to hers. She gives in with a small sigh and whimpers as she melts into my body. Her tongue meets mine as our kisses dance together in perfect harmony. I devour the sweet taste that has been absent from my life for so long.

As we break apart for air, Macy's lips find my neck, leaving kisses, licks, and nipping behind. I find myself growing harder with each touch, and without intention, I realize I have started rocking against her lips in search of friction and release from the tension building inside of me.

Without hesitation, Macy meets my movements with her own, riding the pleasure along with me as she pulls my lips back to hers. As our kisses and touches intensify, I am reminded how intoxicating she is to my system. The words she spews out of her mouth may be irritating as hell to me but having it open to devour is an entirely different high. I bite her pink, pouty lower lip, which trembles down her body, feeling her goosebumps dance across her arms.

Grabbing ahold of her legs and wrapping them around my torso, I carry her towards the couch before planting myself down. She continues to straddle me as I sit down, never breaking our lips from each other. My hands continue to explore each inch of her body before asking for permission to remove her shirt, and to my surprise, Macy nods silently in agreement. As soon as her top is out of the way, Macy reaches for mine.

As her lacy bra pushes up her peaked breasts and threatens to spill over the top, her beauty takes my breath away. I am struck by how beautiful she truly is. The feral desire to worship every inch of her consumes me as I run my rough hands over each curve. I slide my hand under her bra, grabbing and twisting her nipple. The guttural moan escaping from Macy encourages me to continue as it rings throughout the cottage.

I continue to deluge attention to her chest, teasing and licking her nipples until they are fully peaked and begging for more. Macy continues to rock over me, sliding her wet cunt over my rod, fully erected in my pants. I use my thumb to run lazy circles on her clit through the fabric of her shorts. I am teetering on the line of losing control, but I force myself not to sway. This woman has no idea what she does to me.

"Fuck, baby. Please. I need you," I whisper desperately, my hot breath caressing her peaked nipple.

"Prove it." Macy teases between moans.

Without indecision, I reach down to unbuckle my belt and unbutton and unzip my jeans, lifting her just enough to push her shorts to the side. The sight of her wet pussy takes my breath away while she slides down onto my fingers without prompting.

"You look stunned. Did you forget what I felt like?" She taunts, knowing full well I have not forgotten a single moment we have shared together.

A small laugh escapes my mouth. "No, baby, this is just my version of paradise, and I want to savor it. Every inch..." I say while sliding another finger to her hilt, slowly and deliberately moving inside of her. Each movement allows me to savor every inch of her warmth and wetness. I bend my fingers inside of her as she moans and writhes under my touch while I suck a nipple into my mouth. "Did you forget how well I can please you?" I tease.

"I am so close, Lucas. Please." She growls out a plea while riding my three fingers. I am close to finishing myself as pleasure courses through my body, but I don't want to rush this. I want to squeeze every drop from her perfect cunt as she comes undone above me.

Then she says it. Macy says the words to bring my world crashing down around me. "You know this means nothing, right? Just an orgasm. It doesn't mean I want to get back together."

I pull my fingers out of her, causing her to whimper in desperation. While I knew this wasn't my ticket to a relationship, I didn't want to be a toy she used and then threw away. Maybe meaningless sex can occur with those chaotic hook-ups, but it's not what we are, what we can be to each other. Macy is my sun and moon, and I can't fuck around with that. She will never be a blank face to me, especially in situations like these.

"What?" I angrily spit out. I hope she says she didn't mean the words how they came out, as if it doesn't mean something to her too. How could she see me as meaningless fun? Desperation and hurt coat me as I look back at her. My anger is rising with each passing breath.

"Luke..." she pleads.

I lick the fingers I just had in her, cleaning them as desire tries to creep back in. Her sweet taste makes me question what I am about to say for just a second before my heart takes over. "No Mace. That is not right. This is not how I see this, us. This isn't just fucking." My heart aches as I feel it starting to shatter within me. I am dancing on the line of anger and embarrassment. I may desire to rebuild our relationship through respect and love, but the desires between us tonight took over more than I should have allowed them to. I am ashamed of myself for letting it get to where it is right now. I can feel my cheeks heat, reddening from my shame and embarrassment. I start to feel as if having her on me is seeping too deep into my soul, beginning to feel claustrophobic within these cottage walls.

I wrap my arm around her waist to lift her off my lap and onto the couch next to me. I stand quickly to button my jeans while looking down at her sitting on the couch, breathing heavily and with confusion in her eyes. Defeat hits me as I fling my arms out while my voice gradually raises. "I can fuck anyone, but I have only ever worshipped you." I exhaustively express.

Unable to stand and look at her defeated eyes any longer, I turn to leave. "I'm going to go. I will see you tomorrow."

Before I shut the door, I remind her about the three dates I desperately want and let the door slam behind me. Sadness washes over me as all I can think about is how badly I want her back in my life. Each step towards my truck is painful, like walking in hardening cement, pulling me down with it. If I knew she wouldn't come outside, I think I would sit right here, on this dewy grass between the wildflowers, letting my heart and brain catch up with each other. My hands are shaking as I open the truck door, and tears threaten to release. I can't let her see me like that, with such passionate emotions, when she is so willing to push me to the side. I already embarrassed myself tonight, there is no need to add to it.

Chapter Seven

MACY

A **deep, exhausted ache pulses** through my body as I wake up this morning, memories of last night flooding back to me with each breath. As I groggily lay here, desperately trying to convince myself it was all just a dream - a dream any girl would like to live on their own. A dream inflamed me to my very core, but a dream, nonetheless. Unfortunately, it wasn't a dream. It was a real-life saga where I carelessly screwed up again.

I knew better than to let things escalate to that point with Lucas, but he was right there. As each breath hit my skin, his fire-filled gazes made heat roll up my spine, making me feel alive for the first time in years. His rough hands gripped my thighs and hoisted me up like I weighed nothing. As my legs wrapped around his waist, I was cast under his spell.

I knew better than to let it get that far, but he was just right there. I could feel his breathing chest hit mine, and I saw the fire in his eyes. The feel of his rough hands wrapping around my thighs and pulling me up made me feel more alive than I have in years. When I wrapped my legs around his waist, I knew I made it home. I could no longer deny the feeling that a piece of me had been missing since I left for New York. I'm not willing to say I have any emotional feelings for him but having our bodies that close to each other was a spark I couldn't put out.

I have tried to convince myself leaving was my only way to escape this small-town life. Convincing myself the bustling paved sidewalks of New York is where I belonged. I craved the ability to see the world beyond these endless fields and the same five faces at the bar every weekend. I didn't necessarily decide I was just going to leave in the middle of the night. Even I can admit the exit could have been much more graceful. You can tell yourself leaving is an act of bravery, but when you look back, it's easy to find leaving was just the act of running from your problems. There is no bravery in that.

Knowing Luke woke up to an empty bed after a night of mediocre arguing years ago fills me with guilt and regret. As I was doing it, I knew he deserved better. Better than waking up alone while all of my belongings were silently removed. It was the only way to make Luke let me go and to allow him to move on without me once I was out of the picture. And eventually, he would.

As much as it pains me to think about how I left Lucas, the pain stings worse when I think about doing those same actions to my parents. I'm not saying they weren't supportive of me because they always have been, but they would have called me on my bullshit. They would have forced me to be an adult about chasing my dreams. Since I couldn't tell them, I quietly saved money for months and continuously applied for jobs in New York. Once I was finally hired, I found a Craigslist ad for a tiny but expensive apartment and rented it, sight unseen. My start date for my job left me no choice but to leave quickly.

Strategically, the night before I left, I hastily packed my essentials in a suitcase hidden in the cleaning closet. I picked a fight with Luke the night before in hopes he would decide to go stay at his friend's house for the night, making my escape easier. The selfish thought causes a sarcastic chuckle to escape my lips in this small, lonely cottage. Selfishness was always my downfall and the true difference between Lucas and myself. He remained selfless while I was consumed by my own dreams and desires. Highlighting the stark difference that ultimately led to our separation.

As I made my way to the airport that morning, I couldn't help but wonder what his reaction would be when he woke up. Angry? Sad? Confused? A million thoughts consumed me as I thought out every reaction and the following aftermath. I only allowed myself to dwell on it until I stepped foot on the airplane. From then on, I had to leave it all behind and get ready to start my new life. I ignored every phone call, text message, and email from everyone back home for the first month. Even when Abi reached out, I couldn't bring myself to respond. The fear of being alone in the big city without a backup plan would consume me, and if I emotionally allowed myself to return to Texas, I knew I would.

So instead, I sent one text to my parents, assuring them I was safe and continuing silencing my wavering opinion on bravery. I immersed myself in my new job, making new friends, and finding my favorite pizza spot. Six months passed before I reached out to all of them. The first conversation with my parents was strained, each word they spoke was laced with anger and disappointment. The hurt they expressed regarding my secrecy and lack of communication with everyone at home was the hardest part. I never entirely gave anyone, including Abi, the reason I did it the way I did. Instead, I focused on my new life I was building in New York. I found the best divorce attorney I could afford and have been trying to divorce Lucas ever since.

"Enough reminiscing, Macy." I scold myself as I force myself out of bed to make coffee and find my phone. A small part of me hoped to see at least one missed call from Lucas. Hell, I would settle for one missed text, but instead, my screen is blank; only social media notifications are left mocking me. Maybe it really was a dream, I thought while trying to keep my hope at bay.

As I stumble down the short hallway and into the kitchen, the sight in front of me brings me right back to reality. Each item we scattered as the kitchen counter was wiped clear still lay on the floor. Spilled coffee was never wiped up, and my shirt from last night lays next to the couch, taunting me the most. "Nope, it wasn't a dream, Mace. This is your reality," I comment to myself with a growing ache in my heart.

I begin to pick up the scattered items, trying to deliver a facade of order back into the cottage. But my heart isn't ready to erase the evidence of our moment last night. For the first time in years, I sit on the ground and allow myself to break down and cry. Right there on the kitchen floor, I wept every tear I could muster, mourning everything I had lost. A path of destruction follows me wherever I go, proving I am just as lost today as I was seven years ago. Worse of all, the one man who promised he would never leave me has walked out on me without a second glance. As he looked into my eyes last night, the level of pain I thrust into his heart was much more significant than I wanted to believe. Any anger or reaction from Lucas was acceptable as I hadn't given him any answers all these years. Each point of anguish was my fault and is something I will have to live with forever. I deserve every ounce of retaliation, anger, and him walking out on me. Not a single action over the last seven years has given me any clout to be treated better, I can only thank myself.

The memory of Luke's eyes when I told him it was 'just an orgasm' haunts me. I knew he didn't see it this way, and deep down, neither did I. There was no other choice than to shut down both of our emotions. I didn't want to hurt him, but I also couldn't lead him on. As he stormed out of the cottage, a piece of me broke, making me unsure if I would ever be whole again. Why did I always choose to hurt him? Why am I still attempting to gaslight myself into believing I do it 'for him?' I'm not doing shit for him, and I need to remind myself of this.

As the door slammed shut behind him, the sound echoed throughout the empty cottage, and a shiver ran down my spine. I scrambled to grab my clothes scattered around me before hastily redressing and hurrying outside. By the time I stepped out on the porch, all I found was his disappearing taillights in the distance. He wouldn't have seen me and thought alone cuts me to my core. The pain intensifies as I realize this moment will haunt me for years to come. All he saw was me pushing him away, but deep down, I question why that was my first response. All he sees is me discarding our love like a piece of trash. This tall, charming man who once loved me unconditionally has witnessed me rejecting him again after all I have done is abandon him over the last seven years. He shouldn't expect anything more from me than disappointment.

I wish he would have turned back one last time before turning onto the road. If he did, he would have seen me standing outside, tears streaming down my face, silently begging him to come back. I hate the thought that Luke may believe I didn't chase after him. But I wasn't fast enough. I never am when it comes to us, no matter how hard I try.

Salty droplets of tears leave a trail on my skin as they stream down my cheeks. Heavy breaths echo around me as I gasp for air. I realize it has been a long time since I allowed myself to release all the emotions surrounding the ending of our relationship. I had no understanding of how much weight I was still carrying as an overwhelming release soak through my body. I can't ignore how much this release was needed anymore as all of my emotions we realized, smacking me in my face with intensity. The more I look back to when I left Luke all of those years ago, I have to admit to myself I never grieved the way I should have.

As any Southern woman knows, sometimes you have to just put your big girl panties on and move on. It is too late for regrets now. I jump into the shower to rinse off the stink from last night and pack up my laptop. Redbird's Cafe was the ideal place for me to set up shop and continue working on my writing. This cafe is mainly for the old men in town to catch up on the weekly gossip, but Abi mentioned they have the best coffee and free WIFI. I walk through the gossipers giving me side eyes as I head to the back corner, away from prying eyes and a free electrical outlet. Plus, I was sure Lucas would come looking for me if I stayed at the cottage.

The table I pick is a mix of old and new. You can tell it is newly built, but there is a rugged feel to it. This is not something you order from Amazon. This is a solid and high-end statement piece. It reminds me of the tables at Meryl's, but not exclusively identical. As I look around, it is clear they are not mass-produced. Each table seems just a little different. As I went to sit, I noticed that the chair must be made in the same place as it has the same rustic but new feel and is in the same wood tone. "This looks good enough for today, doesn't it, Mace?" I say to myself to pump myself up for the day ahead.

After getting settled at the table, my stomach releases a loud growl, reminding me I haven't eaten this morning. I grab a coffee and a pastry while old women and men from the community come up to me and express how 'pleased' they are I made it home. I'm sure they are trying to be friendly, but those fake smiles exasperate me, grating at my remaining patience. I finally make it back to my table as it becomes evident how rustic these tables and chairs are. The indents on the top cause my laptop to wobble every time I touch it. Frustrated, I trace my fingers along the weathered wood, feeling the round, seared indentions adorning each table and chair. These marks seem to be the calling card of the builder, but significant enough to make a mental note to inquire about them from Abi.

Chapter Eight

LUCAS

Despite my burning desire to feel Macy's body against mine, nothing about last night was solely for satisfying physical needs. Would I have enjoyed it? Absolutely. Would I have let it keep going? Without a doubt, yes. I also know there was no way I could continue if we weren't on the same page. I have loved Macy most of my life, but to hear her say those words to me shattered me in a way I never thought possible.

As I pulled out of Hamilton Ranch last night, I thought I saw the outline of Macy's shadow lurking on the front porch, but I convinced myself it was just wishful thinking, a mirage in the distance. It was physically painful to leave last night. Not because of the yearning physically but because I wanted to push the subject. Is this really how she felt? If so, how is that possible? We have spent our entire lives living and loving each other, and no amount of miles would convince me she moved on that easily. I wore down her defenses this past week, and I had no plan to slow down. We both needed space last night and that is what I gave us.

As much as I tried, I was never able to move on from Macy after she left. My friends, Abi, and hell, even her parents encouraged me to start dating again, but I couldn't bring myself to do it. Sure, I broke my year-long celibacy streak, but none of it was the same. Nothing gave me the hunger to chase the sated high with them.

The way I craved Macy was like a drug addict- always chasing the high and looking for my next hit. Every girl I brought home from Meryl's had one thing on their mind: breaking me and making me open to dating again. But every time, I had to convince them the only thing we were was a good fuck, and that was it. They never believed me until I asked them to leave my house or when I started getting dressed at theirs. My friends couldn't understand why I refused to snatch up one of the town's "unicorn" girls - you know, the perfect-on-paper girls who moved here after college or lived in the next town over. Each failed to give me the rush I was chasing.

So, I waited. Even when a new set of divorce papers were delivered to me to sign, they went straight to the trash.

Regardless, I waited.

As I have done many days before, I stop by the white cottage to drop off Macy's coffee. Today, though, I reach for the doorknob, and it is locked. I knock tentatively as dread spreads throughout me, making my mind race, searching for possibilities. Is this her way of dismissing me after last night? After a few seconds, I knock again, waiting to hear the click of unlocking the door, but it never comes. I am tempted to use my spare key, but after our disastrous night, I'm not sure that is a wise move. I defeatedly sit her coffee on the porch and head back towards the farm to finish up my chores. Later in the afternoon, I swing back by the cottage again, but there is still no answer, and her cold coffee still sits at my feet. Despite the gut-wrenching thought Macy could have run again, leaving her parents and myself behind, I decide to stop by Macy's parents' house to drop off a new display case I made for her mom. In an attempt to not ring any alarm bells, I ask Loch if he has seen his daughter today.

"I saw her leave towards town early this morning and haven't seen her since. Why do you ask?" Her father, Loch, responds.

"I, uh... stopped by to grab that hammer from the cottage, and she never answered. I wasn't sure if she was still boycotting me. I didn't want to walk in if she was there." I stumble in, saying as I look around their tiny kitchen, dodging eye contact to avoid him realizing something was problematic.

"I thought you got everything out of the ol' cottage?" Loch raises an eyebrow at me, silently challenging me when he knows I am lying.

I couldn't stop myself from smiling a small smile when I looked up at Loch. "I did. I forgot you knew that," I chuckled. I should have known better despite not looking him in the eyes. He would know my true intentions.

"I never forget anything, boy. You should know that." Loch's expression turns serious as he looked at me with sadness in his eyes. "Do you really think it is wise to keep chasing after that girl? I'm not going to tell you what to do, son, but having to pick you up from Meryl's when you were drinking your broken heart away is not something I want to do again." I know his words are sincere because he is the one who always elected to pick me up wherever I was. I also see him as my father figure and me as his son. I may not always like what he says to me, but I never doubt the truth behind them.

An emotional lump forms in my throat as I busy myself by filling my thermos with more coffee. "I don't know how to stop, sir." I know he can hear the anguish in my words, but as we have discussed many times over the years, Macy may be his offspring, but he understands her actions were unnecessary. I'm not blood to either of Macy's parents, but I am damn close.

Like the angel she is, Macy's mom, Tessa, walks into the kitchen while I sift through the homemade chocolate chip cookies in the peach-shaped cookie jar. The exact cookie jar Macy and I accidentally dropped when we were teenagers. Despite Tessa's consistent reminder to do rough house outside, we were wrestling when the cookie jar fell to the ground. There were no injury marks except one on the bottom back portion of the jar. I know Tessa has noticed it since then, but she never said anything. Whenever she was tired of fighting one of us, she would cradle the cookie jar in her hands, with the injury mark facing us. She was good at being passive-aggressive when she wanted to be, which always made us straighten up.

"What are you two talking about in here?" Her cheerfully soft voice fills the awkward silence.

"Lucas was just telling me how he forgot some tools in the cottage," Loch answers, his voice unamused by my antics.

"Hmm, Loch, I thought you grabbed everything before Mace moved in down there," Tessa repeats, mimicking Loch's comment, as she furrows her brows, looking puzzled. Her warm brown eyes, matching so closely to Macy's, stare back at me.

Intense emotions are brimming to escape subside within me. "Yeah, well, I was hoping neither of you remembered," I admit with a sheepish grin.

"Well, there was your first mistake. I know everything, Lucas Wright. Both of your lives would be easier if you just believed me." Tess teases me as she walks around her kitchen, cleaning up behind both Loch and myself.

Loch redirects the conversation, asking Tess about where Macy ran off to. "Tess, do you know where Mace went this morning?" Loch asks, giving it away I am the one to initially inquire about her with a quick glance towards me.

Knowing Loch is trying to point out again that I am looking for Macy, despite my better judgment, I know I have to step in. The last thing I need is for either of them to tell Macy I was looking for her. "Hey now, I just needed to grab a tool, I don't care where Macy went." I declare, throwing my hands in the air like I am on trial. We all know my words are a lie, and all three of us start chuckling.

"Not sure where she went, but I do know that girl doesn't go far from her coffee these days. If she isn't in the cottage, I would put money on her being at the coffee shop." Tessa replies.

"Well... that's good." I slowly interject, hoping for a smooth transition away from this topic. "But I'm not here to be nosy. Tess, I finished up your display cabinet. Do you want me to bring it in or sit it in the shop?"

"Oh, honey. You can just leave it in the shop. But make sure it's away from Loch's manure pile. I wouldn't be amused if I had to wipe some off of my new case." Tess instructs.

"Yes, ma'am," I say with a small smile as I start walking toward the front door. "Anything else y'all need from the feed store?"

"Grab me a slice of that lemon cake from the coffee shop." I hear Loch call out, but I can hear the humor in his voice.

"I won't be stopping by there, Loch." I tease as a smirk covers my face knowing damn well I will be bringing him a piece of cake back with me later today.

As I pull into a parking space in front of Redbird's Cafe, I notice Loch's old, beat-up truck.

With a deep breath, realization comes over me, knowing however our conversation goes will determine the fight I have moving forward. Stepping inside, I look around for Macy, but I don't see her right away. It isn't like there are a lot of people here since it is in the middle of the afternoon, but as I step up to the counter to order Loch's cake, something catches my eye. Hidden in the corner, I see Macy sitting with her laptop and at least three cups of coffee surrounding her.

"Can I get two slices of lemon cake, one in a to-go box and another of whatever Macy is drinking?" I ask the sulky teenager behind the counter. After she looks up from her phone, the realization that I am about to approach Macy stings her senses. I have no doubt that after I walk away, she will notify the gossip lines.

I hover over her, watching as she concentrates on her writing and has one of her plump lips between her teeth. The irony hits me as I note Macy has never been someone to hide from others, but here she is, doing exactly that. What happened to my sparkly, life-of-the-party wife to make her hideaway? "How am I supposed to bring you coffee if you're already sitting at a coffee shop?" I interrupt her thought, causing her to slightly jump in her seat.

"What is wrong with you, Lucas?" Macy slowly looks around while taking out her headphones, still shaken up by my presence. "I think, by me hiding from you, it's supposed to tell you not to bring me anything."

As soon as I take a seat across from Macy, the barista brings over another coffee for Macy. I catch the small eye roll followed by a faint smirk. Macy's delicate hands wrap around the hot mug sitting between us. The silence between us is palpable. I don't miss the nervous tick as her hands rub circles on the indent in the table. The small, mindless act causes a flashback to our previous life, where she would often struggle with anxiety. When we were teens, she would tap her pencil school desk until I was forced to reach over to stop her, placing my hand on hers. Macy has always had these ticks to help ground her to reality. The urge to grab her hand again, giving her comfort and calm her impulsive actions. "Why did you decide not to write at the cottage today?" I ask, breaking the quiescence.

"Hoping I wouldn't have to have the conversation with you that I know you want to have. It looks like my plan isn't going to work." Macy admits, still denying me any eye contact.

"It's not a big town, Mace," I mumble under my breath, still looking at her, waiting for the eye contact I want so desperately. Macy is the first to bend to the pressure and finally looks up at me. She goes to sit down her mug when it wobbles a little bit, almost toppling over.

"Can anyone tell me why this town only has tables with weird rings in them? It causes balancing problems." Macy loudly grunts, causing the barista to glance over at us. I push to ignore her question, wanting to distract her from other topics.

"Go on those three dates with me, Macy. That's all I am asking for." My plea is borderline pathetic. The words hang heavily in the air between us while the clanks of mugs ring out, and a fresh whiff of coffee is released with every new pour.

"So, we can have another repeat of last night? That turned out well." She teases, attempting to distract me from my mission.

"Last night wasn't a date. We got a little ahead of ourselves." The red sneaking up her neck and onto her cheeks proves she is thinking about the same thing I am. "I'm not asking you for any other reason than I want to spend time with you. I want you to see the man I am now." My heart clenches as she darts her eyes anywhere other than at me. There is so much she doesn't know about me- her family- than she thinks. The world moved on after she left it in ruins. Macy isn't doing herself any favors by not learning about those things while she is here.

A small laugh escapes her lips. "I think we both know putting us together isn't a good idea, Lucas. Please just let it go."

I stand, frustrated and disappointed, as I lightly hit my fist on the table. "I will see you tomorrow, Mace." I throw money on the table for my purchases and grab Loch's lemon cake before heading out the door.

As I push the door open, Macy's indignant voice yells after me, "Hey! Where are you going with my cake?"

Turning back with a smile, I reassure her, "Babe, this is for your dad. He would kill me if I didn't bring some back for him."

I hear her grunt of frustration as I continue out the door and make my way to my truck. Before putting my truck in reverse, I close my eyes and take a deep breath, laying my head against the headrest. This game of cat and mouse has been going on for days now. Continuous days of me trying to get those three dates. Days of watching her push me away. After days of me continuing to show up with hope, today is the day she lets me in, even if only a little bit.

My next four days look almost identical to this day. As promised, I stop by and give her a coffee refill, and try to make small talk long enough to get something in return. After realizing her eyes brighten when I ask about her writing, I quickly rush to this topic since this is the best way to get into her mind and have her talk back to me. The glimmer in her eye proves she loves writing, and this has been her outlet of release. Each day, before leaving the cottage, I always ask about our three dates. For four days, she says no. Personal self-preservation determined I will only allow myself to ask for seven days. After those seven days, I need to refocus my efforts. As I leave each day, it becomes more difficult to see this turning out positively. It feels like I am at the top of a rollercoaster, and it is about to take the plunge. What I don't know is if it will be a good or disastrous plunge. Seven days, Lucas. Continue for seven days.

Chapter Nine

LUCAS

watch the sun set on this Saturday evening as I head to Meryl's to meet some of my buddies in the local bar. The sound of country music drifts out onto the street as I make my way to the door. Tonight is their weekly country dancing night and the anticipation of the first sip of cold beer pulls me in. My buddies and I like to stop by this local hangout frequently, often catching up with each other from the week and watching our friends strike out when attempting to pick up someone to take home. The one thing often overlooked when you live in a small town, you have known 99 percent of the people in the bar since you were a toddler. I might think a girl is cute, but I also can't help myself from thinking about the time she accidentally shits her pants in middle school. Knowing those dark secrets about someone often leads to a pause in taking them out. That doesn't stop most of us, but it is one of those quirks you wish you could forget.

I step through the door and instantly see my group of friends sitting around some of those rugged tables in the corner. It isn't hard to find them quickly since they are often the rowdiest bunch. The smell of cigarette smoke and stale beer surrounds me as I take in the neon lights that have been hanging on the wall well before I started coming here. For a bar where you can no longer smoke in, the smell still seeps into your clothes and there is a permanent haze throughout the air. Each piece of charm adds to the intimate ambiance of the place, my shoes feel sticky as I stumble through the crowd.

All the regular guys are here tonight, and many have brought their wives and girlfriends along with them. I realize it will be a crazy night as I take in the amount of empty beer bottles already littering the small tables. Some of my friends live out of town, and I only get to spend time with them on nights like tonight, so I try to savor these moments as best I can. Since it is dance night, the bar has pushed the tables tightly against the wall. If you didn't arrive early like some of my friends, it would be considered standing room only.

I quickly order a beer while Angie stops by our table to get everyone their next round. In moments like this, not having a significant other hurt a little more. My friends are used to me being the odd man out, but since having Macy pushed back into the forethought of my mind and seeing her every day, it feels even more strange than usual.

"How is it going having Macy around, Luke?" My friend Hayes tries to shyly ask. I know him too well to know there is nothing shy about him. He is our local bull rider friend, often stopping through town before heading back on the road to chase his next ride. He grew up with our mutual friend Chase but quickly found his spot in our tight group.

I chase down the anguish clogged in my throat with another swig of my beer before I turn to look at Hayes. "I mean, it hasn't been easy," I reply with forced detachment. Internally, my heart swells at the thought of her while simultaneously remembering our awkward night at the cottage. The rumination of her automatically causes my pulse to race as my eyes pass over the crowd, wondering if she has stopped by the bar tonight. "But there is nothing I can do about it though."

"Man of so many words," snipes my friend, Ryder, slapping me on the shoulder and laughing. Little do they know, I have a lot to say - to Macy, first and foremost. Another negative of living in a small town and knowing my friends for decades is that each of them has seen me at my best and worst. Each one of them took care of me in the dark days after Macy left. Whether they were keeping me company, trying to set me up on dates, or just buying me a beer, each of them filled a void for a few months. They showed up for me, and I will never forget it. Despite all of those things, I am trying not to say too much about how I am feeling with Macy back in town. I wonder if they will be able to move past our history or if they will shun her from the group. Moving forward, I want to show a positive attitude about it in hopes my friends will follow behind me.

"Well, speak of the devil," Chase says suddenly, drawing our attention towards the entrance. I don't need to turn and look - there are only so many devils they could be referring to - but I do anyway. I see Abi walk in first and know Macy can't be too far behind her. My heart skips a beat when I catch sight of her. She's wearing cut-off shorts and a crop top that barely covers her midriff. I snake my eyes down her body as I see she has her old cowboy boots on. Those boots take me back to some of my best days and nights. I remember the Christmas she received this specific pair, being ecstatic about her shoe addition, before quickly getting them scratched up and running through a field a few weeks later.

Despite not needing boots for so many years, she walks in owning them. Abi scans the room until her eyes land on our friend group at the table. She grabs Macy by the hand, dragging her to us. Chase is standing, blocking her view from me, so it takes a moment for Macy to register I am also here. My heart starts racing even faster as she meets my eyes, my cock twitching enough to remind me how I am always pulled to her. My nervous energy regulates as I take another sip of my drink.

"Mace," I say softly, tipping my chin at her.

"Hey, Luke." She coolly replies, shifting her eyes from mine and flagging down the waitress.

My friends take in the exchange, sensing the tension, waiting to see who will make the first move. I can feel the beady eyes of the entire bar staring at us. I don't plan on giving them a show tonight, but as always, I will follow Macy's lead. Our eyes meet again as Strawberry Wine by Deana Carter comes across the speakers. A sly smile rises across her face as she turns to Chase, taunting me as she does.

"Chase, we should dance," Macy says quickly, grabbing his hand and pulling him to his feet. My friend looks at me with wide eyes, silently pleading for advice on how to handle the situation. I quickly nod my head and give the approval, knowing stopping them would only give the bar the spectacle they're pining for. I find it humorous as Chase is the last one to dance with someone he doesn't know, preferring to stand in the shadows until he gets to know someone.

As the music blares through the crowded bar, my best friend and my wife dance circles around the dance floor. Jealousy creeps over me as I watch Chase twirl my wife with ease. Despite knowing Chase would never lay a hand on her, anger pulses through me. I am sure she did a lot more with men while she was in New York, but seeing it flaunted in front of me causes me to see red. My fists clench tight and then loosen, trying to lessen the tension and calm myself. I drain the rest of my beer and catch myself squeezing the bottle so hard it threatens to shatter in my hand.

Hayes, Chase's childhood - and now my- friend, notices my agitation and quickly replaces my empty bottle with a fresh one. Without hesitation, I chug this beer as well. I follow Macy and Chase spinning around the dance floor, unable to look away, in fear another guy will take advantage of her. Watching her with my friend is one thing, but if I saw anyone else's hands wrapped around her, I wouldn't be able to control myself. Macy is shining like a beacon of light as she laughs and sways her hips in beat with the music. It may be my jealousy and rage, but I swear I see Chase pull her even closer to his body with each spin. The way her body rubs against his like she used to against mine, raising her arms in the air, showing the underside of her tits out of her cropped white shirt, snaps my last bit of control.

Without thinking, I stand and grab the nearest girl to me. "Bell, do you want to dance?" I ask with barely contained fury. There is no secret as to why I am asking her to dance, and I know there will not be any confusion about whether she is going home with me tonight. A small smile creeps across her face when she reaches her hand out.

"Of course, Luke. You are always my favorite dance partner." We make our way to the dance floor while I hear snickering coming from my friends at the table. I pull Bell close to my body as we dance. We move in sync to Boot Scootin' Boogie as I twirl Bell around like a top and even dip her part-way through. Bell laughs along with me, willing to give the rest of the bar a show with our dancing as I can feel Macy's jealous glare following us around the floor. Every time I look over at her, she plasters a fake smile to hide how much she hates I'm doing this.

As the next song starts, our motions slow to fit the new tempo of the song. Out of instinct, I pull Bell closer to me, but she quickly picks up on my hesitation. Bell understands I wanted to dance to get a reaction from Macy, so when she leans in and whispers to me, I am not surprised. "Luke, you don't have to hold me that close tonight." Her tentative smile confirms I picked the correct girl to dance with tonight.

"Why would you say that?" I ask through clenched teeth and frustration. I don't want to hurt her feelings, so I want her to be leery of my words. My heart starts to slow as the music and dancing start to calm me, but also because I know I am making Macy feel the same jealousy I have.

"Because I know I'm not the body you want embracing yours." Her words hit me like a punch to the gut, but before I can react, I feel Bell tug me closer to her. She is trying not to make this something it isn't, not to add any drama to the night. I decide to stop peacocking for Macy and focus on the friend who is doing me a favor right now.

Towards the end of the song, Bell rests her head gently on my shoulder when I see an unprecedented movement to my left. I see Macy storming out of the back door, going into the alley behind the bar. I look at Bell, and because she is such a good friend, Bell gives me a supportive smile and encourages me to follow after Macy. I push through the heavy, industrial back door and into the cooler night air that welcomes me, along with the strong smell of trash from the dumpsters in the alley.

The door slams behind me when Macy quickly turns towards me. I hear a guttural grunt come from her. "Please just leave me alone, Luke." She pleads. Her voice is aching, searching for air while also wanting to show how angry she is with me. As mad as she is at me, I am just as frustrated with her. Two can play this game.

Despite always striving to give her whatever she wants, that isn't an option tonight. "No."

"No? No?" Her voice is filled with exasperation and frustration, echoing in the empty alley as it slowly raises in pitch. Her anger is seeping from her, but I don't back down in my stance in front of her. Her hands are shaking, and her breaths are heavy as she starts to pace in front of me, pulling her hair off the back of her neck in an attempt to cool down.

"Ok, Luke, I give up. I am trying so hard to heal from my abrupt move from New York, trying to understand my new role as a 24/7 daughter again, and the last thing I want is to try and figure out what to do with you. And don't give me that look. You know what I am talking about. So, let's just get it all out right now." She pauses long enough to take a deep breath before continuing with a softer tone this time. I hesitantly take a small step closer to her, scared to move too fast and spook her. "Please don't get closer, ok? I'm sorry I left. I'm sorry I have put you in a position where you don't feel like you can move on because you never got closer. But Luke, I left you. This isn't up for debate. I don't want to be with you anymore. I have grown too much to come back to this life." The anguish in her voice tells me she means the words she is saying and truly just wants me to move on. "Please, I am begging you, just let me go. Let me live my life so you can go back to living yours." Her voice lowers to a whisper, cracking with emotion as she pleads to fill the empty space.

There are no words I can say to stop each gut punch she spews at me, so I opt to say nothing as I take a step closer to her when she turns to look down the alley for the influx of music seeping from the bar's front door. "And why are you still working at my parents? Can you tell me that? Are you so desperate to hold on to me you won't go find another job?" The deep sting of those words breaks me out of the concentration I have on her words, and I take a step closer. Does she really see herself on this high of a pedestal to think I am still pining after her, waiting for her to come running back to me? I may still deny her divorce papers, but I quit chasing after her before she returned home.

My emotions are stuck in my throat as I try to speak. I fear that my emotions will give away too much on how her words stung me, but I know we have to push forward. "No, Mace, I don't still work out there to hold on to you." My voice was barely above a whisper as I try to push forward. "If you would pull your head out of your ass for two minutes, you would see how completely different everything around here is. Have you considered asking your dad why he still lets me work out there? Have you asked your mom how she is keeping busy while your dad is out in the fields, and you are off in New York doing whatever in the hell you want?" My frustration is boiling under the surface as I clench my fists to channel my anger to anywhere other than spewing words. "Have you Mace? I am guessing no because if you did, you wouldn't be asking me these questions. If you did, you wouldn't be so damn confused by any of this. But you are so caught up in your own world that you have no idea. How you have been, and still are, acting is one of the most selfish things I have ever seen."

I stop talking and look away while I try to control my emotions coursing through me. My temper threatens to appear, but I force myself to stay calm so maybe she will listen to my words. When I look back at Macy, she is utterly speechless, just standing there looking at me; tears start to fill her caramel-colored eyes. The emotion hits me once again, but I refuse to hold back anymore. "The people in this town have always loved you." My voice cracks as I speak, the weight of my love for her almost too heavy to bear, shoving my hands through my hair just to give them something to do. "This includes me and while I wish I didn't, I can't help it." Tears start to leak and fall down her cheeks. I stop my urge to reach out and wipe them away. "I have always loved you and I don't know how to stop. I don't want to know how to stop. Don't you get it?" I could yell and fight with her, but that has never been the best way to communicate with Macy. She is stubborn, infuriating, and sometimes impossible to deal with, but I know her better than she knows herself. I can't yell at her, or I risk causing greater damage.

My heart races as I take a few steps closer to Macy, my hand pressing against the side of the bar as I bracket her to the wall. Her chest is rising and falling quickly as her breaths come in quick, shallow gasps escaping her, dancing on my face as I lean in close to her. The sweet, fresh aroma of flowers wafts through the air, combining a delicate rose and tangy citrus, creating a feminine and alluring fragrance. Her fragrance outshines the alley and trash smell as I attempt to memorize it for future reference. Her mouth is slightly parted as I look down and realize she is not wearing a bra under her short t-shirt. The cool breeze causes her nipples to pebble while my desire for her intensifies. This isn't why we both escaped into this alley, but my desires quickly push away our previous conversation.

I struggle to control myself, fighting the urge to slide my rough hand under her top and feel her peak. I could take her right here if I wanted to if she wanted me to. I step even closer, making our chests meet while still caging her in to not allow her to run again. Out of instinct, my hips shift up against hers, causing her breath to hitch as she looks at my lips. A low growl releases from me as Macy runs her tongue over her pink lips. Does she want me to kiss her? Her dilated eyes give away her arousal as her hips move forward to meet mine and grip my belt loops, holding me in place.

I know there is so much I need to say, let her know about, and clear the air, but the temptation is slowly winning me over. I could devour her right here and not care who saw or heard us. I could make her mine all over again. In a low, controlled voice, I finally firmly speak. "Let me make one thing clear, Mace. No matter what you do or say, nothing will deter me from fighting for you to the bitter end. You can say whatever you want." I place my palm on her cheek, cupping it in place but not missing how her head leaned into it. "Dance with whomever you would like, but at the end of the day, I know all you are trying to do is push me away. You hated seeing me dance with Bell just as much as I hated seeing Chase's hands all over you. You can pretend and say you weren't watching us over Chase's shoulder, I will say you are lying. I saw you, just like you saw me. You wouldn't have felt envious if you still didn't have a small portion of you that still cares about me and doesn't want to see me with anyone other than you."

"Luke, I didn't even pay att—" Macy starts to protest, but I cut her off by placing my finger on her lips, feeling how wet they are from her licking them.

"Bull shit, Mace. I saw you keep looking over at me when I was dancing with Bell. We both hated seeing the other one in someone's arms. So cut the shit and go on those three dates with me. Please, just give me this one thing." I plead, pushing my body next to hers, eliminating any remaining space between us.

The lust falls from her face, and her tough exterior resurfaces. She holds her eyes on mine, like trying to calculate what to say next. My eyes ping-pong between hers, waiting for her to give in. "Fine." Macy quickly blurts out, finally succumbing to my requests. She ducks under my arms, caging her to the wall, and starts walking away, searching for one last bit of defiance.

I can't help but chuckle to myself at her stubbornness. Fine, my ass, but I am not going to push my luck tonight. "I'll pick you up at 11:00 am on Saturday, wifey," I call after her.

She continues to walk away but throws up her middle finger in the air as a final goodbye. Damn, I could watch that ass walk away from me all day long. I love this woman even when she is feisty. And since now she has agreed to go on these dates, I can't wait to show her how much it means to me. Scrubbing my hand over my face, I turn back towards the door, returning to my friends.

Chapter Ten

MACY

As much as I tried to evade Lucas the past couple of days, he always seemed to find me.

A part of me believes my parents or people in town have been feeding him information on my whereabouts. I even sought refuge in the tiny bookshop, but he still managed to find me. The owner must have tipped him off since Luke still showed up with a coffee when outside drinks are usually not allowed, making it clear arrangements were made beforehand.

All this running and hiding didn't get me far since it is now Saturday and I find myself standing in front of the very limited wardrobe I brought from New York. Luke has refused to tell me what our plans are for our date, leaving me no other choice than to guess. Our date is during the day, which eliminates the little black dress I brought. I regret not going to Dallas earlier this week to find something more suitable for an 11:00 am date, but I just didn't have the desire to give Luke any hope with my efforts.

This dilemma only leaves one option. Texting Abi.

Me

> Abs, I have nothing to wear for my date with Luke. HELP !!

Abi

> Mace, you are one of the most stylish people I know. You have something.

> What about something like this?

Me

> Absolutely nothing like that.

Abi

> On my way.

Despite her distaste for exercise, Abi gets to the cottage quicker than expected. As she bursts through the front door, her voice echoes down the hall, already offering suggestions for hair and makeup. "Hey, Mace, I am here to rescue you. What was your first choice?" Abi's breath is heavy, a true sign of her lack of exercise.

"I was going to go with the black top and jeans. Would you know what we are doing today, Abs?" My curiosity spikes in hopes she spills the beans while distracted.

"I cannot confirm or deny anything, honey, but you can't wear this outfit." Panic flashes across her face as she starts making an inventory of the clothing I have strung around. My panic shows with the different piles of clothes, rapid heart rate, and sweat gathering under my hairline. "I brought you a few things I thought may work."

"So, you're really not going to tell me what I am doing today?" My anxiety increases with each passing refusal. Is she not telling me because she knows I will hate it, or will it make me question my wall of refusal to fall for Luke again?

Abi sighs as she hands me a stack of clothes. "Listen, I am Team Macy in this, but Luke did ask me what I thought of his date idea. You are going to love it, so you need to relax. It will be a very laidback day, so you need to dress accordingly." Her light squeeze on my arms gives me some release of emotion, but I also don't always love surprises.

"If it is as chill as you are acting like, can I just wear my sweats and a tank top?" Hope causes my voice to rise an octave as I stare down at my friend, taunting her in hopes I can get her to tell me what the plan is.

"Start with the pink dress. It will make your eyes do amazing things!" For the next 30 minutes I try on different outfits and Abi helps me perfect my makeup. She insists I bring something to pull my hair up with, leading me to believe we will be spending time outside. At this point, the fight to solve the mystery is worth more effort than I'm willing to give it. I succumb to Abi's directions with a smile on my face.

At 11:00 a.m., I hear a light knock on the cottage door. I open it to find Lucas standing there, holding a coffee for me and an empty vase. His eyes widen in surprise as he takes in my appearance, looking me up and down. His mouth is hanging open before he realizes it, and he closes it shut quickly. "You look beautiful, Macy. I brought these for you."

I may have taken note Luke is eyeing me up and down, but I am doing the same thing. My gaze roams over Luke's figure, taking in every detail of his appearance. Up until this point, I have not allowed my eyes to linger, but today I can't stop myself. He stands tall and strong, his broad shoulders and defined biceps straining against the fabric of his well-fitted green shirt. My eyes trace the vein lines running under his skin, pulsing under the surface of his skin, and I can't help myself when I lick my lips in anticipation. He is gorgeous and undeniably attractive in his own weathered way. Every shirt should be made to fit a man's shoulders and pecs the way Luke's does right now.

My eyes drag further down, catching sight of Lucas' tight jeans that I know, without a doubt, will be molded perfectly around his toned legs and ass. While I fight the urge to ogle him, feeling my cheeks starting to get hot, I insist I keep my looks in check, never looking too much. If I take him in the way I want, I'm not confident my willpower won't snap. As my eyes climb back to his face, I realize he now carries a devilish grin across his face.

Shaking myself back to reality, I turn my focus to the items he is holding in his hands. His firm, rough... okie dokie, Macy, get your mind out of the gutter. I clear my throat, my prompt to focus on the task at hand, drinking the coffee he brought me. "Thank you for bringing me a coffee this morning. I panicked since you didn't show up earlier today." I say gratefully, embarrassed. I admit how I anticipate his presence every day. "I do have to ask about the empty vase, though."

His mischievous grin widens as he replies, "Do you wish I stopped by earlier? I saw Abi's car out front and figured it was girl time. I will next time, though." He snaps a playful wink at me while he continues to tease me. "But you will understand the vase part later. Be patient."

"Presumptuous much?" I tease right back.

Luke doesn't miss a beat as he reminds me I have agreed to two more dates with him.

My eyes widen while my eyebrows shoot up in surprise. "What if this date goes horrible, and you realize it isn't worth it?"

"Yeah, that won't happen. Now, let's go." Luke confidently demands as he sits the vase on the entry table, grabbing my hand to drag me to his truck. As much as I don't want to admit to it, the moment he touches my hand, a spark snakes throughout my body. He has always been able to give me butterflies without trying, but I was hoping this would wear off over the years. I allow him to drag me to his truck as I break my personal promise to not look at his ass in these jeans. As soon as I do, I know I am in trouble. Seeing him like this makes me realize how much trouble I am in.

"How's your book coming along?" Luke finally breaks the silence on our way out of town, drumming his fingers on the steering wheel in time with the low music playing in the background.

"It's okay," I reply. I need some inspiration. I am stuck on a couple of chapters I don't know how to move past."

"What kind of a book is it?" he asks, but instead of believing he is trying to insert himself into my life, I can tell he is asking because he cares. It is refreshing and eases the tension I have been carrying. My shoulders lower as I take a deep breath, releasing it slowly.

"Isn't a type of book you would read," I say evasively, scared to share too much but embarrassed to write this kind of novel.

"How do you know? You sound pretty confident about my reading habits." Luke challenges me with a hint of amusement laced between his words.

"Let's just call it a hunch feeling," I assure him, humming along with the music.

I lean forward and turn up his radio, avoiding his question altogether. In the past, I have told people about my book, froze, and eventually abandoned it. This time, I am protecting it at all costs.

Before I know it, we turn off the two-lane highway and head towards Bryanville. "Is this where you kill me, Luke?"

A chuckle breaks across his lips, "No, babe. This is just where our date is." He flashes his smile at me while my core warms under his gaze. Plus, if you end up dead, I will too since I can't tell Loch I killed his daughter."

The truck rattles down the dusty road, sending plumes of dust flying behind us. I am instantly taken back to the many nights we would drive these same back roads, listening to country music and enjoying each other's company. I remember the way he would slide me over his bench seat in his handed-down truck and rest his palm on my thigh, tracing circles with his thumb.

We sit in silence for several minutes before Lucas finally turns off the dirt road to a vast field of bluebonnet flowers. As he shifts the truck into park, he swivels towards me and gives me a shy smile. Hesitation seeps from him as he calculates whether I will follow along with his plans. "Will you grab the blanket sitting on the floorboard for me? I will be right around to grab the door for you."

Before I can even respond, Luke is out of the door and opening the back door to retrieve a large basket and a bottle of wine. I quickly grab the blanket as he opens the door for me, offering his hand to help me out. "When did you become such a gentleman?" I tease.

"I never stopped, sweetheart," he mumbles as he leans in to give me a small peck to my temple. I try to slip my hand out of his, but instead, he tightens his grip before leading me into the field.

"Are we allowed to be out here?" I ask nervously, glancing around as if someone is about to jump out and kick us off their land.

"Yep! I talked to Mr. Benson to make sure." Luke assures me with a smile.

We walk hand-in-hand through the endless fields of Texas' State flower. Their delicate petals sway in the gentle breeze. The vibrant blue stretches out in front of us, creating a sea of color against the green grass. Many people assume Texas is not unique or pretty, and even those who live here forget since the beautiful parts seem to blend in and make them unnoticeable. For the first time since being back, I let myself appreciate what surrounds me. As much as I loved living in New York, there is no denying the natural charm surrounding us.

Lucas must have noticed my awe as he stops and allows us to take it in. My concentration is broken when I notice he is lightly rubbing his thumb over my knuckles as a sign of endearment. I give him a small smile, communicating to him we can keep walking. Eventually, we come across a clearing where a small pond lays still and serene.

"Will you lay down the blanket for us?" Lucas asks. As I look up at him, I can see the excitement in his eyes. In the moment, I consider this could have been our life, if I hadn't left. Despite the hell I have put him through, Luke still loves me with the same intensity as when we got married. Emotions threaten to clog my throat, so I quickly retrieve my hand back from him and lay out the blanket on the freshly cut grass.

"Here is the food if you want to start taking it out while I open up this bottle of wine," Luke speaks, breaking me from my thoughts.

"Of course, what did you pack us?" I quickly reach for the food, trying to shake off the weight of nostalgia.

"Just a couple of sandwiches, no mustard, I promise." He teases me with a small wink at me when I look up from the humor in his voice.

"At least your memory hasn't been replaced by those grey hairs you have coming in." I retort playfully. It is amazing to me that even after all this time, Luke still knows me so well - even how I prefer my food. I look up at him, noticing his hair is now longer than it was when we were together. Surprisingly, I love him with longer hair. His hair flips out under his hat, providing shade from the burning sun. It takes everything in me not to reach up and slide his locks through my fingers.

"Shit Mace." Luke chuckles as he shakes his head in disbelief. "I know you would have some grey hair, too, if you didn't stay so caught up on your hair appointments." I laugh because I know he's right. His veined, muscular arms trap my attention as he uncorks the wine bottle. It's even more clear the muscles you get in the gym are not the same you get working on a ranch every day of your life.

Lucas takes a seat next to me and pours both of us wine into the plastic cups. He inspects both sandwiches to make sure I get the one without mustard. He knows I hate it, but he loves that nasty stuff. I have accidentally bitten into one of his sandwiches too many times, leaving me hesitant to take a bite without his inspection first. Even when I was in New York, I always second-guessed biting into a sandwich with no Luke in sight.

We settle into a comfortable silence, watching the flowers sway in the breeze and watching fish jump in the nearby pond. I know there is so much Lucas wants to say, but he is trying to be patient, trying not to push me too fast. I slip my shoes off and allow my bare toes to sink in the blades of cool grass as I wiggle my toes, further grounding me to where I currently sit.

"Listen Luke," I begin, breaking the silence which has become deafening between us. "I think we need to talk about the other night." It's a conversation I don't necessarily want to have, but it is a conversation we have to have to move forward. He turns to face me while finishing his sandwich before responding, his tension skyrocketing as his posture tightens in front of me. Fear and hesitation flicker across his features as he waits for me to lead the conversation.

Chapter Eleven

LUCAS

"What about it?" I stammer, struggling to maintain eye contact with Macy. A piece of me is embarrassed I allowed myself to lose control and put us in that situation. Another part of me has considered she may also regret that night. Can she still be attracted to me, a rough-around-the-edges type of man? Did she just get caught up in the moment before realizing who she was doing this with? I understand I'm experiencing self-sabotage, but I can't ignore the possibilities. Am I a mistake in her eyes?

"I am really sorry about how everything happened. I didn't mean to make you upset." Macy diverts her eyes from me, her voice softer than usual. Her nervous tick of running her fingers through her hair being her dead giveaway.

"You didn't mean to make me upset, or you didn't mean to say how you felt out loud?" I can't help but push back a little, desperate for clarity about the night. It's exhausting constantly trying to decipher her words and actions and place them in my life accordingly. I wish I could dive into her mind and know, with certainty, where I stand with her. Is she putting up this facade to protect herself?

"Both?" Macy sighs before turning to make eye contact with me. "I never want to make you upset, but I also shouldn't have said it out loud. It was more of a reminder to myself to not get caught up in the moment. I knew you wouldn't see this situation the same as me- as just sex, so I shouldn't have led you on."

"Is that really how you saw the situation, Mace? You fell into our rhythm pretty well, if you ask me." I probe, keeping my eyes on her while I watch her squirm under my glaze, anxiously messing with the hem of her dress as the breeze sways her hair around.

"I want to. Being back here is so confusing for me, Luke." Her voice wavers with emotion as she continues. "It is like my brain and heart are not talking to each other, constantly fighting with how I should act. It would be so easy to fall back into all patterns and actions. Like nothing ever happened, you know?" She confesses with a small smirk and shrug of her shoulders. I struggle to determine whether her words and facial expressions are genuine or if she is telling me what she believes I want to hear.

"There is nothing we can do to change what happened." I declare, trying to keep my voice steady. "I, for one, wouldn't change any of it. Even if I could barely button my pants to walk out the door," my comment takes her by surprise as we both share a small laugh. "Our story has never been easy, and I don't think it ever will be. I will never regret you, Mace. I have tried to move past you, but I can't seem to get you out of my system." I reach over and slide a piece of her dark hair behind her ear, keeping it out of her face. "That's why I am pushing for these dates so heavily, not just for my sake, but also for yours. I told you I just want three, and I am going to stand by that Mace. I am hoping this gives me closure just as much as you do. This will all lead to a broken heart or love. There is no in-between for us. So, thank you for doing this for me."

We sit together in a long silence, both lost in our own thoughts. Suddenly, I hear a low sniffle. When I look up, Macy is watching the pond while a small tear slowly rolls down her cheek as she takes a deep breath. "Don't cry, Mace." Instincts kick in as I perch on my legs, cupping her face between my hands. I swipe my rough thumb across her cheek, wiping away the lone tear. Our gazes meet as we stare at each other, both of us feeling the weight of our complicated history between us.

"I really am sorry, Luke. I shouldn't have left that way all of those years ago, but I didn't know how else to do it. Nothing else would have worked. I wasn't brave enough to do it differently." I can feel the pain in each of her words. As much as I wished she would have approached me and been honest with me, I also know I would have physically stopped her from leaving me. The only way she would have left would have been under the cover of darkness.

I just wish she wouldn't have done that to her parents, though. Those people are some of the best people in the world and they deserved more than that. To know how much Loch's health has deteriorated in the last couple of years, having Macy around to help with mundane tasks would have done a lot of good. Both of her parents needed her support, but with her absence, they struggled to keep up. I did my best to care for them, but juggling the ranch and taking care of everything on my own was not easy. When Macy left, she left a Macy-shaped hole in their hearts.

"I know. And so do your parents and Abi. It was just difficult to go from having someone in our lives we saw and talked to daily to just being gone. Not taking our phone calls. We were just in shock... we weren't ready for you to disappear." I see her wipe away another tear as it rolls down her cheek. "Come on, let's go pick some flowers to fill your empty vase."

I stand up and put out my hand to help her up. She eyes me hesitantly before reaching for my hand. "Lucas! We can't pick these flowers. "She protests as I lead her towards the wildflowers blooming in the field. "It's illegal! Getting me thrown in jail is not the way to get me to stay in town." She alleges as her delicate hand wraps tighter and continues to follow me.

I shake my head because she is exhausting. She has no faith in me, and I swear it has been her life mission since the moment we met to test me. "Sweetheart, that is not true. It is a made-up law to keep kids off their property."

"How do you know? What if you're just saying it's a lie to trap me? My daddy would never forgive you if that was your plan." Her lingering small Texas twang has been peeking out when she gets irritated with me or insists on fighting with me. I won't mention it to her out of fear she will get spooked, but boy, do I find it sexy as hell.

"Do you want me to call Dillon Lang?" I challenge.

"Why in the hell would you call Dillon?" Her voice is rapidly increasing in volume, but humor dances across her eyes.

I can't help but pull her closer, my thumb unconsciously rubbing circles over the back of her hand. A habit I started when we were teenagers. It is funny how one seemingly casual comment can bring you back to reality so quickly. It is so easy to forget when someone leaves, they miss those little things that happen in their hometown. People grow, get new jobs, move, and die. These are all things that many don't think about until they are back and the new reality hits them. It stings that Macy has found herself in this situation, but hopefully, she is in town long enough to learn all these things. I can feel the emotion rising as this realization hits me, and I quickly turn to start walking away from Macy. "Did Abi not tell you he is now the county Sheriff?"

Her laugh fills the small field we are standing in and echoes off the pond behind us. "Mr. 'I bet I can take out 15 mailboxes before the cops figure out who is doing it, Dillon Lang?" Macy jokes, recalling a popular prank the kids in high school would do.

"The one and only, babe," I confirm, reaching my hand back towards Macy, and her hand slides in casually. I can't help but pull her closer and rub circles with my thumb over the back of her hand. It is a token of comfort I have always caught myself doing over the years. "The same Dillon Lang who wrote 'Getting away with murder isn't that hard.' in our high school yearbook."

The memory of Macy arguing with Dillon in the third hour about how he couldn't put this quote in the yearbook comes flooding back to me. "I can't believe I forgot he did that. I am running an ad in the newspaper for his next birthday." A loud chuckle escapes my mouth as I picture Dillon's face when he opens the newspaper that day. Our laughter and playful banter fill the air, providing a sense of familiarity and comfort as we continue walking through the field.

We continue picking bluebonnets for several minutes as the soft breeze carries the sweet smell of wildflowers around us. Once we gather enough flowers to fill up multiple vases, we head back to the picnic blanket and while I am not ready to leave, I also don't want to push her too far. I could sit and talk with her all day, but at some point, she is going to realize I have taken her entire day and will demand I return her back to the cottage. I would rather suggest leaving myself than have to hear her request to go home.

"Are you ready to head back so we can put these flowers into the vase?" I ask, trying to hide the hint of disappointment while fiddling with the long stems of the flowers I am holding. As I peer towards my wife, a surprised and disheartened look falls across her features. Her pink lips part while her eyes dart around my face, almost as if she is searching for something. I can't help but wonder if she was disappointed by my suggestion, enjoying our date today.

"Oh, yes, we probably should." She anxiously tugs her long hair behind her ears and starts walking away from me. I have to jog to keep up with her as she starts packing up the blanket and food. I notice how she quickly takes a swig of wine from the bottle before putting the cork back into it while turning and seeing me, watching her frantically move around the grassy area.

"We don't have to go if you don't want to." I blurt out, regretting the mention of leaving. "I didn't know how long you wanted to stay. I didn't want to take away too much of your time if you were ready to go." I reach out and grab her wrist since she won't look at me, nor will she acknowledge what I just said to her. "Mace, please look at me." I plead. Slowly, she turns to face me, a mix of hurt and defiance meeting me. Her eyes have tears peeking through, but her tight shoulders tell me she is fighting how hurt she is. I pull her closer to me and gently tip up her chin so she has no other choice than to look at me. "We don't have to go. I would prefer we didn't."

"Why would you suggest we do something you didn't want to do, Luke? These are your dates." Her look of frustration being spoken through her words and body language does not escape me.

I release a deep exhale, trying to remain calm. "I didn't want to hear you say you were ready to go back to the cottage. Okay? Self-protection kicks in after a while." I try to say this is in a nonchalant, uncommitted way hoping Macy admits she wants to stay, but I can hear my desperation.

My words seem to have no effect on her as she pulls away from me, heading towards the truck. Her warm, soft hands slip away from me, and the heat still lingers on my skin. The urge to reach back for her and pull her closer rages throughout my body. I hurry to beat Macy at the truck door, opening it for her, despite her ignoring the hand I try to lend her to help her into the cab of the truck. I close the door behind her and take my place behind the wheel. I can feel the tension as I start to drive us out of the field. I was hoping this would be a romantic date, but it appears I've only disappointed her again. I settle in my seat as I drive her home, hoping I can turn things around between us. With each mile, I consider slowing down or taking the long way back to her cottage just to buy more time with her.

slowing down or taking the long way back to her cottage just to buy more time with her.

Chapter Twelve

MACY

The silence in the cab of this truck is deafening. The unspoken tension is hard to ignore while I fiddle with the hem of my sundress. I was taken aback when Luke suggested we head back to town. Logically, I know spending less time with him is best, but it is hard to deny the joy I was feeling while with him. I haven't allowed myself to relax much in recent years, the hard streets of New York not allowing you to. My ex, James, was more worried about always being perfectly presentable, relaxing, or letting myself shine through, which was not something he appreciated. Even when we left work, our interactions often appear as if we were stuck surrounded by our work peers. I became so used to it that I forgot how tightly wound I was at all times. Today was completely different than that feeling.

Knowing Luke went out of his way to plan this date, working work with Abi so I dressed appropriately is one of the cutest and sweetest gestures a man has ever done. Each thought-provoking act pushed me to melt away any residual anger I had toward him. I got caught up in the magic of it all and found myself forgetting I wasn't supposed to enjoy my time with Luke. The wind not only made the bluebonnets sweep around us, but it started to feel as if it was sweeping away my hesitation.

A small voice inside me yearned to reach over, grab his shirt, and pull him to me, allowing me to kiss him one more time. Remembering our shared kiss a couple of nights ago only sends a surge of electricity through my body as I crave to taste his pillowy lips again and swallow his moans. As I take sneaky glances over at him, I notice his knuckles turning white from the strain of him gripping the steering wheel tightly. My initial instinct is to comfort him, letting myself reach out and touch him, letting him know I am here with him. Instead, I ground myself by feeling the wind fly through my hair as my arm falls out the window.

"Did you have fun today?" Luke breaks the silence when we are about halfway to town. He doesn't look at me, nor does he give any indication of how he feels about today.

"Yeah, it has been a while since I spent some time in the Texas air," I reply honestly. I truly don't know what to say or how to feel. "Luke, why are you still working for my parents?" I don't turn to look at him as I ask it for fear of what I would see when I did. Luke's answer had me on the edge of my seat, but it was when I felt him quickly pull over to the side of the dirt road and throw the truck in park takes me by surprise.

"What are you doing? Why did you pull over?" I demand as panic rises in my chest. Instead of answering, I can feel Luke turn to face me. "If you aren't going to answer me, take me home." I finally look over at Luke as I see him nervously fidgeting his pocketknife in his fingers. He's trying to portray confidence, but his body language betrays him, giving away he is just as nervous as I am about this conversation. "Answer me, Luke. Why?"

"I just am, Mace. I am not sure what you want me to say." His voice fades away, knowing I won't accept this answer.

"Don't lie to me, Lucas Wright. You forget I know all your tells. Why?" My anger grasps at me, trying to rise to the surface. I work to maintain it because I am so desperate for his answer, I don't want to make him fall silent.

"Macy, I can't have this conversation with you. Not here, not right now." Luke's eyes are pleading, his words are strained as he speaks. Looking at him, I know there is something he is trying to tell me through his eyes but can't say verbally. "There's so much you don't know about. Questions you haven't asked. Answers that aren't my place to answer."

"Being vague is not becoming, Luke. Not everything has to be mysterious and complicated. Sometimes things can just be." I pause to take a deep breath while breaking eye contact with Luke. My mind races with the missing words I don't speak. I slowly reach across the cab of the truck and slip my fingers through his, relishing in the warm, rough touch he gives me. His touch provides me comfort when I feel like he is the one who deserves the comfort. He lightly squeezes my hand, letting me know we are in this together. "Am I supposed to wait for you to randomly slip up and tell me why you refuse to move on from the farm?" I try not to let my frustration show, but I'm not successful. I crave his presence and honesty, but at the same time, it terrifies me.

A deep, corrupt chuckle comes from his chest, sending shivers down my spine. "You really think very little of me, don't you? No, Macy. I think you need to start spending more time with your parents.

Relearning who they are as people. Keep up better with Abi because a lot has happened with her, too. Things you don't know because sometimes..." He takes a deep breath as if grasping at the strength to calm down. It doesn't work and only makes me realize the emotion he has towards me and how each conversation is like daggers to his heart. "Sometimes people want to feel love from one another outside of them calling to talk about themselves. Sometimes, people don't have it in them to call and relive something painful with someone else. Especially when that person is emotionally checked out from the life they are living. So don't start attacking me when you haven't asked your parents this question." His disgust is evident by the shake of his head.

"You are just going to assume I don't give a shit about anyone? Do you really think I stopped caring about everyone? Maybe I am asking you because I don't have the nerve to ask my parents. Have you considered that?" Every word he says cuts right through to my core, but I know I deserve the pain. I wish people understood I do care, but I left, and now I don't know how I fit into each of their lives. He keeps acting like I am selfish for not asking questions, but what if I feel selfish by coming home and raising havoc with everyone?

He gives me one last tight squeeze of my hand as he straightens to the windshield and reaches to turn the key for the ignition. "Put your seatbelt on, Macy. It is time to take you home."

Chapter Thirteen

MACY

The truck rumbles down the country road, kicking up dust and gravel in its wake. As we approach my parents' house and the cottage behind it, my anxiety increases. I take a deep breath to steady my nerves as Lucas parks the truck and walks around to open my door. He offers his hand and at first, I hesitate to take it, but eventually give in to his silent request. A spark of electricity zips throughout my body as I let my hand linger longer than I should. As we make our way to the front door, I can't help but feel the familiar awkwardness of a first date. As much as I want to hate him, he can still give me butterflies, unlike any other man.

As we step onto the cottage's porch, I turn and face him, signaling I won't be asking him inside. But as I look at him and contemplate the awkwardness we are in, I can't help but start laughing.

"Why the fuck are you laughing at me right now?" Luke's face shows his annoyance at my reaction and the situation I keep putting us in.

"I'm not laughing at you, I'm laughing at this." I gesture my arms and spin while looking around. The flat Texas plains are dotted with cattle and horses grazing peacefully. The tall grass sways in the wind as I spot an old oil rig looming in the distance. It smells like the home I grew up loving but chose to run from when I felt like that was my only way. My parent's house sits across the field, and I can't help but wonder what secrets lie within its walls when I'm not around. The warm breeze makes my dress tousle in the air as Luke's glare softens just a small amount, resting on irritation and not anger.

"I'm nervous like this is our first date," I say anxiously, "but we have been together for almost twenty years, in one way or another."

"I'm hoping this is our second first date, sweetheart." A small, playful smirk crosses his lips as he calls me 'sweetheart,' a term of endearment used to make me melt into a puddle at his feet but now twinges on mockery. This man is mocking me, but he is too charming to care. I'm still mad at him, but ever since he told me maybe I should be asking the other people in my life what is going on I have had a haunting feeling he is right.

"How did we go from having a cute picnic, getting mad at each other, yelling in your truck, and now having this cute moment at my door?" I ask, trying to keep myself grounded in reality and not caught up in a fairy tale dream. I try to frame it as a tease, but Luke sees right through it.

"That's what we do, Macy. We always have." Lucas takes a step closer to me. His familiar warm, mahogany scent envelopes my surroundings, overwhelming me. I can feel his presence take hold of the air as I fight the urge to look up into his eyes, afraid of what they may say back to me. From the way his hands are balling up into fists at his side, I can tell he must be stopping himself from either punching the wall or reaching out to touch me. He chooses neither, showing remarkable self-control.

My gaze drops as I take in his dirty, used boots and then take stock of my own clean ones. It is like two worlds colliding- one that lives with the land and one that tries to run from it. I guess running doesn't get your boots dirty, I think, as the thought makes me laugh to myself. Despite the paths we took, we both ended up here, standing on this rugged porch, trying to figure out our lives in real time.

"Are you going to look at me or just admire how clean your boots are?" I can hear the humor laced in his voice and while I don't want to look up at him, my pride won't allow me not to.

As I lift my gaze up at him, I take in the new wrinkles popping up on both sides of his eyes. Luke's skin is a little more worn than when I left him so many years ago. I notice that while he used to stay clean-cut and religiously shaved his beard away, he now lets it sit for a few days at a time before just giving it a trim. And just my luck, he is sexier with scruff brushing against his jawline.

"Here I am. Looking at you. What else do you have to say?" It takes everything in me not to reach up and run my fingers through his short beard, imagining it brushing against my thighs. Heat flushes my cheeks, giving a hint of what I am thinking about.

Luke takes a small step closer to me, the toes of each of our boots almost touching. His eyes never stray away from mine as he exhales deeply, I can feel his warm breath envelop me. My heart starts racing as he bends down towards me, our faces almost touching. "We are going on our second date next Saturday. Be ready at noon."

Out of all the things I expected Luke to say, out of all of the things I wanted him to say to me, this wasn't one of them. Those wrinkles become deeper next to his eyes as his smile widens in his beard. He slowly takes a step away from me and gives me a wink as he turns to walk away from me. God, I love watching this man walk away from me.

"Wait, what? Where are you going?" I call after him.

"I don't kiss on the first date, sweetheart," he replies over his shoulder. "Like I said, be ready at noon on Saturday. I'll let Abi know what you need to wear." He shoots me a wave over his shoulder, never turning to look at me until he gets to his truck, opens the door, and climbs in.

The smile he gives me through his windshield as he puts his truck in reverse is enough to make my panties melt away. I stand with my mouth open, just looking around for Ashton Kutcher to jump out and tell me I was getting Punk'd as he finally hits the country road and heads toward his house.

As I make my way back into the cottage, I can't help but think that while our date didn't go perfectly, it certainly gave me inspiration for my book. My book has been silently taunting me for days, making my previous lack of inspiration much worse. After the way Luke looked at me as he drove away, I am definitely in the mood to write some steamy romance scenes... or maybe even two.

Chapter Fourteen

LUCAS

With any day spent away from the ranch, it feels like a week's worth of work piles up and needs my attention immediately. The new calf in the back pasture needs tending to, as we approach spring, the newest batch of crops must be planted soon. Tessa has mentioned needing a few shelves built before next weekend's Trade Days up North. With the thought of Tessa, worry creeps in for Tessa, Loch, and Macy. Macy may believe she understands the world circling her, but there is so much she's missed. It's not as if I never considered stopping my work at the ranch, but after Tessa and Loch took me in as a teenager, I couldn't imagine turning my back on them. They didn't have to take care of me the way they did, and I will spend the rest of my life paying them back. Growing up with an alcoholic father and an absent mom, I didn't have a basis for what a good, healthy relationship or hell, even a healthy person, looked like. Loch taught me how to work, and Tessa taught me how to love. I can't imagine where I would have ended up if they didn't save me.

I still remember the look on Macy's face when her parents told her I was moving in with them. Macy and I didn't run in the same circles, with her being one of the popular cheerleaders while I was the boy from the other side of town who couldn't afford to go to games or the movies like the other kids. Macy made the best of it, and eventually, we became best friends. While I had a crush on her from afar, when I moved in, that crush moved to love quickly, and there was nothing I could do to stop it.

I could never forget the first time we kissed in the back pasture, it took me over a year to gather the courage to make my move. Over time, Macy gradually started wanting to spend more time with me, and finally, one night, I got my chance to kiss her after getting stuck in the mud during a large rainstorm. We were both covered in mud and laughing together as we tried to get unstuck. The way she shined despite being sopping wet and covered in mud will be something I will never forget. Macy looked beautiful and as we walked back to the truck, Macy grabbed my hand and pulled me closer to her. In that moment, all I could think about was how badly I wanted to taste those plump, pink lips of hers before cradling her neck in my hands as I pulled her closer, making her body mold around mine, tipping her face closer to my own.

If I didn't think I loved her before that moment, I knew I did then. My world stopped as I forgot all about the mud in my boots, how Loch was going to yell at us for putting ruts in his field, and the complications that would come from my living with them. All that mattered was the feeling of wrapping my arm around her waist and the simple moan that escaped her. From that moment on, my world revolved around her, and I knew I would reroute my life to orbit around hers. And this is exactly what I did.

As I drive through the ranch gate, my heart races in anticipation, hoping I will get a glimpse of Macy outside the cottage. But as I scan the area, all I see is the familiar sight of the barn and the surrounding fields. With a sigh, I make my way to the barn to tend to the livestock. I tinker around the barn for a while before I realize I need an excuse to go to the cottage to see Macy. I haven't been able to stop thinking about her standing in front of me, nonverbally begging me to kiss her. I decide to use the same tactic that worked before- bringing her coffee and cake.

As I look down at myself, I see how dirty I have become in the couple of hours I have been working. I briefly consider going home to change before seeing Macy, but I quickly dismiss the idea, knowing I would just get dirty again on the farm. While I am stalling from knocking, I hear music playing from inside, causing me to knock a little louder than I normally would. I hear a faint "come in." I slowly open the door, my eyes falling on Macy as she's sitting on the couch with her hair pulled up in a messy bun and her bottom lip caught between her teeth. She seems lost in thought as she types at lightning speed. Dark circles envelop under her eyes and as I glance around, I see remnants of dinner and breakfast surrounding her, along with an empty wine bottle and a mug of coffee. I clear my throat to get her attention, holding out a fresh coffee and a slice of cake.

"Mace, don't take this the wrong way, but you look like hell. Did you go to bed last night?" A small amount of worry is laced within my words. I can't decide if this look is charming or concerning, either way, I hand her my treats.

A quick, deep breath puffs from her mouth, causing a loose piece of hair to fly up, just to fall right back into her eyes. "No," she admits. "I am regretting it now, though. Is that coffee for me or are you just teasing me?" Hope rises within her as I take a step toward her.

I playfully roll my eyes and shrink the space separating us. "I'm not sure how hot it is. I got it in town. Let me know if you want me to warm it up for you."

Macy assures me it is perfect and thanks me with a small smile. As we sit in comfortable silence, my mind races with thoughts of how to spend more time with her. My desire to spend more time with her fights the consideration that she may count it as our second date. "Um..." I lift my cowboy hat to rub my hand through my sweat-stained hair and replace it. "I have to go fix some fence. Do you want to go with me?"

My question is a clear surprise to Macy. "I would, but I have been making strong headway in my book. I'm kind of afraid to break my concentration too much." Shockingly, I believe her disappointment by the way she keeps looking between her computer and myself.

"Oh, so you are writing again." I tease. "That's good. You don't look so distraught over it like you did the last time I saw you trying to work on it."

Realization dawns on her what happened the last time I saw her, and a blush starts creeping up her neck and back down. "Yeah, well, I feel like I am in a better headspace than I was that day," she admits.

It feels like she is trying to have a different conversation with me with her eyes boring into my soul. A million conversations bounce between our glares. "Can I read it?" I finally ask.

Macy's face contorts in panic as she slams the laptop closed, shaking her head, attempting to shut me down. She stands from her seat and begins picking up her scattered pens, half-eaten food, and empty cups of coffee.

I can't help but give a small laugh, causing Macy to shoot a glare my way. "Now, I'm not a writer, but isn't people reading what you write the point of writing, Mace?" I ask, trying to diffuse her fear.

"Maybe for some authors, but I'm not a real one yet, so it doesn't count," Macy responds, flustered as she floats around the room, ignoring any glance at me while my eyes still follow her around the room.

I shake my head at her logic, arguing with her would just make her more flustered. Whatever delusional world she wants to live in, let her live in it. Instead, I try to change the subject. "Come on, let's go outside for a bit," I suggest, tipping my head towards the door. "Go grab those clean boots and put a smile on your beautiful face. I'm going to warm up your coffee." I say while I pick up her laptop and grab a couple of pillows from the couch.

Macy follows me to the door, still grumbling under her breath. "Where are you taking my laptop, Luke?" She says as she leaps towards me as if to save me from jumping off the Grand Canyon.

"I'm taking it out to the truck, along with these pillows. You can sit and watch me work like you used to." I lean down and peck a small, chaste kiss on her cheek as I walk around her, not missing the goosebumps rising on her arms.

I hear her snide remarks all the way down the hall while I shut the front door behind me. Within minutes, Macy is walking to the passenger side of the truck, and I can't help but look over at her and take her in. She looks effortlessly beautiful, not worrying about changing out of her ragged cut-off shorts and worn sweater. She couldn't leave without putting on her trusty boots, still a country girl at heart. With a hidden smirk, I put the truck in gear and drive us to the back fence so I can mend it.

****

I haven't worked on building fence with an audience in years. The last time Macy sat out here with me, talking my ear off, was the last time I didn't do this alone. It is a satisfying change of pace, having company as I worked.

At first, when Mace left, I found solace in being out here by myself. Just me, my thoughts, and getting my anger out with every push of the driver. That quickly grew tiresome, though, and before I knew it, I resorted to blasting music to distract myself and get through the mundane task. One can only spend so much time thinking and rethinking one's life before falling into a path of self-doubt and self-criticism. It wasn't until a couple of years later I started to convince myself otherwise. Both can be true, you can be a good human, just not be the person someone needs at the time.

But today was different. Today, I had my wife sitting in the bed of my truck, typing away. The clicking of her laptop keyboard was all the music I needed, providing the perfect background noise as I worked. Sometimes, when I went to get another post, we would make eye contact when I walked up to the bed of the truck. Other times, she would be too caught in the moment to look up at me. Her and those teeth biting into her bottom lip shoot a spark down my body every time I see it.

Last night, when I got home from work, my mind kept wandering with images of Macy's dress flowing in the wind, those secret looks she kept giving me, and even her flash of frustration she held on to while I drove us back to the cottage. Oddly, thinking about her irritation only turned me on more. Her actions were proof she still cared, even if it was something other than me.

As I gripped my hard rod, I couldn't help but picture her kneeling in front, gripping my thighs as she took each inch of me between those fiery lips. Would she still be able to take all of me or has this unique superpower left her abilities? The things I would do to find out.

Now, I keep seeing her biting her lip, only highlighting my shower tonight will include that look on her face as I picture being on top of her. I want to feel her raw, messy, quick. I want to feel her in the way I have for so many years. I need to have her wrapped around my cock, tightening with each thrust, arching her back off the mattress while taking her hard nipples into my mouth. My desire to hear her scream my name as I finish in her cannot be measured. I want to give her inspiration for her book firsthand.

As I finish driving the last fence post into the ground, exhaustion washes over me. Building a fence in the Texas sun used to not wear me out as quickly as it does now. Despite my fatigue, there's one thing that never changes - a quick jump into the cool water in the back pond just a few feet away from where I stand will immediately cool me down. All day, I have stolen quick glances her way, eating up how perfect she looks sitting there, each look feeds the desire I have for her. Before I turn to pack up the truck, I beg my medium-hard dick to calm down because the last thing I need is her to see and ask me about it.

With all my supplies gathered, I turn and make my way back to the truck. Luckily, Macy kept moving the truck down the fence line as I worked, shortening my walk to the truck. As I glance over at her, I see she has settled against the old hoodie and pillows I brought and has drifted off to sleep. The soft rise and fall of her chest and the relaxed expression on her face are a welcome sight after a long day of work.

I should have known she had fallen asleep when I no longer heard the constant typing on her laptop. But I must have been lost in my own thoughts, noting what I will be doing during my shower tonight to keep up with her typing. To see all the care and worry relaxed out of her face, her deep breathing overtaking her, I realize maybe I won't be thinking about her biting her lip later tonight instead, I'll picture how peaceful she looks right now.

I don't dare wake her up since I know she stayed up all night working on her book. I can't help feeling tempted to sneak at her laptop, reading part of her story. Despite the temptation, I know her trust is fragile right now, and I don't want to jeopardize any progress we've made in our relationship.

Instead, I start undressing myself - unbuttoning my shirt and throwing it on the tailgate, kicking off my boots, unbuckling my belt, and sliding out of my jeans, just leaving my boxers. I quickly slide my boots back on before taking them off again once I'm at the edge of the water. The cooler weather reminds me the best way to get in is to jump off the extended dock, quickly shocking my system without hesitation. As I dive deeper into the water, I let it wash away the sweat and dirt covering my body. As I resurface, I take a moment to simply float and admire the beauty of the fields and trees surrounding this piece of heaven.

"This is how you decide to wake me up? Telling me you are done working for the day by making me look at your abs?" Macy's voice startles me out of my serene state, momentarily forgetting she was in the truck. Turning around, I'm met with a sight that takes my breath away, a glow surrounds her and as she gleams with a radiant smile.

"You could always join me. Plus, sleeping this late in the day will make it difficult to go to sleep tonight." I taunt, noting how she is watching me as I paddle in the cool water.

"Like hell will I be joining you." Macy scoffs at my suggestion. "Do you have any idea how cold that water is going to be?"

"Actually, yes," I reply with a smirk. "Considering I'm already in it, I think I know more than you do. Now get in here." A few strides through the water and I reach the dock, looking up at Macy. "Join me, it will be fun." I continue with a pleading look into her eyes.

Macy pretends to contemplate for a moment before shrugging her shoulders and giving me a brighter smile. "Oh shucks, I forgot my swimming suit. I guess I can't..." The mischievous glint in her eyes encourages me. I want nothing more than to call her bluff.

"It's not like you have never skinny-dipped in here before. Now get your ass in here and prove to me you still have a little bit of country still in you." My dare doesn't go unannounced as she continues to glare at me, challenging me.

She knows I poked the bear and dared her to do something only a crazy person would do, the water is freezing, after all. She also knows she can either get in willingly or I will throw her in here myself. At least if she chose, she would have dry clothes to put back on afterward. Macy rolls her eyes as she turns to see my clothes sitting on the tailgate of my truck. She first pulls off her shirt, then her boots and shorts, before making me realize this whole time, she wasn't wearing any underwear. This makes my eyebrow quirk as she glances up, watching me trace each curve. Before I can realize what is going on from the naked-pussy-trance I am in, she reaches up and pops her bra off, letting it fall to the grass. "I swear, Lucas, if this is too cold, I will never let you live it down." A small yelp escapes her as she splashes into the pond, the cold water enveloping her.

Emerging from the water's surface, Macy's face is contorted in shock as she attempts to adjust to the frigid temperature. She slowly swims towards me, paddling in place while directly in front of me. "Cold?" I ask with a sly grin.

"You're an asshole! You know how cold it is!" Her words are laced with annoyance and amusement.

"But yet here you are, aren't you?" I retort playfully.

Macy swims closer, wrapping her lean legs around my waist. I managed to calm my body down from the first glance I gave her but feeling her pressed against me causing a fire to ignite through every inch of me. I pull her closer, wading in the water for both of us. Her shocked face interrupts my thoughts as she leans away from me, but not enough to escape my arms. "Why do I feel you having boxers on when I am completely naked, Lucas Wright?"

A low, boisterous laugh escapes me as the realization dawns on her. "I never once said I was naked, Mace." I pull her back, closer to my embrace, needing her to feel my hard body enveloping hers.

"But you told me to skinny dip..." Fake anger becomes her, trying to make me feel guilty about my actions. Then, a sly, devious smile appears on her face as I see fire in her eyes. Is her look from fire, anger, or arousal? She squeezes her legs tighter around me, making me strain against my boxers while she rubs up and down my length before leaning back. She floats on her back while her breasts break the surface of the water just enough to tease me and drive me wild. In response, I raise my arms to skim the water's surface, taunting her as if I'm going to touch her. I can't help but notice the sharp intake of breath as my hands come dangerously close to her body before pulling away. Without hesitation, I quickly submerge myself into the water, taking her with me.

As soon as we are beneath the surface, her arms wrap back around me, inching up to my neck while her fingers glide through my hair. Under the water, everything is different. We are not two adults living a complex, entangled life. We are simply two teenagers taking a quick dip in the pond after making love in the back of my truck. Underwater, she still loves me the way I will always love her. Underwater, I can almost feel her lips against my chest. Just the thought makes me want to stay submerged for eternity. I continue to rub my hands up and down her torso, taking in each piece of skin she will allow me to touch.

Eventually, I am forced to take us back to the surface. The water cascades off Macy's skin in rivulets. Something happens to me I wasn't expecting, not a physical reaction or even sexual, it's an emotional connection that reminds me of who we were and who we could still be. This moment reminds me who I need to be for her moving forward. So much has evolved in the last seven years. I have grown so much in that time, owning my own successful business which allows me more time on the ranch. The work on the ranch has become more of a hobby and less of a means of livelihood. I fight the desire to tell her these things and explain my inspiration behind it all. A piece of me knows if I tell her, she will make it about her. Not in a selfish way, but in a way that would make her think I did it for her. I did it for myself and my own growth and fulfillment, improving myself for Mace was an added bonus. I turned my passion into a business that started out small but now provides for me in ways not many understand. I did it for me when my world was so dark and scary after she left. The uncertainty of me working on the ranch led me to find my passion.

I'm caught up in my own thoughts when I feel a hurried movement as Macy dunks me back into the cold water. Just like earlier, I grab hold of her and take her with me. This time, I feel her trying to push away from me, releasing her toned legs from my waist. I let her go, but only because I have plans on my own.

As we both come up for air, I notice she is frantically swimming away from me. But not fast enough for me to not catch her. As I do, I dunk her into the water again. As she sinks down, her fingers entangle the elastic of my boxers, pushing them down with her. I feel them float away below me, adding the thrill of being naked in this pond with Macy. There is no more hiding just how hard I am for her.

"You little brat!" I groan playfully as she swims towards me again, attempting to dunk me once more. Our laughter fills the air while I pretend to swim away from her. This time, I am also skinny dipping with her, and I have no intention of playing nice. As she climbs onto my back, I grab her waist and pull her to my front. Using all my strength, I lift her above my head before throwing her into the air, causing a splash a few feet away from me. When she returns to me, a sense of familiarity washes over me. We've done this countless times before. I remember there is one thing she has to do before we get out.

"Go swing on the rope that goes over the pond." The familiar look of a dare crosses my features.

A quick laugh escapes her while she wraps her legs back around me. "You have lost your damn mind, Luke. I'm not going to climb a tree naked!"

"It's not like you haven't done it before... all of the time," I remind her with a smile. My lips graze my shoulder, and I resist the temptation to leave small kisses all over her body.

"Maybe, but now I'm older... and I try to pretend to be more mature."

"You're full of shit, Mace. Get up there." I whisper in her ear, squeezing her harder against my body, not leaving any room for wonder about how my body involuntarily responds to her.

"What do I get in return?" Macy intertwines her fingers back into my hair laying at the nape of my neck.

"Other than making me lose my boxers? What do you want?" I remind her of her previous discretion.

Her finger taps her lips, as if pretending to be contemplating this conundrum. "Hmm... what could a girl want?" She leans closer and grazes my ear with her lips before whispering her request. "If I climb up that damn tree naked, you have to sing a song at the upcoming Taylor Swift karaoke night." She gives my ear a small bite, making any remaining electricity shoot through me. My dick twitches, causing it to brush against her folds, reminding us both how much I want her.

"Oh, that's it?" We may be wadding in a cold pond, but I know her heat better than anyone. I don't press my luck and allow my body to do what it is begging to do. I give one baseless thrust between us, making her gasp and give me a whimper. This just proves our bodies still know each other intimately, even after all these years. If we get too close to one another, both will act accordingly. "Are you afraid I won't follow through?"

Macy never shifts her eyes from mine, her warm chocolate brown eyes keeping me locked in place. I can't help but admire the way her hips sway with each movement, her body a perfect silhouette against the setting sun. She snaps her lips closed, fighting the release of a moan. "Follow through with what?"

"My singing of course." I follow this up with a wink and coy smile before thrusting my hips one last time before submerging us one last time into the cold water. As we come back up, her laugh fills the area around us while swimming away.

"Fine Luke! You win, I will do it if you sing." She continues swimming until she reaches the dock ladder and I see her naked form glimmer as she pulls herself out of the water and walks away from me. "But when you do, I get to record it and hold it as ransom for the rest of your life."

'Rest of your life' shocks me as I take it in, a mixture of excitement and fear. This is really the first time she has talked about a future with me, and I will take every moment I can get from her. I watch as she climbs the tree, grabs onto the rope, and pushes herself off, swinging over the vast pond before falling in with a laugh.

We both swim towards the dock, but she pauses before climbing out. I was hoping I'd get a glance of her ass in my face, if only for a second, as she climbs out. "Get on up there Luke, I'm getting cold." Macy slaps my ass while I swim past her.

"Oh, so you want to see me naked?"

"What fun would it be if I didn't, Lucas?" We both laugh while we climb out. I jog over to my truck to retrieve my hoodie - the same one she snuggled up against earlier - and pull it over her head, shielding her from the cool evening air. She releases a small shiver as I pull her towards me to warm her up enough before she reaches down and grabs the rest of her clothes. I can't help but notice the way her eyes roam my naked body as I walk back to the truck.

After today, there may be no turning back.

I'm hopelessly in love with her.

Passionately and hopelessly.

Chapter Fifteen

MACY

can't help but wonder if Luke's constant reminders and urges to talk to those around me have finally sunk in the way he intended. The last few days have whisked past in a haze between the family gatherings and pouring myself into writing my book. I have periodically stopped by the library, where Abi works, to do small check-ins before leaving to keep the old women's pesky "shh" at bay. Today, when I stopped by, she was about to take her lunch, so I took this opportunity to drag her to Redbird's for a quick coffee and some old-fashioned girl talk.

Of course, she's prodding for more information about my first date with Luke. At first, I tried to gloss over the less pleasant sides of our date, but she could see right through me, and I ended up spilling every detail. I wouldn't say she took my side, nor would I say she took Luke's. Understandably, she secretly wants us to get back together if only so I move back, but I also know she will always present as Team Macy. As I tell her about us swimming together at the pond, she becomes overly giddy with the situation I have gotten myself into. Her squeal brings wandering eyes our way. Despite my attempts to deny it, I couldn't help but feel the same way about that day. The day felt like we were both back to just being Macy and Lucas. Two teenagers having fun and falling in love on the way. Dunking him as I did gives me too many flashbacks to the life I used to live, and there was no denying my hormonal urge fighting to take over when I had my legs wrapped around him.

The heat rose in my cheeks as I recount the experience with Abi. The blush betrays me as I tried to hide how much I enjoyed my time with Luke. I never wanted to let go and feeling him between me tested all my self-composure. I could also gauge he was having a hard time composing himself as well, which heightened all my senses. I knew if I gave a centimeter to him of a green flag to continue, he would have. I wanted it, but I can't have it. Isn't that the thing, though, sometimes, getting what you want is what destroys us.

Part of me wanted nothing more than to give into my primal urge surging between us and let him take me on the dock, splinters or prying eyes be damned. At that moment, nothing else mattered except feeling his heat close to me and feeling his touch dance over my skin. Reality intervened, and I knew we couldn't give in. It was endearing and sexy as hell to watch Luke struggle to keep his composure. For nostalgia and fantasy's sake, I wouldn't have denied us being in the bed of his old farm truck. Parents should never underestimate what teenagers are able to do when left alone. Hell, one time, we fucked in the cab of my dad's John Deere tractor on the side of the road. I will never look at a tractor the same again. These little secrets and moments add up and become part of who you are, and the thought terrifies me the most.

Abi pushes and prods, determined to coax out my feelings about that day, but those are feelings I am not ready to feel or acknowledge yet. Her smile grew wider with each blush creeping across my cheeks. Her smile was like a beacon guiding us to a dangerous precipice. We are driving directly towards a cliff I am not ready to fly off of. Abi was relentless, and at the end of the day, I could never escape her grasp.

Finally, I manage to steer the conversation away from Abi's questioning and into a safer topic - my writing. I hadn't been upfront with what I was working on, but she somehow knew exactly what I was doing in my spare time. A shiver of fear runs through me at the thought of failing again and having to face the humiliation. Then what? I wasn't purposely trying to hide it from her, but seeing the disappointment in your loved one's face when you tell them about this project you were bragging about is never coming to fruition. Experiencing this before carried enough humiliation to last a lifetime.

Despite my hesitation and fears, Abi provides invaluable insights into what readers are drawn to these days - their preferences in book covers, favorite tropes, etc. Working in the library, she has a wealth of knowledge that some pay thousands of dollars to hire someone to research these topics. Her daily interactions will greatly benefit me in this process.

I even found myself hostage to her and her chocolate cake I love so much. Somehow, Abi convinced me to hold my first book signing at the library, getting free publicity in return. I agreed, though secretly unsure if that day would ever come. Perhaps this agreement will push me to complete my book solely for a slice of her cake. One thing you can say about Abi, she knows how to corner you to do what she wants. I love her for it, even if she thrusts me in the hot seat.

When we step back out into the spring air, Abi grabs my hand and drags me to the center of our little town. The grassy area is picturesque, reminiscent of the white gazebo in Stars Hollow. It is easy to picture those quirky characters like Kirk, Taylor, and Miss Patty sitting on a bench, waving at the townsfolk who walk by. If only I could run into the movie-version of Jess Mariano, the moody writer we all know and love (if you know, you know).

Abi and I sit on the park bench, enjoying each other's company in comfortable silence. As much as I wanted to savor this peaceful moment, I knew I had to ask the difficult questions that have been weighing on my mind.

Taking a deep breath, I turn hesitantly to Abi. "Can we talk about something, Abs?" I catch myself biting my fingernails as I sit in fear of what she will tell me. Am I capable of handling what has to be said?

"Of course, babe," she replies, her expression shifting from curious to concerned. My nerves start to build, and I look away from her gaze to find the courage to continue. "What's going on?"

"When I left… I'm really sorry. I should have told you what was going on. I should have…" My words falter as Abi tries to interject, but I continue. "No, please let me finish. I may chicken out if I don't say it right now." I can see Abi nodding slightly out of the corner of my eye. "I'm really sorry I didn't come to you and tell you what was happening. I know you would have jumped in to help me in any way you could, but that was the biggest reason why I didn't say anything. I needed to do this on my own." A lump forms in my throat as my friend reaches over and takes my hands in hers. I truly don't deserve someone so good.

"You deserved so much more than how I acted afterward. It was unacceptable," I continue, fighting the trembling in my voice. "I ignored your phone calls. I even ignored my parents' and Luke's. I shouldn't have treated you that way. If anything, I should have at least called you back after a couple of weeks; instead, I disappeared." Tears well up in my eyes as I confess my regret and self-hatred. "You deserved so much more than what I gave, and for that, I will forever hate myself." I exhale a deep breath, a breath I didn't even realize I was holding.

"Can I speak now?" Abi asks. Partially joking, partially trying to read me and where I am with everything. I nod reluctantly, my heart is racing with anticipation and fear of what my friend may say. Her own breath releases a long sigh before she speaks. "At the time, I don't know if I understood why you did it. Why wouldn't you tell your best friend what was going on? It didn't make sense to me at the time, and I admittedly took it personally. All I saw was pure devastation, which spread overnight and was a blow to all of our lives. Nobody knew how to handle it, and we were... we were lost, Mace."

I reach over and grab her hand, squeezing it gently as my form of approval continues. "After a while, I had to move on with this giant, Macy-sized hole in my life. I didn't want to, but you wouldn't call us back. Eventually, life went back to the new normal while learning to forgive you. I eventually came to believe you had your reasons, and you would tell me them when you were ready." Abi continued, her gaze shifting from me like I had any right to be upset by what she was saying. I deserved this and so much more from her based on how I reacted.

Abi looks over at me with tears brimming in her eyes. "I loved you, Mace, and I still do. I knew you would eventually let me in. Can this be the start of fixing this?"

I nod silently, knowing it is time to finally tell someone the whole truth.

"Lucas was working so much and then when he would get off, he was too exhausted to spend any time with me. He had always been there, you know." I begin, my voice trembles as the memories flood back. "I felt like he was trying to distance himself from me, and the only thing I could think of was to hunker down and protect myself. We talked about trying to get pregnant, and while I agreed, I couldn't stop thinking about how I would feel like a single mom because Luke was never around. I couldn't fathom bringing a kid into the world and having their dad not around. Of course, I tried talking to him about it, but he only gave me excuses and said he was trying his best. And maybe he was doing his best, but I couldn't see it. Or maybe I didn't want to see it because deep down, I knew something wasn't right."

Tears stream down my face as Abi reaches over to wipe them away. "I knew if I told anyone, they would dismiss it as me being paranoid or looking for problems. I truly wasn't. So, I decided I had to leave. From that point forward, everything I did was to prepare for my move. All the money I was saving, all the conversations I knew would soon be our last for a while. All of it." Getting this off my chest while telling Abi the truth released a weight I held heavily on my chest.

"How did it go once you got to New York?" Abi asks, her voice filled with empathy.

A wet laugh escapes me. "Horribly. I was miserable from the moment I arrived and realized I made a huge mistake. I didn't fit in there at all, but I was so deep into my decision I was too scared to come home and admit defeat. You should have seen the horrific and overpriced apartment I was living in. It was disgusting." I add, attempting to lighten our heavy conversation. Both share a smile with each other as I have a flashback to the bugs coating each surface.

"Then, one thing led to another, and before I knew it, I had made a new life for myself there - friends, a new boyfriend, a job... none of which matched who I was back in Texas. I didn't want the old me, but I craved any sense of familiarity. After a while, I created this new persona I could hide behind. Everything fell apart in an instant, and, well, now I'm back home."

Abi's voice is gentle and understanding as she warily asks about my return plans. I can tell she didn't want to ask the question, but it was an answer I would need to figure out sooner rather than later. I lean back and take in the familiar sights and sounds of home, the rustling of leaves, the distant sound of children playing in the background, and the comforting smell of freshly cut grass. Both try not to meet the other's gaze.

"Honestly, I don't know. I convinced myself everything would be the same as it was when I left. I am quickly realizing that's the furthest from the truth. What did I miss from your life while being gone?" I can feel a twinge of sadness in my chest as I think about what I missed during my time away.

It is Abi's turn to laugh as she places her head on my shoulder. "You didn't miss much, the same shit, different day. I dated a couple of guys, none too serious, obviously," she says while showing me her empty ring finger and shaking her head with a wry smile. "I did think this one guy, Mark, was going to turn into something, but he had a wife and a couple of kids in a different state. I dropped him immediately, but boy, did he try to get me to stay."

She releases another deep exhale, almost as if she is trying to exhale the memories from her brain. As she continues, Abi has more enthusiasm in her voice. "I got my job at the library and kind of love it. I have really tried to focus more on community events and getting school-aged kids involved. I have even started a book club not only for the adults in town but also for the high school kids. To be honest, the one with the kids is my favorite." She says with a sparkle in her eye. "So much is new to them, they aren't jaded by the real world yet. They still believe in fairy tales, and it takes me back to a simpler time."

I smile, knowing how well-suited Abi is for motherhood. She has always been at ease when surrounded by kids. "Do you have a book club I could join? You know, with my type of books?" We both know what that means, but the exaggerated wink really sets it in stone.

Abi laughs and playfully nudges my arm. "Of course, I do, but your mom comes to it sometimes, so maybe we wait until it is a book I know she won't read."

"Bluck, ew, Abi, I don't want to think about my mom reading those books!" The thought of my mom reading those books makes me uncomfortable. Abi's grin becomes mischievous.

"Well, she does. It does make seeing your dad's happiness the following day feel a little different." We both fill the courtyard with laughter as I mock throwing up.

"Have you had these conversations with your parents yet? With Luke?" My friend asks as our laughter dies.

"I have tried to ask Luke my questions, but he always clams up and tells me I need to talk to you and my parents. He also won't give me too much about what has been going on with him, outside of how much he still wants me and how he is convinced these dates are going to bring us back together." I say while trying to contemplate what this could all mean.

"Do you think his plan is working?" Abi probes, raising an eyebrow.

"I wouldn't say it's working, but our first date wasn't terrible, and we have our second this weekend. By the way, Luke said to ask you what I should wear." I roll my eyes, knowing Luke has enlisted Abi's help.

Abi suddenly sits straighter, crossing her legs under her with a sly smile on her face. "Oh, I am glad you are asking. I have been thinking about this. You need to wear jeans, a cute sandal, a small heel will be fine, and the purple v-neck top you wore the other day. It would be perfect."

Curiosity gets the best of me, and I can't resist asking, "If I begged, would you tell me what we are doing?" I lean against her, resisting the urge to lay my head on her shoulder.

"Not a chance in hell would I tell you, but you will love it. I'm not sure if you have ever done this before unless you did it in New York, but either way, I can't wait to see what Luke pulls out of his hat for this date idea."

My heart clenches as I brainstorm on what this date will entail. "Now I'm more scared than I was before asking you," I admit, my voice betraying my growing nerves.

Mischief covers her face while her eyes sparkle with delight. "No Sweets, you will love it. But I do have one request." She states while squeezing my hand again.

"Do I even want to know?" I ask cautiously. Dread fills my belly as I see her smile grow.

"Will you just give him one kiss afterward? That man needs something exciting to think about," Abi pleads.

I release what could be the loudest groan in protest, not realizing she would push me to this topic. "I will not be kissing him, sorry Abs."

"You don't have to use tongue, a nice, small peck would go a long way." Abi pouts, bringing her hands to her chest, pleading with me.

"I won't even commit to a hug, so I think committing to a kiss feels unrealistic." I protest.

"You know, you never were the fun one out of the two of us." She teases while wagging her finger at me and standing up. "Okay, I better get back to work. Miss Angela gets grumpy if I am gone too long, and she has to actually speak to people." She shakes her head in amusement while leaning down and kissing my cheek. "What is the point of working with the public if you don't actually like the public?" Abi turns to walk away from me while laughing at herself.

"Oh, Abi, I have one more question," I yell out as she is walking away from me.

"Give it to me!" She urges, turning to look at me.

"Why is Luke still working for my parents?" The smile fades from her features as she stops in her tracks.

"Babe, that is something you need to talk to your parents about. I can't be the one to answer that." She says gently, but I can see the pain in her eyes.

"Ugh! Luke keeps telling me the same thing." A dramatic whimper escapes me as I fling my head back, resting it on the back of the bench.

"Then maybe that is what you should be doing." She suggests with a sly tilt of her eyebrow, communicating she would not budge on her response. I flash her a quick middle finger before she turns and walks towards the library, laughter following her.

Chapter Sixteen

LUCAS

The sun rose early on Saturday morning, a warm glow covered the ranch as I rushed through my chores. The scent of hay and sweat filled the air as I worked, already anticipating the plans I had for the day. Since I am on a time crunch this morning, I have no choice but to use the stall shower to bathe myself as quickly as possible. Ideally, I would have had time to go back to my house for this shower, but I figured there wouldn't be time to do that, so I planned ahead. Since I had been working this morning, my work gave my mind a break from my increasing nerves about our date.

I couldn't shake off the feeling Tessa and Loch knew what was going on. Tessa was oddly insistent I didn't help Loch load the trailer for their trip to Trade Days. She even stopped me from working late to fix a display case she accidentally broke. When I pressed the subject, she gave me a knowing smile and told me she didn't want me too tired for the day ahead.

Pulling up to the cottage, I glare through the front windows, seeing Macy pacing back and forth in the living room. She looks nervous as she fiddles with the pinky ring she is wearing, still stunning in her tight jeans and v-neck shirt. I lightly knock on the door, wondering if Macy will end up backing out of our date.

With a quick swing of the door, Macy stands there, glaring at me. I can't help but to take in her beauty. We both seem jittery despite already fulfilling the first date of three we agreed upon. I raise a hand to graze the back of my neck while she reaches up and pushes a piece of hair behind her ear, still taking me in. When she asks if her outfit was okay, I quickly reassured her how beautiful she looked.

I reach my hand out, wondering if she will lace her fingers between them. As she does, I lead us both towards my truck while I open the door and help her in the passenger seat. As I put the truck in reverse, her stare catches my eye. "Why are you looking at me like that, Mace?" I ask, trying to smile to comfort her.

"Because I think I like the version of Lucas with facial hair. It suits you." Her cheeks turn a shade of pink as if she was embarrassed, I caught her watching me. Her smile grows wider as I reach across and squeeze her hand, causing my smile to spread as well. If this woman likes my facial hair, then I am never getting rid of it.

"When are you telling me where we are going?" Macy asks, breaking the silence.

"Ah, that. Well, first, we are going to go grab lunch at the new Mexican restaurant outside of town. What happens after lunch, I can't tell you yet." She shakes her head next to me, but I can't tell if it is out of annoyance or excitement.

As we leave lunch, our stomachs are full, and our spirits are high after seeing Mrs. Kendall get day drunk with her daughter-in-law. Luckily, her husband, the local sheriff, was able to come pick them both up before things got out of hand. If he hadn't Macy and I were going to have to escort them home, something neither of us wanted to do. As we drive down Main Street, we pass by the newly renovated storefronts now filled with various restaurants, shops, and boutiques. It's a far cry from the dilapidated buildings that used to line this road before an out-of-towner bought the whole block. While there were mixed feelings about this, no one can deny the bustling energy it brought to town.

"Remember when we used to cruise down this street every Friday and Saturday night?" I ask Macy as we park in front of a Paint-Your-Own-Pottery studio. "Now, there would be too many people sitting outside to witness the hell we got into."

"Of course," she replies with a fond smile. "Who would have thought this is the same road? It has so much life in it now. Can you imagine all these people watching us cause chaos down here? They would have run us all out of town." A small giggle comes from her, likely picturing what they would have looked like. As teens, our friend group loved to spend our nights lining the streets, walking down the line, talking to friends, and stealing beers as the police drove circles around us. Looking back, we had no idea how great our lives were, too busy planning what we would do once we graduated high school.

I help Macy out of the truck and guide her inside the pottery studio. I can't help but take in her rush of excitement while she looks around the small room. "Oh, I have never done this; I am so excited!" she exclaims giddily.

"That's what I was hoping for, Mace," I whisper in her ear, causing goosebumps to rise on her skin. I'm going to think about those goosebumps for a long time.

Maggie, the studio owner, appears as if summoned by our conversation. She greets us with a small wave before locking the door behind us and explaining the steps in painting our own piece of pottery.

Once she is done with her speech, Macy and I walk around the room, looking for the perfect piece to paint. "I had this idea," I suggest nervously. "We don't have to do it, but I would like us to." As soon as I came up with the idea, I knew it may be the perfect icebreaker to tell her about something that happened while she was away.

Macy looks up at me, patiently waiting for me to finish my thought. "What if we both chose a piece and painted a memory we have with each other? Something to keep in mind, but still loose enough to paint what we want." Macy stares at me with a neutral face. In a panic, I continue to ramble about ideas before I feel her petite hand land on my arm.

"Luke, please stop rambling, it's just me." I can hear the tease in her voice as she watches me flounder in front of her. "Anyways, I will play along with this idea, despite me knowing you are fishing for compliments from me..."

My gaze shoots to her as she speaks, my heart racing at her unexpected words. This wasn't my plan - I only wanted to force her to think about a happy memory with both of us. But before I can stop her, Macy bursts into laughter and grabs my hand. She pulls me around the room, looking at the pottery.

"I'm kidding, Luke," she says between giggles. "You looked so flustered, I couldn't help but mess with you." Rolling my eyes playfully and slide my hand around her waist as I follow her around the room like a lost puppy.

Together, we decide to paint mugs. I chose a more traditional but tall mug, while she chose a fat-mouthed mug that could only be held with two hands. Even our mug choices are vastly different, reflecting our individual personalities. As we paint for hours on end, we talk about everything from memories and dreams to gossip I can share with her, knowing Maggie is still on the other side of the wall. It was nice since we were both relaxed being there in each other's company. No tension. No discussing how we went wrong or what I hope happens at the end of these three dates. We were just ourselves... simply existing.

"Ugh! Did this town decide to make a mandate to only have uneven tables in this town?" Macy exclaims, trying to balance her cup on the wobbly wooden table. Her tone makes it apparent this is something she has recognized before.

"No, Mace," I say, shaking my head with a smile. "You just keep putting it in the notch on the edge there." I try to turn her focus to the round circle, but she waves me off, assuming I am making fun of her.

Macy shoots me a playful pout before looking around the studio before rubbing her fingers over the ring embedded in the table. "Are the rings part of the new mandate as well?"

"There is no mandate, Macy." A large smile crosses my face while I shake my head, unable to keep the amusement out of my voice. This girl is so close to one of the town's biggest secrets but has no idea.

We continue talking about random topics as we continue to paint. I can't help but notice how her laughter fills the space, a sound I haven't heard in a long time.

"Ok, I think I am done," Macy declares, leaning back and crossing her arms. This small movement causes her tits to pop up from the v-neck in her shirt. I remember Abi telling me she told her to wear this shirt, and now I understand why. Abi wanted to torture me, and her plan flashes right back at me.

A few moments later, I carefully sit down my finished mug, placing it back onto the wooden table with a quiet clank. The used brushes soak in the jar of water, the vibrant colors muting and blending together. "Ok, on three, let's show each other what we chose."

A small nod from Macy prompts me to begin counting down. "One... two... three." We both turn our mugs around simultaneously. My attention is drawn to hers as she takes in mine. Her mug includes a pond illuminated with moonlight and stars at her parents' house. It is the perfect moment to symbolize our nights spent under the sky, talking and laughing on a blanket or in the bed of a truck. We would sit on the water's edge and count the fish as they jumped, breaking the still surface. Those are some of my favorite memories too, but those are not the ones I chose to share today.

"I don't get it," Macy says, pointing at my mug. "When was this?" Her eyebrows squint together, showing her confusion the longer she reviews my pottery.

I take a deep breath, trying to build my nerve to share this secret with her. I knew I was going to today, but sitting here now, I can't shake off the fear plaguing me. "So, Mace," I start, attempting to swallow a golf ball-sized lump in my throat as her gaze is locked on mine, searching for answers. "I came up to New York to see you. It was about a year after you left." Memories flood my mind, recalling how long it took to build the courage needed to go see her.

"Wait, what?" Macy's expression shifts from confusion to surprise as she processes my words. "What do you mean you came up to see me? I never saw you." She does not mean to, but her voice begins to rise the more she speaks.

"I know," I admit, shifting my eyes from hers while shame floods me. All the courage I built up was not enough for me to approach her once I found her. "This painting," I point to my mug, making sure she understands which scene I am referring to, "is from the moment I saw you walking down the street, talking to a woman I assumed was one of your new friends. You two went into a coffee shop while I was on the other side of the street, watching you." I pause, only realizing how stalkerish that sounds. "In that moment, I understood I couldn't compete with these new friends, fancy coffee shops, or the laughs someone could hear echoing from inside. So, I left." My voice trails off, the weight of the memory still heavy on my heart, almost making it difficult to breathe.

Chapter Seventeen

MACY

A loud humming noise surrounds me, making my ears ring from deep within. It's the kind of sound that resonates in your bones and makes you forget everything around you. I know exactly what day he is talking about. I went to grab coffee with Brooke, my roommate at the time. The air was tension-filled as I sat down in this small cafe and broke the news to her. As much as I was thankful she took me in as her roommate when I first moved to New York, our differences were too drastic, and moving out was my only option. The outing started with laughs but quickly turned South as she realized I was friend-breaking-up with her. Needless to say, it didn't go well. I know it was this day because, for the first year and a half, I didn't have any other friends I would have walked down the street with, and then it took me about a year to tell her how much I couldn't stand her. I remember walking down the streets, dodging tourists left and right, but feeling desperately alone, the weight of my decision heavy on my shoulders.

Now, here I am, years later, listening to Lucas telling me he was there that day. I don't know how I would have reacted if he had approached me, but I can't help but wish I had been given a choice. He saw me as someone with friends and had already moved on, but in reality, I had nobody and never felt more alone. Why would he travel that far just to let me walk away? On the outside, did I really appear to have everything together despite struggling internally? He succeeded in visiting but still didn't choose me. Undeniably, it hurts my soul.

"But…" I struggle to find the right words as my ears keep humming and my heart pounds. "But why wouldn't you stop me? I know you said you felt like you couldn't beat my life then, but I don't understand why you would fly so far and not say anything." My surroundings still circling me while I fight the urge to pass out. None of this makes sense.

"I was hoping I would see you or you would see me, and everything would fall into place." Pain and regret fill his expression. "Whether I had to move up there or you were moving back home, I wanted us to work out. In that moment, I knew my argument for us to do either was not realistic. I knew I had to go home and be more than the boy who fell in love with you. I had to turn into a man who could provide for you and all your dreams. I wanted to provide for you in a way I couldn't then." His silence is deafening around us as he pauses, looking down at his hands. "So, I came home and tried to figure it out... I guess I haven't felt like it was enough yet..."

I stare at him slack-mouthed, unsure of what to say. I was flattered at his intentions, angry at his silence, and sad for what could have been.

"Lucas..." I sit there, still too stunned to move. "What? Did anyone know about this? Did my parents know? Why didn't they tell me? Who else knows? Abi?" With all the questions I want to ask, I am confused about where to begin.

"Yeah, I mean, Abi knew..." Luke nods in place, scared to say too much. "Abi used her sleuthing skills to research where you could be working, which is kind of creepy when I say that out loud. Either way, she was able to figure it out by the photos you were posting and restaurants you were tagging."

"Wow, definitely not creepy or anything." A sarcastic laugh fills the small space as I think about Abi's investigative skills. Deep down, I am grateful for her help but hurt she didn't reach out to tell me either.

Luke's arms flexed as he reaches to run his fingers through his hair before looking back at me, heartbreak filling in his eyes. "I'm pretty sure your dad figured it out when I asked for a few days off and asked him to watch after my house while I was gone." He states, calmly trying to decipher how I am feeling about the events he is telling me. "It was probably a process of elimination," he pauses, scratching his well-kept beard before tugging at his hair, making it disheveled. "If I were to guess, he told your mom. I doubt, at that point, Tessa would have reached out to Abi, but I don't know. We were all lost when you left and didn't know how to react. Especially when interacting with each other."

"I'm sorry I didn't see you. I feel horrible." I murmur, fiddling with my hair while avoiding his eye contact. Tears are prickling in my eyes, not sure I'm ready to let Luke know how touched I am. "She wasn't a friend, she was my roommate. We had a fight, and I moved out right after. I hadn't made any friends at that point. It was just me." I release a shrug as if trying to let that time in my life run off me. "I can't tell you how I would have reacted if I saw you. I was not in a great place. I wish you would have stopped me."

Luke reaches across the table and slowly glides his fingers through mine, giving it a light squeeze. In his own way, this is his way of telling me we were in this together.

"I never gave up on you," he reassures me. "All I ever wanted was to be enough for you if I ever got another shot."

I clear my throat as I feel emotion clogging it, about to burst from me. "It wasn't as if you weren't enough for me, I was a lost soul. When you got home, did you figure it all out?"

"I feel like I'm close," Luke replies, his own voice husky from his affection. "But it's difficult to know if I would ever be good enough for your love. I have been focusing on building a place for you to land if you choose to do so. I want to be the place you choose." We stare at each other, tears filling his eyes as we both try to keep everything at bay. "And I'm not saying you can't do it yourself, of course. Or you would have needed me, feminism, and all of that, but I wanted to be an option. Hopefully, you can see I am close to being an option for you."

His words sting as I shake my head. I give in and let my tears stream down my cheeks, unable to hold it back any longer. "Lucas, I never worried if you were enough for me," I confess, squeezing his hand, still enveloping mine. "I ran because I didn't feel like I was enough for you. I felt so stupid for leaving after believing my plan was foolproof. Then, it all fell apart in the end. I considered coming home and admitting I made a mistake, but I'm stubborn. At first, returning felt like it was too early. Then, it felt like it was too late, and I failed. In the end, even if I did come back, I had already turned my back on everyone. I didn't deserve any of the love and friendship I knew I would receive. So, I stayed."

"We were both running from each other and ourselves at the same time?" Luke says after several quiet moments pass. I meet his eyes again to see the humor now shining on his face.

"Yeah, Luke, I think we were." I can't help but return his smile and squeeze his hand this time. Before anything else can be said, Maggie comes around the corner, trying to act like she didn't hear our whole conversation, and asks if we were ready for her to fire our pieces. Luke and I both stand and start getting our belongings together.

"How long does it take to finish?" Luke asks as he reviews his mug one more time, making sure everything is perfect.

"I tell people two weeks to be safe, but I can probably squeeze you in faster if you need them sooner?" Maggie's eyes flicker between the two of us, silently asking if I would still be in town in two weeks. I stare at Lucas, but the question in his eyes forces me to give a faint nod. With no immediate prospects, I don't see myself leaving in the next two weeks.

Lucas looks at me with surprise. "No worries, Maggie, I think two weeks will be sufficient, don't you, Luke?" A breath escapes him while he lets my words sink in. All I receive in return is a stern nod and one more squeeze of my hand.

After leaving the pottery studio, we slowly walk to Lucas' truck, not in a rush to end the date, taking in the small town that holds my heart so deeply. "Are you ready for me to take you back to the cottage? I don't want to keep you away if you have other plans. Or, I mean, we could walk over a few blocks and get some ice cream or really anything you may want. Are you hun–"

"Luke, you're rambling again." A giggle escapes my lips as I playfully nudge him with my shoulder, hoping to relax and soothe his rushing mind. "If you are ready to be done, then that's fine... but personally, I was having fun. If you wanted–"

Before I can finish my sentence, Luke takes ahold of my hand and leads me down the street. Despite knowing everyone is watching us with curious eyes, holding hands, and smiling with each other, I have no desire to break the spell we are under. Luke and I share ice cream before roaming through the bookstore, me showing Lucas my favorite books. Luke even jokes they'll soon have my own on the shelves. As I am grabbing too many books to take home, I overhear Luke asking the cashier about any specials they have for local authors and what would be required for a book signing event. This man has such unwavering love and faith in me.

I can't wipe the smile off my face, even after we leave the bookstore, Luke effortlessly carries my bags. Maybe those sexy muscles of his are coming in handy. We continue to walk and talk, relearning each other the best we can. Before we realize it, we have eaten dinner, and Luke is driving us out of town. This time, I have the window rolled down to feel the joy of country air on my face. After the first date, I rolled down my window out of anger, tonight is different, though. Our hands remain intertwined unless necessary. Even when we get back to the cottage, we sit on the tailgate of Luke's truck and gaze up at the stars together.

Once I yawn for what feels like the hundredth time, Luke proclaims it's time for bed. As we approach the door, I turn to face him, standing closer than necessary. "Would you like to come in, Luke?"

Luke wraps his arm around my waist and pulls me even closer. "As much as I want nothing more, I don't know if it's a good idea." His delicate touch brushes over my cheek before lightly tucking strands of hair behind my ear. "But don't think for a second it's because I don't want to. Because I do. But I don't want to ruin our good day by rushing things."

I can't help but look away from his intense gaze, his eyes piercing my soul, sending flames across my skin, and settling in my lower belly. I can't believe I am saying this, but I am disappointed. While I understand where he is coming from, I was hoping he wouldn't listen to that instinct. "Is it moving too fast if I ask for a kiss?"

Luke doesn't use his words to answer me, instead lacing his hands through my hair on the base of my neck, using his thumb to tilt my face towards him. Swallowing my gasp, Lucas leans closer to me, barely brushing my lips with his own. His timid touch takes me by surprise since I know he is craving more, just like I am. Desperation shivers through me quickly, fisting his shirt, I pull him to me. His hands are snaked around me, making me mold against his body. Groans escape us both when I slide my hand under his shirt, mapping his muscles. When Luke uses his tongue to separate my lips to enter, he simultaneously shatters any remaining willpower to fight off our third date.

I am falling for my husband, and I don't know what I'm thinking.

Chapter Eighteen

LUCAS

abandoned my shop a couple of hours ago, seeking refuge in the warmth and comfort of my living room. I can hear the fire crackling next to me as I relax into a soft leather armchair with a book in hand. The slow acoustic country melodies emitting from my record player add to my cozy atmosphere, giving me the perfect background noise. I hold a glass of whiskey, its amber liquid swirling gently with each sip. A storm rages on outside, causing rain to hit my windows and the wind whipping the trees around. The rain has brought with it a cold front, allowing me to use my fireplace one more time before we face the consistent Texas heat.

As a man who spends their day working on a ranch and then in my shop, many would be surprised to see me read, despite not trying to hide it. In all honesty, it has always been my pastime, even when Macy was still here. Currently, I am switching between two books - one for leisure and one for "business" reasons. Those "business" reasons just so happen to be a book I grabbed from the library about how to write a romance book. Why? Well, Macy is writing one, and I want to help her in any way I can. I don't know where she is in the process, but if I can understand the creative process and publishing steps, I will be able to better support her. That is, if she lets me.

My usual preferences are thrillers or historical books. Because of that, I tend to be on edge when I am engrossed in a book. When I hear footsteps on my front porch, instincts kick in to find my pistol. Logically, I know if someone wanted to break into my house, during a freak rainstorm wouldn't be the ideal time. Unable to find my pistol, I grab my pocketknife sitting on the coffee table and gently sit down my book. I know my jumpiness comes from just finishing a book about a home invasion.

When the tapping on my door persists, I cautiously push the curtains to the side to see if I recognize the person on the other side. Once I do, I quickly swing open the door to see Macy standing there, water rolling off her and puddling on my porch. The light from my entryway falls delicately across her features. My eyes roam up her body, she is physically shaking from the cold, and the breath I was holding whooshes from me as I take in her swollen and red eyes. Instincts kick in when I reach out to grab her and bring her to my chest.

"Mace, what are you doing out in this weather?" I ask with concern, pulling her even closer to my chest and rubbing her hair soothingly. "Come in where it is warm. What is going on?"

"Lucas..." she sobs, trembling in my arms as I usher her inside. "How did I not know?" Her last word is interrupted by another heavy sob. Unsure if she is shaking from the cold or upset about something else entirely, I help her out of her dripping raincoat and wrap her in a blanket off of the couch. "How did I not know Lucas? I should have known."

"How did you not know what, baby?" I ask, kneeling in front of her and taking her cold hands into mine. She snuggles into the couch, angling herself towards the fireplace. I peel off her rain boots, causing water to pour out of them.

A soft, wet chuckle escapes her as we watch the water seep onto the floor from her boots. Her voice is apologetic and sorrowful as she apologizes for the mess, a pained smile crosses her face as she takes me in, calculating whether I am upset about the water.

"How long were you standing out there, Macy?" I ask, trying to infuse some humor into the situation. My hands return to hers as I trace aimless circles over her knuckles, hoping to provide comfort.

"Long enough to realize it was too cold to stand out there that long," she replies with a small grin, looking down at my hands wrapped around hers. "I didn't know where else to go."

"You can always come here, Mace. You know that." I assure her with a sense of pride swelling in my chest. She could have gone anywhere but came to me instead. I can't help but wonder if this reflects her walls slowly lowering for me. "Do you want some tea or coffee?"

"No, not right now. Thanks, though," she responds shyly as if just realizing she is sitting in my living room.

"Talk to me, Mace. What's going on?" I reach up and tuck a loose strand of hair behind her ears and watch as a shiver runs down her body. A tear rolls down her pink cheek. I catch it before it can trail too far down her cheek.

"Well..." She swallows and looks away. I can see tears filling her eyes again as she tries to keep herself calm. "I was helping my dad get the horses in the barn before the storm hit." Macy begins, taking a slow, deep inhale and exhales as if buying time before she has to finish her comment. I squeeze her hand to provide encouragement. "And I asked him why you were still working for him."

Her eyes flick to meet mine briefly before looking away, another sob escaping her lips. "Oh shit, Mace." Without hesitation, I pull her into my arms and we both settle on the floor, wrapped around each other. I provide warmth and comfort as the weight of reality hits me - this is why she can't control her emotions.

"I didn't know, Luke. How did I not know my dad was dying?" Macy sobs on my chest as her world crumbles around her. There's nothing I can do to stop it other than giving her the space to mourn. "He has cancer, and treatment isn't working. How did I not know this, Luke?" If I had any power, I would use it to stop this pain for her.

"Macy, look at me," I implore, cupping her chin and gently lifting her face, forcing her to meet my gaze. I need her to see me, really see me, before anything else. "Mace, he didn't want to keep it from you. Please believe that. I am so sorry." At the time, I never considered I should have tried calling Macy to tell her, at minimum, to convince her to call her parents. Looking back, I understand Macy wouldn't have responded well to this information, but I fear by reaching out to her, maybe she wouldn't be in the state she is now. Could I have prevented all of this if I called her when Loch and Tessa told me not to?

"And that is why you are still working for him? He said he put the deed of the farm in your name so…" Another weep flows from her, but she continues to hold my glance this time. "… So, you can step in when it is just my mom."

"Yeah," I confirm with a nod, feeling a wave of sadness wash over me. "He felt like it was best. I tried to buy it from him, but you know how stubborn he can be." We share a small smile while she gently nods her head.

"I've fought him on this since it all came up, but since he won't budge, I started doing extra things around the farm to make up for it," I explain.

"Thank you," Macy whispers, tears still streaming down her face. "I will never understand why you never wavered with them. With everything I have put you through… you could have walked away from them. If you did, it may have been easier to close the wound I caused."

"Yes, Macy," I say softly, "I could have, but I didn't want to. You know those two are like my own parents. It hurt, but deep down, I knew it was the right thing to do."

Macy's eyes fill with tears again as she looks at me. While she is still emotional, she does not seem as manic as she was when she showed up at my door. "Why didn't you tell me? Why didn't Abi?"

I sigh, knowing even if I had tried to reach her, she wouldn't have answered. "Would you have taken my call even if I tried? Or Abi's?"

A sad smile fell across her face. "No, probably not."

"That's what I thought." I pull her closer to me again and place a small kiss on her temple. I take in her familiar scent of vanilla with a hint of rain. Despite her shivering body, her body still fits perfectly against mine. "Can I get you some dry clothes to change into?" I ask, concern evident in my voice. "You can stay here as long as you want. You can wear mine, or I can run to the cottage and grab some of yours..." I hesitate, "You know if you'd rather not wear mine."

Her voice is muffled against my chest as she speaks. "Can I borrow some of yours?" My chest aches with anticipation, knowing I'm about to see my wife in my clothes after almost a decade. The thought brings back so many bittersweet memories, but I fear if she thinks of them, she will run away from me.

"Of course, Macy. Let me start the kettle of hot water then I will go get you something." She nods in agreement and untangles herself from my embrace.

The removal of her heat almost causes me to reach back for her. She is a drug I can't escape or stop chasing.

As I stand, I lean down one more time to brush a light kiss on her cheek and head to the kitchen before heading upstairs. When I get back to her, I hand her the clothes I gathered and show her where the downstairs bathroom is. I hear the shower start, so I know she has decided to take a hot shower to shake off the chill and emotions she arrived with.

Having Macy in my house, in my shower, gives me a stab to the heart. I catch my heart starting to race, trying not to allow myself to reminisce on previous nights like this one. I have heard her take countless showers in my life, but none have hurt as much as this one. Her presence provides warmth and fear deep in my chest. The smell of her perfume lingers in the air, providing a comforting scent that fills me with both nostalgia and longing.

I place a tea bag into the steeping water and head back upstairs to my bedroom. I quickly change my sheets and start a fire in the master bedroom. I am offering her a place to stay tonight, or however long she chooses, so I want to ensure she feels comfortable in the space around her.

After I finish preparing the master bedroom, I head down the hall to one of the spare bedrooms. I hear Macy emerge from the bathroom, and I call out to her, letting her know the tea is ready on the kitchen counter. I quickly text her parents, letting them know she's safe at my house. Relaxation floods me as the familiar act feels like second nature in being her protector.

After I finish making the bed in the spare bedroom, I head back downstairs. As I turn the corner, the sight of her stops me in my tracks. This woman is the most breathtaking woman I have ever seen. The sweatpants and t-shirt she is wearing engulf her small, petite frame. Her dark hair is piled on top of her head, revealing her natural beauty without makeup. At this moment, I know I will choose to remember her in this way - standing by my fireplace with a tea mug in her hand and wearing my clothes. The gentle hum of music feels the air as she joins in softly singing along. Hearing the stairs creak as I step off them, she turns to look at me. Her eyes are no longer swollen and red from crying earlier.

"Are you writing a book?" Her voice shakes me out of my mesmerized stare when I look down at her hands and notice the book I borrowed from the library.

Well, shit, this isn't something I wanted her to see. "Um," I nervously scratch at the stubble on my chin while I avoid looking directly at her. "No. No, I'm not. I just borrowed the book from the library."

"Why?" Curiosity laces her question, her eyebrows quirking up as she stares back at me.

"Well, um... I knew you were struggling, and I thought maybe reading some tips could help you with your writing process." I shift uncomfortably and look at my bare feet on my wooden floors. "Just in case."

"What?!" She says in a higher pitch than she did before as she processes what I said. Fear pulses through me as I worry she will see this gesture as me desperately trying to hold onto her rather than genuinely wanting to help her.

"Please don't make me repeat that, Mace." A desperate plea, followed by a hint of humor, escapes my mouth. I don't know if I can be honest and let her know my true intentions again.

We share a lingering gaze at each other as she slowly sits the book back down in my chair and walks towards me, barely nodding her head as she watches her feet move across the floor. Her thin arms slide around my waist as she places her face into my chest. I finally allow myself to exhale, realizing I was holding my breath in anticipation of her response. I pull her even closer to me, and we stand in silence for a moment. Eventually, she pulls back slightly, tears are beginning to start filling her eyes as she looks up at me. "Don't cry, baby. Everything will be ok." I give her a reassuring nod before suggesting we watch a movie.

"What movie do you want to watch?" I ask, taking her hand and leading her over to the couch. She sits down as I grab a blanket, remembering how much she loved to snuggle under one while watching movies.

"How do you feel about watching Sweet Home Alabama?" A wide grin spreads across her face as I realize she knows exactly what she is doing to me.

"You still haven't moved past that movie?" I tease, causing a matching smile to meet hers.

"Nobody just 'moves on' from the best rom-com movie ever made." Macy jokes.

"That is debatable because people should. It's that Ryan Gosling guy, isn't it? That's why girls like that movie so much?" I prod back at her, giving her permission to tease me while communicating I will tease her right back.

"His name is Josh Lucas, and yes. Those blue eyes pull me in every time. When was the last time you watched it?" I can't help but smile as my wife playfully teases me about her celebrity crush.

I start flipping through my streaming services when she pulls her feet closer to her body and pats the couch for me to sit next to her. In my defense, I was going to sit in the chair to not risk scaring her, but if my wife wants me to sit next to her, then who am I to argue? She sips her tea, her lips leaving a faint stain on the mug. Her long legs are stretched over my lap, sending tingles up my spine.

"Oh, I would say a little over seven years ago." A small gasp comes from her when she looks up at me. All humor has left her features as her eyes roam over my face. From the outside looking in, this would look like a romantic night in for a husband and wife. In reality, I'm scared shitless I'm going to mess this up. Macy has relaxed on the large couch as I take in the way she laughs at all the right moments, the way she tucks her stray pieces of hair behind her ear and the way she leans into me during the romantic scenes. It's a good thing I have seen this movie countless times because I am not paying attention at all. All I can think about is how close my hand is to her.

As we get to every woman's favorite movie quote, Macy looks away from the TV and asks, "Why would you want to marry me for, anyhow?" as she tries to mock the southern twang she already has since she was born and raised in Texas, but I don't mention that to her.

I give her a quick wink before following up with, "So I can kiss you anytime I want." At first, all humor leaves the conversation, but suddenly, a loud, boisterous laugh escapes her as her head rolls back. The sound warms my heart as I take in the way her eyes crinkle and her cheeks turn rosy from happiness.

"You are ridiculous, Lucas Wright!" She continues laughing and flattens out on the couch, making herself lay over me even more than she was prior. I freeze all thoughts and breathing until I feel her wiggle on the couch to get comfortable and I realize that this wasn't an accident. She knows what she is doing, and I love it.

As we near the end of the movie, I notice her heavier change in breathing as it becomes steadier and heavier. Glancing over, I see she has fallen asleep against me. My heart swells with love for this woman who is effortlessly beautiful and peaceful in her slumber.

I let her lie there for a few more seconds before I turn the TV off and slowly get off the couch. I reach down and lift her into my arms to carry her upstairs. She nudges her face closer to me, and I hear her release a soft sigh. "Thank you, baby," is all she says as I climb the stairs. I gently lay her in my master bed and pull the sheets back. I tuck her in and lean to give her one last light kiss on her forehead and turn to walk out. Right as I reach to close the door behind me, she quietly says, "Are you not sleeping in here?"

I take a moment to memorize how she looks in my bed before I choke down my emotions before I push out a response. "No, I will be down the hall." She doesn't respond, and her breathing becomes heavy again. I stand in the hall against the door and convince myself it's best to sleep in the other room, but I can't help but wonder if this will be my last opportunity to hold her. I remind myself I am playing the long game as I lay here for what feels like hours, thinking about how it's almost physically painful that I don't get to keep her here with me.

My last thought before I fall asleep is how I will never forget this time with her for the rest of my life.

Chapter Nineteen

MACY

The **morning light filtering** through the curtains is what initially wakes me up from my sleep. At first, I have to remind myself where I am and how I got here. My mind immediately starts racing, replaying the events of last night. Contemplating the decisions I have to make may be the most daunting task I have. As I do, I sink back into the bed and try to hide from the outside world. My world, as I knew it, seems to be crumbling around me, mirroring the turmoil I am chasing inside my head. Should I stay longer at Pigeon Lake to help my parents? The weight and pressure my parents have to be feeling from his illness must be exhausting. Unless he told you, you wouldn't know my dad was sick. I wonder how many in this small community know what he is up against. Would it be better for me to leave now and return when things inevitably worsen? I know he would tell me to keep living my life, but I have a small inkling this isn't what I should be doing. Then, there are practical considerations, such as the job applications I've been submitting instead of working on my book.

After what feels like an eternity, I hear movement from downstairs and realize Lucas is awake. My initial impulse is to snoop through his things while he still believes I am asleep, but the tantalizing smell of bacon wafting through the air quickly derails that plan.

"Bacon," I whisper to myself with excitement, springing out of his bed and beelining for the door. However, as I reach for the door handle, I consider whether I should confirm I look presentable heading downstairs. "Mace, don't be ridiculous." I scold myself. "He has seen you without make-up and in baggy clothes before." As I reach for the door handle one more time, I hastily stop and turn to the on-suite bathroom. I glance at my reflection fand ix my messy hair while putting some of Lucas' toothpaste on my finger, brushing my teeth the best I can. I roll my eyes at myself as I switch off the light and head downstairs.

As I land on the last few steps, I can hear Luke singing along to the music playing on his record player. I remember when I got him that player for

Christmas, right after we got married. He had mentioned he had always wanted one, so I took the plunge and surprised him. The look on his face when he opened my present was one of the happiest looks he ever gave me. Maybe even happier than when he saw me on our wedding day. I round the corner with a smile on my face as he turns around, flipping pancakes in just his basketball shorts. The sight of him interrupts my introspective thoughts.

His tan, muscular body instantly takes my breath away. He is beautiful. He may be more beautiful than he was when we were together. You could always tell his muscles were earned through hard work on the farm, not in a farm. Memories flood back to me watching him load bales of hay while perched on the back of his truck. These moments were considered our secret, stealing kisses, and laughing together before returning to my parents' house. In those moments, we went from friends to something more, a crush evolving into an all-consuming love.

My legs keep propelling me closer to him, stuck in a muscle-induced haze. The way his arms move, flexing with each turn of the wrist, is mesmerizing. As I draw closer, I catch a glimpse of a small line drawing tattoo going up the side of his waistline, but still too far to make out the details. Lost in my thoughts, I don't even see the barstool until I run right into it, stubbing my baby toe and releasing a loud yelp, stopping all movement from Luke.

He turned towards me quickly, concern etched on his handsome features as he rushes to my side, as if I've just suffered a severe injury. My face flushes with embarrassment as I realize I only ran into the stool because I was so caught up in watching him. "Mace, are you ok? What were you doing?"

"I... um... well, I ran into the barstool," I stammer, feeling heat spread down my neck and onto my chest. I laugh at the absurdity of the situation.

Luke joined in on the laughter, but I can tell he's mostly amused by how flustered and red-faced I am. "Why are you blushing so much, Mace?" He pokes my side playfully, making me squirm and try to slide away from him. Our laughter fills the space between us as he teasingly asks, "Were you checking out your husband?" His ability to read me continues to be unmatched.

"No," I protest, burying my face in my hands as I grow increasingly embarrassed under his watchful gaze. "I was too caught up in thinking about the bacon you are cooking."

"Yeah, I bet you were Mace." He continues to laugh at my expense as he reaches out to grab me. He effortlessly picks me up and sits me on the island counter as he inspects my foot. "I sure hope you didn't break your toe while you were checking out..." he paused for dramatics, winking at me before finishing, "the bacon."

I roll my eyes at his playfulness, still laughing as we banter back and forth. It's moments like these that remind me of our past - friendly teasing, the easy chemistry between us, and verbal stings to each other. "I am pretty sure my toe is fine, Luke. Don't be dramatic." I say with a coy smile.

Before I know it, he's already placed a small bandaid over my toe, making sure it is properly covered. "This is almost a reverse Cinderella moment," he says with admiration in his eyes as he pulls my sock back on and leans forward to place a tender kiss on my forehead. The simple gesture takes my breath away.

As he puts away his first aid kit, I cough softly to clear my throat, feeling flustered and embarrassed by the attention I received. He returns to cooking the pancakes, discarding the burnt ones from earlier while he was 'fixing' me. "So, what else are you making over there?" I ask, unable to take my eyes off his chiseled back now I'm up close. The way his back muscles ripple and contract with each movement may be my new favorite form of porn.

"Bacon, as you know," Luke replies with a low chuckle, throwing me a sly look over his shoulder and causing me to roll my eyes at him. "And some pancakes. I can make eggs after this if you want any. I didn't think you would be awake already."

"The sunlight woke me, but then I smelled breakfast, and it motivated me to get down here before you ate it all." Lucas turns to face me while picking up a piece of bacon and stepping closer to me still sitting on the island counter. Determination fires in his eyes as his closeness forces me to spread my legs, making room for him. His hand grazes over my legs, causing shivers down my spine. Luke brings a piece of bacon to my mouth, holding it out for me to take a bite. I hold his gaze as I open my mouth for him and take a bite. Lucas' eyes fall to my mouth, and I catch the sound of a hard swallow. Without realizing it, both of his hands engulf me, pulling me closer to him. As if trying to feed the flame, I release a small moan as I continue to eat the bacon.

The moan breaks him out of the trance and whatever is running through his mind. "Don't you dare moan like that over bacon." Lucas playfully scolds me, laughing as my eyes widen with his comment. "Don't tease me if you can't follow through, Mace." I can't help but laugh at him as I feel him growing between my legs, pushed up to the counter. But something inside me shifts and I can't resist him any longer.

Wrapping my legs around Lucas' waist, I tug him closer to me. My hands roam over each defined muscle on his stomach and make my way around his neck. "Don't tease me, Macy." With those deep, pained words, I realize I don't want to continue this tease. Over the last several weeks, Lucas Wright has slowly torn down my walls, making my desperation to kiss this man consume me. I may not be ready to say those words out loud or to change any plans, but my desire to feel him underneath my hands becomes too much to bare. I comb my fingers through the hair lying on the back of his neck and pull his lips to mine.

All hesitations disappear as I fiercely press my lips to his. A deep, guttural moan escapes him as he wraps his hands around me, pulling me forward to eliminate any remaining space between us. My back arches into him, pressing my hard nipples to his chest. Luke removes his mouth from mine and, with a harmless tug of my hair, pulls my head back, giving him unlimited access to place his lips on my pulsating neck. As he kisses down my collarbone, I can't stop the moan from escaping me. Grabbing his hair, I arch into him even more as I beg for more.

Suddenly, Luke stops, removes his hands from my hair, and looks at me with wide eyes. For a moment, I fear something is wrong, or he has changed his mind. As the smell of burning food fills the air, Luke takes a small step away from me, twists, and turns off the stove that is still cooking pancakes. He immediately turns back to me, gliding his hands under his shirt, which I'm still wearing. His callused hands run up my sides, lightly skimming over my breasts.

With a gentle press of his lips, he silently questions if he can enter my mouth. I open with less hesitation than I had when taking a bite of his crispy bacon earlier this morning. As his tongue dances with mine, I feel the flex of his arm muscles and the tight grip of his hands on me. I lightly twist his nipples, causing a shiver to run through his body as he loses control for just a moment. He always liked it when I did that, and I see it still drives him wild.

As he slides his hands further up my back, he whispers in a low voice that almost goes unheard, "Can I take this off?" I give a small nod, causing him to immediately spring into action, removing his shirt from me. His breath catches as he takes in the sight of my bare chest. He saw my breasts several weeks ago during our debacle at the cottage, but this time feels different. Everything about this moment is different than maybe any other time before.

"Please, Luke," I plead between deep breaths, my chest rising and falling in sync with his. He leans down and gently places his tongue on one of my nipples. Timid at first, but then unleashes all his desire as he sucks it between his teeth. Giving me tiny nibbles before swirling his tongue over it as if cleaning away the pain. His hand reaches up to grab my other nipple, twisting and pulling at it as he switches back and forth between them. A loud, desperate moan crosses my mouth. "More. I need more."

Luke switches to the other nipple while he lays me back on his cold, white granite counter. The sudden chill sends a shock through my body before adjusting to the temperature. Luke grabs his cock, which is so hard it's practically busting the seams of the shorts. He gives it two thrusts before pulling back, looking me in my eyes as I lay spread out across his kitchen counter, fully exposed with my mental and emotional walls coming crashing down, unable to resist his gaze.

"This isn't just an orgasm, Macy," he says with a hint of anguish in his voice. "This isn't about two people fulfilling their physical desires, right? This is...something more?" Realization hits me: I want more than the physical pleasure, the physical and emotional connection only few will ever understand. I want it all from him.

"No, Luke. It isn't just an orgasm for me." The large, warm smile spreads across Luke's face, making him even more stunning. I can feel pressure on the bridge of my nose, the first signs I am going to tear up. This man loves me like no one has. And while I may not be ready to say I still love him, he is doing a damn good job of showing me why I should.

His warm, calloused hands trail sensually over my body, lightly skimming the waistband of my sweatpants. "Can I taste you?" His husky voice sends shivers down my spine as my core tightens in anticipation. I nod eagerly as I prop myself up on my elbows to watch the view. He licks his swollen lips in anticipation and slowly, almost torturously so, pulls down my sweatpants. As he pulls them off from my feet, I look down at him, still up on my elbows. "Let me look at you, baby. I need to take you in." Lucas lowers himself to his knees, placing each foot on his shoulders and spreading me open for him. "I have never seen a more beautiful thing in my life," he murmurs, his fingers tenderly tracing up through my wet folds before bringing them back to his mouth and licking me off. Our eyes meet each other as a million words and feelings pass between us in those two seconds, but it's all we both need to say. "Hold on, wife, I am about to eat you for breakfast."

With that, he moves closer to me, spreading me out with his fingers and leisurely sliding his flat tongue from bottom to top, slowly gliding into me before finishing at my clit and drawing circles with his tongue. A loud moan escapes me as I take in how amazing he feels. "I can't wait to hear you scream my name, Mace. I am never going to let you stop." As he slides in one finger and returns his tongue to my swollen nub, I fall back, laying completely back on the counter, hands in his hair, and pulling him closer to me with each stroke. "There you go, baby. Ride my fingers. Let me finger fuck you. If you don't drip down my arm, I didn't do good enough, do you understand that?" He places a second finger and then a third, relentlessly bringing me closer and closer to the edge. Every movement of his fingers is perfectly calculated, hitting just the right spot inside of me while his tongue alternates between slow laps and teasing nibbles.

As I arch my back and cry out his name, he never falters in his ministrations until I am completely spent, my body trembling with pleasure. I know I am about to explode. It isn't until he places a fourth finger into me that he reaches up and twists my hardened nipple that I lose all ability to hold back. I scream his name louder than I ever have before. He never stops pumping until I am fully down from my high. "That's it, baby. God, you are perfect. Do you have any idea how tight you squeezed my fingers?"

I lay on the counter, trying to catch my breath as he gives me one last lick to clean me up before standing to take in his handiwork. As I look up at him, he is licking each of his four fingers, cleaning them from all of my juices, with a huge smile on his face. He stares at me for a long moment, just taking in each inch of me. "I sure hope you aren't a one-and-done wife. I have big plans for that cunt of yours." He winks seductively before opening a kitchen drawer to grab a rag and starts cleaning me off.

"I'm sorry if I got anything on your counter," I say shyly, feeling bashful after the intense pleasure he gave me.

His laughter fills the kitchen as he leans down to kiss me, making me taste myself on his lips. "Are you kidding me? This is my new favorite part of the kitchen. I may even put a plaque here or something." His smile doesn't waver from satisfaction and pride, his possessiveness blatant.

I roll my eyes as I sit up, still holding my lips to his. The taste of his kiss lingers on my tongue, a combination of heat and sweetness fans the flame within me. With one hand still tangled in his hair, I reach down and slide my hand into his shorts, feeling how hard he has become while he is on his knees for me. A small nip to my lips makes me pull back from him, breathless and eager for more.

"How can I repay you?" I ask, but before I can finish the sentence, Luke is carrying me up his stairs and into his master bathroom. He sits me on the bathroom counter before reaching to turn the shower on, making an instant haze fill the room. He wastes no time in shedding his clothes, throwing them carelessly into the corner. I watch him closely as he returns to his knees in front of me and spreads me open again.

This time, he takes his time to explore me fully, tracing every curve and dip with his fingers and lips. The heat from his breath dances on my skin, sending a shimmer down my spine, making me feel alive and wanted. His words send sparks throughout as he teases me with promises of pleasure.

"You better be careful," I tease back, "this counter may start competing with your kitchen counter for our attention. I don't know who would win."

"I have no problem with ordering a plaque for every inch of this house, Mace," Luke replies with a smirk. "Now, let me take you in like I should have earlier."

I spread myself further for him, not wanting to block anything he wanted to see. His pupils dilate again as he slides one finger through me, teasing my entrance. Arousal coats his tongue as my back arches up.

"Are you ready to fuck my tongue, Mace?" Luke asks with a mischievous glint in his eyes. "Or are you sore?"

Without hesitation, I lean back towards the mirror and use my legs to pull his head closer. A laugh escapes him while setting up the perfect angle needed to fuck me properly. Before I knew it, his lengthy tongue was in me, and I was rocking back and forth on it with no desire to stop.

Chapter Twenty

LUCAS

lead Macy to the edge of eternity while my tongue slips in and out of her. Her screams reverberate throughout my house, echoing off the walls and stirring up desire in every corner. As she reaches her climax, I am certain the entire town can hear her. I eagerly lap up every drop, savoring the tangy, sweet taste of her as if it were the finest delicacy. The taste of her is a shock to my system and brings me to life.

As much as I want to continue indulging in her, my aching cock is screaming for attention. I thought I was going to explode right there, kneeling in my bathroom, when I felt her constrict around my tongue. I give it a few jerks to buy myself some time before picking her up and carrying her into my double-headed shower. My throbbing dick presses between us as I push her against the wall. My hips jerk without my approval as it stands at attention between her wet folds. A guttural groan escapes me as I force myself to place her under the streaming water, unwilling to allow her to get cold. I take in her beautiful form before me.

I lather shampoo between my hands, rubbing my hands through her long, jet-black hair. Despite knowing the moan she gives me is to tease me further toward my release, I do my best to ignore it. As I start rinsing out the shampoo, Macy pushes her ass out, shaking it as she bends further over to taunt me. Her tight ass tempts me more than I want to admit. Grabbing her hips, I pull her closer and press myself between her cheeks, teasing her tight hole. She gasps as she lifts herself on her tiptoes, making her ass stroke me. I can't help but lean over her, placing my palm on the cool tile, letting her ass jerk me off. Wrapping my hand around her waist, I gather her arousal on my thumb, returning to her ass, using the lubrication to circle her hole before cusping the edge and sliding in. I fuck her with my thumb as she continues to slide up and down my shaft. Macy widens her legs, giving me more room, allowing me to reach around her and lap quick circles on her bud.

Her climax hits her quicker than expected as I hold on to her, not allowing her to collapse to the tiled floor. As she comes back to recognition, Macy spins toward me, kissing me roughly. I feel her hand slide down my chest and reach my rod. After a few pumps, realization hits me I will not be able to stop my release if this continues. "Is this really something we should do?" My voice is uncertain and shaky as I contemplate our situation. Taking a moment to take her in, looking at every feature up close, I continue. "I don't want to do the wrong thing here, Mace. I mean, fuck, I want it all with you, but..." She slips her hands around my neck and pulls me closer. "But I don't want to scare you or make you run. Help me do the right thing."

She reaches up on her tip-toes and places a wet kiss on my lips before kissing a pathway down my tight body until she kneels in front of me. With one hand on the side of the shower for support, I almost lose control when she takes my balls in her warm hand. Her pink, swollen lips part, allowing her tongue to dart out to make small circles around the head of my throbbing member. She licks the tip, savoring the small amount of pre-cum that has formed there. A deep moan escapes me while I watch as she looks up at me with mischievous eyes before wrapping her hot mouth around me. The sensation of being able to see her mouth surrounding me only intensifies my need for release. "Baby," I groan desperately, "I don't know if

I will last long doing this." My hips jerk involuntarily as she responds with a throaty groan, making the vibrations echo around my shaft.

"Fuck my mouth, Luke. Make me cry." She says this while looking up at me and keeping her mouth open and tongue laying flat out for me. My hands grip her hair tightly as I thrust my dick as deep into her as possible, slowly rocking back and forth. She eagerly accepts every inch of me, her tongue caressing and working in unison with my movements. Tears fall down her face, encouraging me to keep going and feeding my primal need. It may have been a while since she has taken all of me, but I know she can do it. She has done it so many times that her throat is on autopilot as I slam into it. Seeing this woman on her knees for me, begging me to make her cry, does things to me.

"I'm almost there, baby." I mumble breathlessly, "Will you swallow me or spit it out?" She answers by squeezing my balls harder and shaking her head.

After three more thrusts, a loud scream comes from me as all my cum shoots out in long, bursting streams down her throat. I watch as she swallows everything I give her, and I realize this may be the sexiest thing I have ever seen. Seeing her swallow me was the sexiest thing I have ever seen.

We stay where we are, both attempting to catch our breaths. Once I have recovered, I pull Macy off her knees and into my arms. We may have crossed many lines this morning, but there was nothing I would change. We stand there together, pressing ourselves to each other, allowing our hands to explore the other. Both of our bodies have changed since the last time we were intimate together, so we both need a moment to memorize the other again.

Her hands run down from around my neck and slide down my stomach until they reach the large tattoo on my abdomen. Her hands trace the outline, and questions clearly run through her mind. I feared the moment she would ask about it, but I knew it was time to come clean about it.

"What is this tattoo?" She questions, staring at it instead of looking up at me.

"It is a windmill," I explain. "Like the ones we used to see out by the bluebonnet fields."

She smiles as she remembers those drives, counting the spinning windmills to pass the time.
"I still like to watch them spin," I continue. "So, one day, I decided to make it part of me."

"It's beautiful," she says, still running her fingers over each dot of ink stitched into me.

"Not as beautiful as you, though," I replied with a genuine smile.

A large smile crosses her face as she giggles at me "Is that a line, Lucas Wright?" She accuses me while shaking dismissing me. s.

I shrug at her comment before asking if it worked, earning another laugh from her. I take in her laughter while reaching behind her and turning off the hot water. I smack her ass while I open the shower door and grab a towel. I slowly wipe the towel over her, using the opportunity to take her in more closely. Once she is dry, I wrap the towel around her chest while helping her out of the wet shower, reaching for a second towel to dry myself off. I watch her eyes follow my hands while they run over my body, taking a longer appreciative glance as I squeeze my dick with a smirk on my face.

Standing outside the shower, it is clear we are both thinking about our recent activities. The mood has turned slightly awkward as if neither knows what to do now. "How do you feel about finally eating breakfast?" I ask, breaking the tension.

"Yeah, sounds good," she answers, her voice lacking its usual confidence. I can feel her inner turmoil and it fills me with fear, worried we may have pushed too far, and she may decide to leave me again.

"Let me grab you some new clothes. Do you want anything in particular?" I offer, trying to divert her attention elsewhere.

"No, anything is fine. Thanks." I lead her to my bedroom and hand her a new set of clothes. Her towel drops and I quickly turn away, feeling shy in my own home. "No need to turn around now, Luke. I am pretty sure you just saw every ounce of me," she jokes, attempting to lighten the mood. When I turn to face her, the lightness and smile on her face ease my anxious thoughts.

Before we head back downstairs, I plant a light kiss on the top of her nose, lacing my fingers through hers, leading her to follow me. In the kitchen, I am met with the aftermath of our distracted cooking session, but I can't help but chuckle. "Don't you know you should clean up after you are done cooking, Luke?" Macy teases, a brazen smirk on her face.

I quickly grab the kitchen towel that was previously thrown on the counter and playfully pop it against her backside before she can escape. Her bolt away from me is followed by squeals and laughter, causing me to chase after her like a playful kid. As I reach her, I lift her in my arms and spin us in place. Her continued laughter bounces off the walls in my heart, reaffirming that what I am doing is right.

walls in my heart, reaffirming that what I am doing is right.

Chapter Twenty-One

MACY

Somehow, **someway**, I found myself staying at Luke's house for longer than I ever dreamed of. One day passed, then two, and then a third. During these idyllic days, we simply reveled in each other's company. Some days, I would accompany him to the ranch to "help" him with chores - a guise for simply basking in his physical labor. The sun beat relentlessly on our skin, the smell of hay and sweat mingling together. More often than not, I found myself entranced by the way his muscles flexed and strained as we worked.

While I may have been on my parent's property, I distanced myself from them, still not ready to face the reality of my dad's health. Despite the lingering tension, I focused my time on watching Lucas and allowing him to provide daily inspiration for my book writing. I laugh at myself, knowing all of the ways I was building him into my book. Book boyfriend, my ass, he was my book husband - literally.

After the long, hot days, we would retreat to his house, often sharing a shower, before heading downstairs to cook dinner together. If the night became chilly, Luke would gather wood and kindling to start a fire in his outdoor pit. The flames would dance and crackle, casting a warm glow over our faces as we would sip on glasses of red wine, the taste of blackberries and oak filling our mouths. Plush cushions and blankets surrounded us as we talked about everything from our childhood memories to our hopes and dreams for the future. As the night reached its end, we would climb his creaky stairs together, hand in hand, slipping under the covers for a peaceful night's sleep.

I had forgotten how much I loved the simple joys of sleeping next to someone. During the nights I had to leave his side to use the restroom, he would often tighten his grip around my waist, making my departure difficult. His incoherent mumbles would often result in a sleepy laugh, as I noted to tease him the following morning. Every morning, as we shared our coffee, I would make jabs at him about his sleep habits. Despite doing this, I know nothing made me feel safer or happier than when he fought me to leave him. It was the silent pecks to my bare shoulders through the night that made me remember how I fell for him to begin with. We never crossed the line of having sex with each other, but neither of us went very long without the other's mouth covering all the sensitive areas of our bodies. Night and day, we navigated the plains of both of our bodies.

On my fourth day of living this fake life with Luke, I have a feeling if I don't leave now, I may never leave. I'm wondering if I'm just caught up in the moment or if I truly want to just stay here in his arms forever. It's a tale as old as time, isn't it? Is the grass greener on the other side, or have you forgotten to water the grass you already have? Confusion laces my brain as I take a mental note to come back to this.

The air is thick with the smell of burning wood and the warm glow of the fire dancing across our faces. I take a sip of red wine while Luke is nursing a cold beer. We watch as the smoke circles around us before disappearing into the darkness. The stars shine above us, accompanied by the soothing chirping of crickets in the distance. In moments like these, my worries and anxieties fade away, replaced by a serenity I haven't felt in years.

I want to bottle up this moment to capture it forever, a reminder to savor life's simple moments.

As if sensing my turmoil, Luke kneels in front of me, his kind eyes full of understanding, looking back at me. His eyes tell me he knows I am internally panicking about our status and this life we have had this week. "What are you doing, Luke?" I ask, my voice trembling with my simmering emotion.

Before he responds, I already know. He is there to comfort me, reminding me that no matter the challenges, he will walk through them with me. "Looking at you."

"Well, it is kind of creepy, you know that, right?" I say, taunting him in an attempt to lighten the mood. The patient, steadfast man is the Lucas I fell in love with. In these silent moments, his looks tell me he is there to stay, whether I am or not.

A broad smile erupts on his face as he looks down at me, taking me in as I lay in his sweatpants and hoodie. His glare leaves a path of heat up my body. His smile forces me to depart from my spiraling thoughts, giving me a small sliver of peace. "I'm just looking at how beautiful you are."

"That is what you keep telling me. I think it is up for debate." I shake my head as if to ward off his advances, giving his shoulder a small shove, almost causing him to lose his balance from sitting on his heels.

The flames highlight the sparkle in his eyes. "No debate needed, wife." His fingers lace through mine, taking my glass from my hands and sitting it next to him.

As he calls me "his wife," a sharp pain infiltrates my body, causing me to gasp. I look up at him and see the unwavering love in his eyes, love that refuses to falter. Before I can speak, Luke stands to his feet and reaches for me. As I rise to my feet, he wraps his strong hands around my thighs, lifting me up as I instinctively wrap my legs around his waist. My fingers tangle in his hair to pull him closer, our lips crashing together in a passionate embrace. Every emotion hidden in his eyes is now conveyed through the taste of his lips. His nose dips as he slides it under my chin, nudging my face back to give him access to the sensitive spot on my neck. With a small flick of his tongue, a small whimper escapes me. His tongue continues to glide up before giving me a playful bite to my earlobe, sending shivers down my spine.

"I need to taste you one more time, Macy." His words reverberate through me as they have an almost haunting tone to it. As if he knows our time is ending. "Can I?" he pleads.

As he says, 'one more time,' panic coats me. Would I be ok with just one more time? Right now,

I don't think so. Has he re-examined our relationship and only wants it to be physical moving forward? I know our hormones caused this to start as only physical, but more has developed within me with each morning I woke up next to him and each night we sat around this campfire. He walks us towards his house and up the stairs as I continue to cover his neck with kisses and nibbles. With each step, low moans and hums escape both of us, anticipation growing with each step. I can feel him growing under me, my desire building and leaking from myself.

Lucas carefully lowers me to his bed, our gazes never breaking from the other. The panic that this may be his last time to touch me makes me frantic, wanting to pull him to me. My panic begins to subside as I see the love in his eyes, causing me to tear up. At this moment, saying goodbye to him feels unimaginable. The first time was difficult to comprehend, but doing it again may break me beyond repair. "Don't cry, baby. I'm right here." Luke reaches down and wipes away the single tear as it glides down my cheek, catching it before it hits his sheets. "I'm not going anywhere." Emotion coats each word he says as he continues. "Just in case I never get to have you this way again, I never want to forget how I feel right now. I'm going to want to remember this moment."

The panic returns to me as I sit up on my elbows, reaching for his shirt to pull it off him. As I continue to raise his shirt, he carefully wraps his hand around mine, slightly shaking his head when my eyes meet his again. It is so slight, if the moonlight hadn't been floating in from outside, it would have been undetectable. A light push on my shoulder makes me lay back fully again. Luke doesn't say anything, slowly sliding off my remaining clothes, never breaking his stare at me. I hear the thump of my clothes landing on the floor, leaving me bare in front of him. With a small bend of his fingers, he beckons me to sit up for him. Without hesitation, I oblige. His eyes trace over the beautiful shadows casting over my pale skin as he begins to slowly remove his own clothes. The tension rises with each second he watches me. His clothes are thrown in the same pile as mine, giving me the ability to stare at his muscular form. It rivals any Greek statue found in a museum, a realization of how he is all mine as long as I want him.

Luke slides his hands under my calves as he props both legs up, my hunger for him glistening as I am spread apart. My arousal seeps from me as he licks his lips in preparation. "You're perfect, Mace. I have never seen a more beautiful woman in my life." Lowering to his knees, his strength pulls me closer to him, causing his mouth to almost border my heat. "Absolutely perfect, Macy Wright."

His use of my married name makes me release an audible gasp, taking my breath away as his intention tonight is to prove I'm his wife and nothing less. As he makes his claim on me, my impatience flies through me, needing him to dissolve the remaining space between his mouth and me. I attempt to use my leg to wrap around his neck to pull him closer, but Luke refuses to budge. "Don't rush me, Mace. You can't rush what I am about to do to you."

Any ability to respond is stolen as he slowly blows his warm air on my soaking pussy, my back arching off the bed. Luke flattens his tongue while giving me an unhurried swipe from my asshole to my clit. His desire pumps through each flick, eating me up like this may actually be his last time tasting me. After he cleans up the mess I have already made, the sensation of his tongue making small circles on my sensitive peak causes my core to clench in anticipation. Instinct kicks in as I reach for his hair, pulling him even closer to me. Everything has such a heightened sensation, driving me wild with each flutter of his tongue.

"More, Luke," I beg in a desperation-seared plea. "Please." I can feel his smile as he never lets up salivating over my shimmering pussy. A small bite at my tip sends my pleasure rushing to the finish line, a deep, loud moan falling from my lips. I never let go of his hair, knowing it was the only thing grounding me.

He leans back on his feet and reaches for my ankles. "Can I try something, Mace?" My juices shine across his face as if a badge of honor of his time between my legs.

A breathy 'yes' rushes out of me, knowing I would let him chop me up into pieces if that meant I could scream his name in pleasure just one more time.

"You don't have to say yes." Luke pushes me, conscious of how my arousal may fuel my approval. I continue to nod my head slightly, giving him permission to pull me further down the bed, ass hanging off the edge of the bed, placing my feet on both of his shoulders. My ass is fully in the air, nothing to hold me up other than Luke's shoulders. As I look up at him, between my legs, his eyes cause a heat to dance over me. "Do you trust me, wife?" I nod again, providing the final reassurance for him to slip one set of fingers through my wet heat pulsating for him. His mouth comes back down to my clit, alternating between rubbing circles over it and nibbling at it.

I am in such a state of pleasure I barely catch he has removed his fingers from me and swipes my flowing fluid lower, hitting my puckered hole. The shock causes me to jump, but relaxing as he swipes more down my line. "Breath, baby. I got you." As he says this, his long, thick fingers push back into me, curving to hit my glory spot and return his tongue to me. With his other hand, he slowly circles my second hole, rubbing my fluid over it, helping me relax. It has been so long since someone was willing to do this to me. Past boyfriends refused, thinking it was gross, never understanding how turned on it made me. As I climb the peak of pleasure, his finger slowly enters my back hole, sliding in and out, deeper and deeper. As anticipated, the pressure builds my arousal even higher while I gasp for air. Before I realize it, Luke is adding a second finger, causing two fingers to pump in and out of both my pussy and ass hole. His tongue still gives me circular laps.

"Macy, do you have any idea how much I thought of you while you were gone?" His voice is rough and filled with longing as I concentrate on the words he is saying. "You consumed me in a way that wasn't healthy for a long time. I never want to let you go again, you know that, right?" The weight of his words intensifies as he continues to pump his fingers in both holes at a pace that leaves me unable to respond. The tingling sensation spreads through my body, but it is nothing compared to the love and admiration I can feel radiating from him. Every movement he makes is filled with passion and desire. Between each of my moans, I hear a small whisper from him, "I never want to let you go again." So quiet I know it wasn't intended for me to hear.

"Tonight, I want to tell you all these things without any words. Can I?" His words send me over the edge, hitting my peak and shattering around his fingers. His movements are relentless as he continues, allowing me to come down from my high with ease. Pulling back, his eyes meet mine, communicating the satisfaction he feels in being the one to make me feel this way. "I am going to worship your body in a way I never have before. I need to memorize every dip and freckle to memory. The way you squeezed my fingers as I finger fucked you tells me you want me to do it to you as well."

He pushes me back up the bed, giving him the ability to make good on his promise as he continues to take me in and memorize every whimper that escapes me. My lips trace lines down his neck, biting his ear and tracing a line back up his neck. He fans my legs wide, allowing himself access to climb between them, hovering over me. "I want to make love with you, Mace, but I won't if you want to slow down. But I need you to tell me. I don't want," he pauses as his eyes bounce between mine. The pain and desperation I have put him through is evident. "I don't want to mess up anything."

"Making love sounds perfect, Lucas." Without hesitation, he lowers himself even further on me, his hard length swiping through my folds, making me aware of each vein and the small mushroom tip as it continues to stroke through me. A grunt slips from his lips as he teases the edge of my opening. The tension and anxiety feel reminiscent of when he took my virginity so many years ago. That night, it was slow, both wanted to learn each other's body as quickly as possible, knowing we had been dancing around this for ages. Despite wanting to take our time, wanting to feel him inside me had been something I had thought about countless times. Feeling our sweaty bodies grinding against each other was just as erotic as I thought it would.

My hips buck against him, causing his tip to barely break the seal of my heat. In an attempt to tease him but also to give in to my need to feel him, feel him give himself to me tonight. A wide grin widens on his face, proving he knows me better than I think and understands what I am trying to do. I can't help but wonder if he is thinking about our first time, just like I am.

He quickly pulls back from my entrance as he shakes his head, grazing around me. I struggle to understand what he is doing until I hear a crinkled tear echo around us. I hadn't considered he may put a condom on, awkwardness floods me as I lay here. The action takes me out of the haze just enough to clock it into my mind to decipher later, but as I feel him line himself back up with me, his lips slowly cover mine. He takes my lips in his and owns me in every way.

Finally sliding himself fully into me, he takes a slow pace, allowing me to stretch around him as my body remembers his. As I make room for the man I have always belonged to, in one way or another, I wrap my legs around him, giving him more leverage to slide further into me. Luke pauses over me once he reaches his hilt, I can see him trying to slow down to prevent a premature release. As he settles into the moment, my lips return to trace lines down his neck, making it to his shoulder blades. Luke slowly starts thrusting into me, reaching his hilt before pulling back out. We rock in tandem, allowing him to wrap himself even further around my heart. When he said he wanted to make love with me, he meant it. He took his time with me. Collecting each moan and heavy breath in his mouth. We hold eyesight throughout, never considering breaking that bond. A silent conversation I will never forget.

"Luke, I am so close." I groan out, his agonizing pace twisting my core once more.

"You don't think I know that, Mace?" His voice as a slice of humor in it, as if mocking me for thinking he doesn't know me better than I know myself. "You have latched onto me, unwilling to let me go until you are ready." We rock back and forth, I run my hands up his abs as they compulse with each thrust. "I'm coming with you whenever you are ready."

With those words, I have no choice but to let this man shatter me from within. I feel as if my body is now shards of glass lying around us, unable to comprehend what it just experienced, not holding back to keep itself together. With one last pump from him Luke is screaming along with me. I have never missed the ability to feel his cum spray in me more than I do right now. I want to feel him seeping out of me, marking his claim the best way he can. We are both limp as his thrusts slow down, our sticky bodies lying together as we both try to catch our breaths. This moment was like a religious experience I didn't know I needed. As promised, he allowed his actions to speak to me without using words, telling me where he stands with me.

Eventually, Luke slides out of me before going to the bathroom to dispose of the condom. As he returns, I see a cloth in his hand. Spreading me open, he places the warm, damp material between my legs to clean me off, giving me the royal treatment and more than I deserve. Whether this man takes me passionately or savagely, he will also treat me with soft hands to express his love to me.

We lie tangled up within each other. As much as I have loved being in Luke's home and peeking at what life could look like, I know it is time to face the demons at my parents' house. "I need to go back to the cottage tomorrow, Luke." I am fearful to break the bubble we are in, but something in me tells me he knew this was coming, and the reason he wanted to take his time with me tonight.

A deep breath passes over my bare shoulders, "I know, Mace." He attempts to hide his disappointment as he speaks those words, but I know it is there.

Knowing I have been honest with him, we both fall asleep in each other's arms, too afraid to say anything else. I worry I am making a mistake by leaving, but also a mistake if I don't leave. Nobody gives you a handbook on how to deal with your estranged husband when your feelings start to appear again.

Chapter Twenty-Two

MACY

The next morning, I wake up again to the smell of Lucas making me breakfast downstairs. What did I do to deserve this man? I know that once I get out of his bed, I have to follow through with my last words last night. I have to go back to the cottage. During all this time I have spent with Luke, our conversations have provided me with greater clarity on how to handle the pointed questions and conversations I have to have with my parents, especially my mom. Fear wraps around my heart, not knowing where this is going to go. I don't know if my heart can take another bombshell like the one about my dad. Despite these fears, Luke has continuously alluded to the fact I don't have a choice in the matter.

Before sitting up, I take the opportunity to roll over to smell his sheets, knowing it is a core memory I want to keep until I am here again. I slowly make my way downstairs, hearing the humming of Lucas following along with the record playing. I'm going to miss these mornings. Hell, I'm going to miss these nights as well. As I round the corner, Luke looks at me, his wide smile shining bright and making his small cheek dimple to peek through his facial hair. I will choose to remember him this way: boxers resting low on his hips and a sly smile on his face.

"Morning, babe. How did you sleep?" He asks, still cooking on the stove and making his way around the kitchen without any thought. Sliding across the floor in his socks, Luke places a playful kiss on my lips before going back to taking care of me.

"Pretty good. How did you sleep?" Stretching my limbs one more time, waking them for the day to come. His shirt I am wearing slides up, showing my stomach and catching his eye. A wiggle of his eyebrows shows me where his mind is this morning.

"Outside of fighting you for the covers all night, pretty damn good." Silence fills the expansive kitchen. I look around, really taking in the home Luke has built for himself. Everything is open, giving you a view of most of the downstairs with one turn of the head. I wouldn't say it is modern, but I also wouldn't say it is rustic either. There is the perfect balance of warmth and metals with cool brown wood floors laced with warm gold lighting fixtures and black door handles. The ceilings are high, and the floor-to-ceiling windows are bookmarked with just as tall bookshelves. The giant kitchen island gives the perfect balance in the space when compared to the living room and its windows and fireplace. Without any ability to slow my steps, I reach him and wrap my arms around his waist. I take in his sandalwood smell and listen to his breathing.

Lucas releases a slow, deep breath before speaking again. "What's wrong, Mace?"

"Nothing." Emotion is laced in my words, but I try desperately to swallow them down. I don't dare look up at him. I fear the tears welling up in my eyes would give away. I am lying to him as if he can't tell by my words.

A small peck is placed on my hair as his arms tighten around me, making me flush with his body. "Mace? If you are going to lie to me, you should probably be better at it."

A small laugh seeps from my mouth as I finally break the spell and look up into his light blue eyes. Small wrinkles frame his eyes when he smiles, but he still holds admiration and love behind them. "I just realized I am going to miss sharing your space with you. It will be weird going back to my parent's small cottage." Pausing for a few beats, getting my emotions under control before I continue. "I didn't realize how much I would fall in love with being here."

Without hesitation, Luke tips my head back, forcing me to look into his eyes. His large, rough hands reach up and frame my face. His calluses graze my smooth cheeks, another reminder of our differences. "Macy, you don't have to leave. You can stay as long as you want, you know that, right?" The declaration hits me deep in my chest, forcing me to break his stare and try to shift my body away from his. "Look at me." Before I can protest, Luke firmly grips my chin and turns my face back to him. Tension engulfs us as if any wrong move could topple the entire base. "You don't have to leave, but if you choose to, you can always come back."

"I know." Tears well up in my eyes, making my sight become blurry. His glare pierces me, causing heat to rise on my cheeks, I'm embarrassed and can't keep my yearning in check. A slow rise and fall of his hand on my back gives me the comfort I so desperately need as a chaste kiss hits my nose.

I allow us to pause, giving in to our embrace for a few minutes before eventually pulling back, wiping the remaining tears off my cheek. Luke turns back towards the food he was preparing, giving me the space I need to calm down. "Do you want some breakfast?" I don't have the words to respond, so I just lift myself to sit on the expansive island, unable to not think about the first time I sat in this same spot, that first morning I was here.

We eat in silence, him leaning against the island while feeding me small bites of pancakes between his own bites. I realize not only is it not awkward like it was when I first got here, but it is more peaceful than anything. Sometimes, your greatest conversations happen when you simply share a room with someone.

We both finish our breakfast before Lucas starts cleaning up and placing the dirty dishes into the dishwasher while I jump down from the island to pack up the few belongings I have here with me. Instinctively, I place a chaise kiss between his shoulder blades as I walk by and give his ass a love tap with my hand. His laughter breaks our silence as I climb the stairs.

***

As I am pulling into my family's property, I start to turn the truck towards the back cottage, but I stop myself. Running from the truth is no longer how I want to live my life. I want to live it fearlessly, with knowledge of how everyone I love and care for is doing in life. The fear I will get the same heartbreaking news as my father being sick grabs ahold of my chest, causing anxiety to swell. "Nothing can change until you allow it, Mace," I say to myself.

Turning the wheel towards my parents' house, a small smile comes over me as I realize I am driving through their front yard, and my tracks will annoy my father. He has always been proud of his yard, getting angry with anyone having to turn around and, in return, get into his yard. "Let's give him something else to worry about," I mumble to myself while I throw the truck in park, turn the key, and head up the steps to their front porch.

As I make my way inside, I hear my mom in the kitchen and see my dad sitting at the kitchen table reading the newspaper. "Do people still read the newspaper, Dad?" I give him a light peck on the cheek as I giggle to myself about the dig I just gave him and hear his grunt in return.

"Do people still not realize I hate it when people mess up my yard?" I know he is joking, but as I turn to look at him, I can see the mischievous look he gives me. I am shaking my head as I sit down when he decides to cut straight to the heavy topics. "Glad to see you finally came home. How was Luke's?"

"How do you know that is where I went, huh?" I taunt him, knowing how he would know that, but wanting to hear him say it out loud. "Did he text you again and let you know?"

"Of course he did, Mace, he isn't stupid." My mom chimes in. "Even if he didn't, the whole town has been talking about seeing that ol' truck sitting outside." I look up with wide eyes. Partially afraid of the lecture I am about to receive. I see my mom give me a genuine smile as she hums her favorite church song.

"What's your plan now?" My attention swings back to my dad as I know what I have to say. Dread washes over me, wishing I didn't have to be the leader in this conversation, but Luke has made it pretty clear I will have to ask my parents since they are unsure if I want to hear about it.

"I think it is time we talk about everything going on around here. What have I missed?" Emotion threatens to show up again, but this time, I force down the swallow. Reaching over, I wrap my hand around my dad's, taking in how weathered his skin looks compared to my own. Poor health and lifelong hard work take a toll on you. "I have missed a lot and it is time I fix that."

My mother and father look at each other. My mom turns off the oven, abandoning the dough she was kneading on the counter. When she pulls the chair beside me out and takes a seat, fear hits me even stronger than expected. What would I do if my mother was also sick? What would it mean for my family? For the last few days, I have only processed losing one parent. What would I do if both were gone?

We talk for a couple of hours as I let them know what really happened to cause me to come home, everything I experienced while away, and we even discussed why I left to begin with. These are all conversations I knew were coming, but naively hoped they wouldn't. It is hard to admit defeated, especially when you disappeared like a ghost overnight. Their looks of pride when I gave them an update on the book was a sharp contrast to how they responded to my news I was applying for jobs out of state again.

My parents gave me more details about my dad's cancer diagnosis, even discussing how the decision was made to put the entire farm and assets into Luke's name. I swallow my pride as they remind me I wasn't here to give them the option of transferring it all to me. I also learned even though it wasn't money driven, my mom has started her own business making jewelry. As my mom explained, she needed something to keep her mind busy so she wouldn't hyper-fixate on how my dad was feeling. I understand this, but it wasn't until I forced her to show me her workroom that I found out Lucas had been building her display cases and shelves for the many shows she had attended. My mom gave me an odd look when I acted surprised Luke made these wooden pieces for her, but as soon as I questioned her reaction, she quickly dropped it. I make a note to return to her response at a later date.

It is mid-afternoon before we both announce there is no other life-altering news we need to share. I stretch in my seat, peeking out the front windows, just to see Luke's truck pulling into the driveway. In the past, I would have been uncomfortable with him just walking in, but now that we have spent so much time together, it feels like he is just coming home. It isn't until Luke places a kiss on the top of my head and squeezes my shoulders as he walks past me that I hear my parents release a deep breath, seeing them relax their shoulders for the first time in what feels like a long time. I didn't even know they were carrying that much worry about me within them. I have been selfish in believing my leaving and returning was only affecting me and not causing distress to those who loved me.

"Tess was telling Macy about her jewelry show coming up this weekend." My dad says, breaking the silence of his kiss. I appreciate his change of subject, not ready to talk more about what is going on between me and Luke. If I don't know what it is, describing it to others would be impossible.

"Oh yeah, she makes some cool stuff, doesn't she?" Lucas looks over at me with a relaxed smile on his face. It is as if we are picking up like nothing happened, all of these years didn't exist, and he is jumping into our conversation like he belongs. It is where he belongs.

"Yeah, it is really pretty. I was telling her she could probably sell a lot more online." I glance at my mom, gauging her reaction to this idea. "I have a friend in New York I could build her a website. I think it would be a great way to sell to more people." The mention of New York sends tension between us all as we all look at each other, remembering I had been living there. Before I can let those thoughts take over, I quickly change the subject. "She also told me you have been building her cases and shelves for her shows, Luke." My pure joy for him is overwhelming, excited for this man to be growing in other ways. "That's really cool. You should send a few pieces you built with my mom to sell. It could be a fun hobby away from the ranch."

Without explanation, Luke's body goes rigid, quickly glancing over at my mom, sharing wide as saucer eyes. "Um, Macy. That's a," my dad pauses, trying to read the room before continuing. "That's an interesting suggestion." Every set of eyes refuse to meet mine, my confusion growing rapidly.

"What do you mean? Is it not a good suggestion? Am I missing something?" I press, wanting an explanation of their change of demeanor.

All three of them look stunned into silence, unsure what to see or if they should say anything at all. There is a whole silent conversation I am not part of. The room goes from tension-filled to awkward, but I guess that is part of my punishment for leaving.

Luke clears his throat, realizing it is his turn to speak. "Hey Mace, uh... the karaoke night you mentioned a couple of weeks ago is tomorrow night. Do you still want to go?" Luke asks as if in passing.

I choose to push this entire encounter to the side, knowing I am learning about each of the people I left behind all over again, it is inevitable to not understand inside jokes or the double meaning of things. The returned excitement I have when I think about going out with my friends, Luke by my side, warms my heart. "Hell, yes, I do! I need to see if Abi wants to join us. Should we just meet you there?" My smile returns as excitement builds.

"Yeah, that works perfectly. And if we meet there, you can't try to count this as our third date, but rather a night out with friends. I know how sneaky you can be." Lucas isn't wrong, but oddly, I never considered trying to get out of our third date.

I have given a piece of myself to Luke and let him steer this ship.

My mom returns to the kitchen, turning on the stove and working on her dough. "When is your third date, by the way?" My mom asks as my dad mumbles her name as a warning to stay out of our business. She couldn't care less if she was intruding. The idea she may is funnier to her than anything else. Her inability to be nonchalant gives me the giggles.

"Saturday, ma'am." I quickly look at Luke, not realizing the date was coming so soon. I am taken aback since I assumed he would wait a few days to schedule anything else. I am almost disappointed it will happen so quickly. Not because I don't want to go, but because the thought it may be our last date forever clenches around my heart, giving me every indication I don't want these dates to end. A thought more terrifying than anything else.

"Already? I thought I would get a few days away from you first." My taunting doesn't phase him, he continues to slowly sip his coffee, waiting for me to push back.

"Are you trying to stretch this out longer, Macy Wright?" Humor laces his words as he attempts to tease me back. His long fingers run circles around the top of his mug, pulling my attention to them and causing desire to shoot through me. Remembering what those fingers have recently done to me causes my cheeks to blush.

I know exactly what he is doing, placing his claim over me once again, but this time, in front of my parents. His reminder of who he is in this family is not needed. Trust me, as I watch his ass in those jeans walking away from me as he heads to the front door, I am far from forgetting who this man is to me.

I roll my eyes, attempting to regain control of the conversation. My parents snicker in the background at my desperate attempts. "Don't be silly. I'm not afraid of you. Why not do it tonight?"

His sly smile pulls me in, my eyes begging for him to continue with this game we are playing. He scratches at his beard, again bringing my focus back to his hands. "Ah, well, I have reservations for Saturday, so we can't change anything. And yes, I have already told Abi what to make you wear." He pushes the door open and takes a step outside. "I will see you tomorrow, wife," as he lets the door shut behind him.

There he goes with that wife word again. All it makes me want to do is climb him like a tree while licking every inch, and he knows it. It's all part of the game he likes to play with me. "I think you may've gotten yourself in some hot water there, Mace," my dad provides. His reminder is unnecessary as I attempt to convince myself he is wrong.

"You have no idea, pops." I stand to get some more lemonade, squeezing his shoulder as I pass before swigging down my glass, praying it cures my suddenly dry throat.

Chapter Twenty-Three

MACY

The warmth of Luke's embrace and the nights spent wrapped up in his arms ignite a fire within me, providing me with bountiful inspiration for my writing. My writing trance is broken as Abi flings open the cottage door the following day.

"What are you doing, Mace? We need to head to Meryl's for karaoke night. Karaoke may not be a big deal in New York, but around here..." Abi pauses for a moment, trying to find an appropriate way of finishing her thought. "Well, we have nothing better to do. Plus, we have to secure a table."

"But It doesn't start for another two hours, Abs," I protest, not wanting to acknowledge her too much as it feels overwhelming compared to the writing cave I have created for myself.

"You've been away for too long, babes. This place will be packed in an hour. Get up, and let's get going."

Reluctantly and admittedly annoyingly, I close my laptop and make my way down the hallway to get ready. I opted for a light blue floral sundress and slipped on my old boots. Within 20 minutes, we are darting down the driveway and heading into town.

Luckily, some of Abi's other friends got there earlier and saved us some seats at the bar. As I settle into my seat, Abi turns to me and remarks, "You look different tonight. What did you do differently?" I quickly glance away from my best friend, but I didn't miss her wagging her eyebrows.

I take a sip of my beer before responding, "I didn't do anything different. What do you mean?"

"You just look... happier than you did when you first came back," she observes. I hear all of her unspoken words, understanding she is prodding and reminding me how staying in Pigeon Lake may make me the happiest.

"Well, I am no longer nursing an embarrassed broken heart," I reply with a smile, attempting to drift this conversation off the subject.

"And hiding out with Luke, of course," she teases.

"Of course." I roll my eyes, avoiding her gaze. If she looked closely, she would see the blush creeping up my cheeks. Looking away, I see Luke walk into the bar. Like a bug to a light, we lock eyes from across the room as he makes his way towards me, I feel like we are the only two people in the world. Seeing the joy on his face causes butterflies to erupt in my stomach, and heat builds in my core. It has been less than 24 hours since I last saw him, but it feels like an eternity.

As my eyesight blurs except my sight of Lucas and my hearing drowns out, I realize I may be too far gone. I realize I may be falling too hard and too fast. Abi's voice sounds muffled as she tries to convince me to spill all the details about what happened between Luke and me during our time "hiding out" together. I don't have the willpower to fight her on the subject, all I care about is the stunning man walking towards me.

"Hey babe, do you need another beer?" Luke's warm hands squeeze my shoulders as he pulls a seat closer to me. As he sits down, his hand slides down my arm and lands in my lap before sliding his hand up my leg, teasing my lace underwear. My skin ignites at his touch, and I can't help but immediately start sweating. Fire explodes across my skin as I immediately start to sweat. I am worked up too much for such a light touch. This man barely has to touch me to get my heat pooling between my legs, causing the beat of my heart to become irrationally noticeable.

"Yes, please, if I am getting through the night, I am going to need a lot more alcohol," I reply breathlessly.

"What are you nervous about? I am the one who has to get up there to sing Taylor Swift." A slow, sly smile greets me as I shift to face him. "Unless you are joining me."

"You lost the bet, Mr. Wright. You have to pay up. And don't worry, I even considered bringing my tripod tonight so I can record your performance without any shaky footage." My smile widens as my ability to push his buttons causes me glee.

Lucas lightly drags my hair off my shoulder, causing a second sizzle of fire to envelop me. As he leans in closer, I can feel his hot breath tickle my neck before he reaches my ear, giving it a bite. The gasp I release causes him to laugh lightly into my ear. "If you are recording anything tonight, it won't be me singing, do you understand me, wife?"

My mind is too blurry to give any response, I take in his voice and give myself over to him. All ability to speak has left me, only giving me the ability to nod my head in delight. Before I know it, Luke places his forefinger under my chin and shifts my mouth to his. His lips are so close to mine that I am convinced he is about to show our cards to our friends in the bar, but as I close my eyes, I feel his body pull away from me, taking away his warmth and woodsy smell. I would be embarrassed if it was any other person, but as I open my eyes, he throws a quick wink before looking away from me and giving his attention to the rest of the table. I am not sure I have ever been so sexually frustrated in my life, the option of pure lust combustion a real possibility.

His complete lack of attention on me tempts me to make a scene, but I know silently teasing him will cause greater enjoyment. Knowing this, I grab my phone before sending him a secretive text.

Me

Don't think that you're going to get away with that tease, Mr.

As soon as he feels his phone vibrate, he doesn't turn back to me, that would be too easy. He stretches to pull his phone from his pocket and while reading it, I see him lazily scratch his beard, trying to play it off. Still never acknowledging me, he sets his phone on the table as my phone vibrates in return.

Lucas

Whatever you say, Mrs.

Frustration rises in me when I realize he did not give in to my jab... AT ALL. This dismissal cannot go unbothered. My desire to get a reaction from him urges me on.

Me

> That's all you have to say to me?

The look on Luke's face as he read my second text gives me no more satisfaction in how this night is going to go. After we finally crossed our invisible line, the way he made me feel is all I can think of. I spent four days living with him where we explored and memorized each of our bodies all over again. Four days of steamy showers and new plaques need to be ordered for his house. Four days, which didn't satisfy my unsated body. With a response vibration causing my phone to dance on the table, my quick grab doesn't assist in keeping our secretive stance with each other. I see Luke shake his head from my peripheral vision, still not looking or acknowledging me.

Lucas

> Do you think that your sopping wet cunt would be mad at me if I shoved my dick down your throat instead?

Well, fuck. He jabbed back, all right. I shift in my seat, trying to rub my thighs together as much as I can sitting next to my best friend. Still refusing to look at me, Lucas places his hand further up my thigh, pressing me down to keep me still, denying my attempt to release.

I quickly attempt to stand, knowing I either have to escape into the restroom alone and take care of this or he would follow me, helping me with this immediate issue. As I move to stand up, Luke presses harder on my thigh, denying my ability to follow my plan. "Don't think about it, Mace. As soon as Chase gets here, I am going to make good on my bet, you don't want to miss it, do you?" He growls in my ear, causing goosebumps to spread down my arms, causing him to lightly drag his rugged fingers over them.

"Would it help if I void your punishment?" I whisper in hope, willing to dissolve our bet if he would give in to my desires.

"Not a chance in hell, baby. I have been practicing." I can hear the humor in his voice. Whether his humor is regarding his song choice or my increasing frustration expanding through me, I do not know. Either way, I am maddened. I continue to try and shift in my seat, but Luke continues to prevent me from this action.

Before I can try to stand again, I see Chase, Luke's friend, walk in and take a seat across from me.

I don't know Chase well, only seeing him in this bar a few times. From what I have learned, he works a lot and has a daughter, so I am not sure if that prevents him from being in town more. What I do catch is his quick glare towards Abi. As I turn to look at her, she takes a large gulp of her drink while requesting another one from the passing waitress. I am unable to determine if she is happy or disappointed to see Chase. I lean in to ask Abi what those looks were for, but before I can, Luke stands, pushing his chair away from me. "Chase, you ready? You're late."

Chase's facial expression looks confused while he looks towards many of us, but once he stops at Luke, Chase just shakes his head, dismissing Luke's question. "Yeah, I know I'm late." His gruff, deep voice catches me by surprise. His strong hand lifts, and he wraps it around the back of his neck, almost kneading away his worries. "I was waiting for my sister to get to the house to babysit. Plus, I told you no, Luke." We all look at each other, wondering what this conversation could be regarding, hoping this peculiar tension doesn't continue the rest of the night.

"Yeah, I know you didn't want to, but, like always, I ignored it, knowing you would still come through for me." Luke stands and slaps Chase's shoulders. "It's time to shine big boy." Lucas starts walking to the stage, stretching his arms as if he is about to run a marathon. I love seeing him feeling at ease with his friends and being himself. Many females have sung their favorite Taylor Swift songs all night, but Luke would be the first male. As I look back at Chase, I notice there has been no movement and he relaxes back to drink his beer, Abi continuing to sneak sly glances at him before returning to nurse her drink.

As the pulsing beat of End Game fills the crowded room, I feel of mix of excitement and apprehension. Luke stands ready with the mic in his hand and a determined look on his face. Before he begins the song's first line, he calls out at Chase, "Chase, don't miss your part, asshole." I look at an unamused Chase making it clear he will not be hitting his part of this impromptu performance.

I can't help but giggle as the music continues, and everyone joins in on the chaotic musical number. Luke is singing Taylor's first couple of lines, but once he gets to the rapping portion, it becomes painfully obvious this part was supposed to be Chase's. Yet, he remains still and silent, leaving Luke to improvise and the crowd joining in to fill in where they can.

Just when I think the whole thing might fall apart, Abi stands up beside me, making her way to the stage. She joins Luke, and together they finish the song, their voices raised in an off-key duet. Despite this, both embody the spirit of the pop star herself, performing with passion and energy despite any mishaps.

As the music stops, both take a bow on the stage while the entire bar stands, cheering on both for their performance. Luke keeps his sights on me as he steps off the stage, throwing me a wink, but keeps walking, heading to the back door. Now, I am not sure if this is supposed to be my cue, but I'm a girl on an orgasm mission and will not test the waters more than needed. I eagerly stand to follow him, Abi shaking her head at me as if she can read my mind.

I throw open the heavy back door, leading me to the familiar alley. If I didn't see the shadow of Luke standing off to the side, I would be freaked out. Why would a grown woman think it is a good idea to go into an alley on her own? They wouldn't. Unless she knew the man she had a crush on was back there. My deep, panting breath fills the alley as I slowly make my way to Luke. The smells of trash and recent rainfall fill the space, giving it an odd mix of joy and disgust.

I reach Luke, leaning against the wall, both releasing a burst of howling laughter, him reaching towards me and pulling me closer. I am in complete awe he made good on his bet, giving me a performance I was not prepared for. "End Game, huh? That's a bold choice." My humor fills my voice, a direct expression of the fun I have had tonight.

"I hope I never have to do it again, so I knew I had to make it count." He reaches up and tucks a strand of hair behind my ear, the heat searing me.

I can't help but rest my hand on his chest, dying for any contact I can have. "Was Chase really part of it?"

"Yeah, I thought I talked him into it, but now I am starting to think he just agreed to get me to shut up." He reaches out, wrapping his hand around my waist before pulling me deep into him, making our bodies mold against each other. "He is the town grump, but I pretend like I don't hear his comments."

"I'm sure it would have been great." With the new closeness, I reach up and land a kiss against his lips. The groan I get in return causes me to tease my tongue on his seam, pushing myself deeper into his kiss and touch. His rough hands slide down from my waist, following the curves of my body before squeezing my ass, almost causing my body to peep from underneath my dress.

My breath catches as he quickly spins us around, pushing me onto the wall. His lips start to travel down my neck before he starts placing light kisses on my collarbone. His firm hands grip my waist as I arch into him while rubbing my thighs together. One hand holds me to the wall as the other snakes up my body, sliding under the top of my dress and popping my boob out. My first instinct is to freeze at his motions, but I quickly start relaxing because being here with him is sexier than any scene I could have thought up for my book.

"Relax, baby, I won't let anyone see you. Do you really think I am the sharing kind when it comes to your body? I am the only one to see these pink nipples again until the day I die. Do you understand?" His fingers barely touch my sensitive peaks, causing my back to arch even more against him. "Look at them, they are standing in salute for me, begging for my mouth."

Before I can give any response, Luke has sucked my peaked nipple deep into his mouth, giving it small nibbles after each flick of his tongue. My head falls back before grabbing onto his thick hair. I catch myself squeezing my lips together, not wanting my moans to echo down the alleyway. What he is giving me is filling the smallest part of my desire, a desire that is mesmerizing and indescribable. It is a need that makes me want to give him every piece of me, even if I have to do it with an audience. "Please, Luke." I moan. His name barely escapes me. "I need more. I need all of you." I am not afraid to beg for him to take advantage of me.

"Do you really think I would take you in an alley like a slut?" His cunning smile splits the air around me. The shake of his head causes his facial hair to scratch my tight peak where his mouth just was.

"Please, let me be your slut," my body arching into him, chasing any touch he will give me. With those words, Luke gets to his knees, replacing his tongue with his fingers on my nipple. His bright eyes look up at me with danger in his eyes. In any other situation, I wouldn't want him to get his pants dirty on this nasty ground, but my arousal is too tight to question him.

His hands sneak up my legs, the anticipation making them shake in place. He reaches my core and pushes his thumb to my clit, a loud moan releasing from my lips. "Any slut of mine wouldn't wear panties when she knows she is going to see me." My dress is crumpled in his hands while he gives me a bite of my inner thigh. "Touch yourself, Mace."

Shocked at first, I slide my fingers down my body, hoping to tease him just enough. I need him to feel the sense of urgency I have right now, chasing a release I am dangling in front of him. As I go to slide my fingers inside my panties, Luke swats at my hand, surprising me once more. "If you aren't a big enough slut to go bare, you don't get to flick yourself bare. Now, touch yourself." Any woman would do as this man demanded if they were in this situation. Seeing him looking up at me, dominating me while holding me in the palm of his hand, making me feral for him.

Luke leans back to sit on his feet while he watches me in wonder. My tiny fingers rush in circles, lapping at my juices, chasing the high only he can give me. "Spread your legs wider, baby." Luke takes an ankle and lifts my foot to rest on one of his shoulders before swiping my hand away from me. "Hold your dress up." As I do, he reaches into my lace panties, which I unfortunately wore, before he rips them in two. He slides my soaking panties into his back pocket, his own souvenir for the night. "There, now my slut of a wife is how I need her. Now, should I clean you up before we go back inside?" With a quick dip of my head, Luke reaches down and laps his flat tongue from top to bottom. I can feel his sharp fingers digging into my legs, holding himself back.

"I missed this taste. I missed tasting you on my lips whenever I wanted you." He continues to sweep his tongue through my folds, my release barrelling towards me. He is eating me as if I'm his last meal, and I wouldn't dare stop him. "Too bad I won't let you come on my tongue tonight." He pulls back and places my foot back on solid ground. As he stands and pushes my tit back into my dress, I see his lips glistening with me. With one last tight lick up my neck, he pulls further away from me.

"Wait, where are you going?" I am distraught with passion. I needed this from him, and while I wouldn't usually mind him edging me, I am wound too tight for that to be an option right now. I haven't had him in less than two days and having him stop sends panic from me. As I look at him, he wipes my juices from his mouth, giving me a wicked smile as he does it.

"Going in to finish my beer before heading home." He grabs my hand and pulls me along with him. I can see my panties peaking out from his back pocket, another way he is publicly claiming me. This statement of claiming me may be his sexiest yet.

"Am I going home with you?" I knew this wasn't the plan, but I'm willing to do anything to have him fill me up, to pump inside me. My arousal doesn't stop leaking from my cunt, sliding down my legs as I walk. I can't help but daydream about him licking my leaking arousal all the way up my leg, truly keeping me clean.

"Nope," he says with a dramatic pop of the p. "I am going to go home and get a good night's sleep because tomorrow's date will take a lot of energy. You would be smart to get some rest, too." He drags me inside, still in a helpless daze.

We both take a seat, Abi giving me curious eyes, causing my blush to creep back up. We finish our drinks with our friends before we all cash out from the bar to head home. Whether it is the heat of being turned on or embarrassed, everyone knows we were just together, which makes my blush spread further up my body. Abi is the only one who gives an inclination she noticed what happened, everyone else ignores any possible exchange.

Once Luke has paid for both of our drinks, he leans down and gives me a kiss. I can still taste myself on his lips. I hear gasps scatter around the room as he whispers to me not to stay out too late. And like that, he is gone. Abi asks for an explanation on our drive home, but I don't have the words to explain what happened. I'm sure the assumption is we

hooked up, but she couldn't be more wrong. My red cheeks should tell her everything she needs to know.

Chapter Twenty-Four

MACY

Knowing I **see Luke later**, there are a couple of things I need to do before he picks me up. The growing tension between us two last night has become so strong and undeniable I truly feel like I am about to combust. Last night didn't ease any heat in me, having to take care of myself after Abi dropped me off. Despite my attempts to keep him at arm's length, I know, for the first time, I am excited for our date. I can't wait to watch him open the door of his truck for me and experience him being a true Southern gentleman. He told me to wear a nice dress tonight, leading me to believe he would be in something other than his tight Wranglers. If I know anything about Luke, it is while he can flip my switch in his tight wranglers, seeing him in dress pants is next level. He always has a cocky swagger to his walk but seeing him in dress pants gives him this aura about him which makes him act even more tantalizing. Before I move on to the main act of the day, I take care of my dishes sitting in the sink, move clothes from the washer to the dryer, and iron my dress for tonight.

None of those chores help heal the burning ache I feel between my legs. The anticipation of tonight's activities is eating me to my core. I check the clock on the oven before realizing I still have a couple of hours before Lucas will be here to pick me up. Upon that realization, I grab my trusty vibrator and head to the bathroom. I run water in the expansive bathtub, adding bath salts and bubbles to level up the atmosphere will push me further off the depths of my orgasm. Turning my music on, I decide to even light multiple candles around the bathroom and turned off the overhead light.

I slowly dip my toes in the hot bath water before registering how while it may be too hot, it will only fuel the heat building in my core. I lay back, taking a deep breath, allowing the aroma to engulf me and allowing my full body to relax. Before getting too ahead of myself, I make sure to shave my legs and wash my body, all leading up to the main act. In my New York apartment, there wasn't room for a bathtub so one of the best things in this cottage is the large bathtub my mom put in a few years ago.

Once all the mandatory measures have been completed, I reach for the small stool next to the bath and grab my vibrator. This specific vibrator was one of my better purchases, it is completely waterproof while also having a curved arm that extends inside of me, retracting on beat with the vibrations. The arm sits perfectly against my clit and feels remarkably like a large tongue lapping circles across you. This is my favorite toy since it will help me reach pleasure the fastest, sating my needs before my date with Luke tonight.

Lucas

I am in a time crunch, trying to leave Loch and Tessa's house so I am not late in picking up Macy when Tessa stops me before closing the door. "Hey, sweetheart, before you leave, can you run down to the cottage and grab the paint I left in the hall closet?" Her cheerful request tells me I can't deny her.

"Yes, ma'am, I will be right back." I take a deep breath as I step on the wooden porch and hop down the steps. I really don't have the time to do this, but I would never not help Tessa when she needs it. I just have to get back to my house to jump into the shower, get ready, and make it back over here by 5:00 p.m. to pick up Macy.

As I reach the cottage, I quickly knock on the front door, but despite seeing the truck Macy has been driving sitting out front, she never answers the door. I start to think she is taking a nap, but I hear her music pouring loudly out of the house. Under the assumption she can't hear my knocks, I grab the key I have secretly kept and head inside.

"Mace!" I call out, not seeing her in the kitchen. My annoyance at her not responding rises, and I feel my time passing quicker than I need. "Macy, I need to grab something for your mom," I yell louder, still walking, looking around for her.

When I hear the music coming from the bathroom, it still has not dawned on me she may be in the shower or bath as I couldn't hear any water running. I tap my fingers on the bathroom door as I hear a breathy "yes" come from the other side. I slowly open the wooden door to only catch the reflection of Macy in the mirror above the sink. I can see her rocking back and forth, making the water splash from the front to the back while her head leans back to the wall with her eyes closed. Her mouth is in a small o-shape when I realize there is a vibrating pattern popping to the surface of the lower half of her body.

I consider quietly shutting the door and leaving her be, but I am a red-blooded man, and there was

nothing I could have told myself that would have made me stop watching my wife get herself off. I step further into the bathroom, her still not seeing or hearing me because of the music when I close the door behind me. I see the candles surrounding her, and I realize she has set the mood for this. If only she would have set this mood while inviting me to join her.

I watch her for a couple of seconds as her breathing becomes more erratic, and I know she is edging closer to her release. "When I helped your dad install this bathtub, I never thought I would get to watch my wife fuck herself in it," I growl out to her while leaning against the opposite wall. My dick grows hard against my jean pants as I fight to touch it.

Macy startles at the sound of my voice and flashes her eyes open. Her cheeks flush bright red as she realizes I have been standing here watching her. She scrambles to grab the toy she was using, embarrassment written all over her face.

"Don't you dare take that out," I sternly say, almost wishing I would have just let her finish before announcing my presence.

"Luke! What are you doing in here?" Her voice reaches octaves I have not heard in a decade.

A small chuckle escapes my lips. "In my defense, I did knock and call out your name multiple times before coming in here." A smirk forms across my face as I see she stops her hand from halting her arousal. I take a significant step closer to the side of the tub. "I didn't mean to interrupt you, please continue. But remember, I am watching this time."

A flash of curiosity, followed by embarrassment, crosses Macy's face. "Absolutely not, Lucas. Get out. You weren't supposed to see this," she protests, but there is a tiny pause in her reaction, which tells me she doesn't actually feel that way.

"Is this how you were preparing for our date tonight?" I ask as we both sit in silence, waiting for a beat to pass. I can tell she wants to lie, but she knows I would see right through it. Taking this as an invitation to stay, I push myself off the wall and slowly start unbuttoning my shirt. unclasping my belt before sliding it out of the belt loops.

Macy's eyes widen even more as my bare, muscular chest greets her, and my hand pulls out my hard length. "What are you doing?" She asks indignantly. "I told you to leave!"

"Baby, I heard what you said, but I don't like following your rules. I know this show of defiance is you pouting since you didn't get your way last night." I take another step closer to her. "Now, can I join you, or are you going to make me stand here and watch?"

"We both can't fit in here." She declares.

"Well, can I at least help you? I can still see your fingers touching your clit, you know."

"I don't need your help. You proved that last night," Macy retorts.

A bigger smile spreads across my face as I kick off my boots and slide my pants down my legs. Taking the final step to the bathtub, I kneel next to it. "Let me help you," I offer.

I can see Macy's internal struggle as she considers how to either get out of this or come up with an alternative ending that is better than she anticipated. "Will you at least let me watch you? I won't touch you," I assure her.

Macy's final mental wall crumbles as she rolls her eyes as she reaches for her toy. "If you want to. But I won't be thinking about you, so don't think I am." Her chin pops up in a show of defiance, but her lust-filled eyes give away everything.

I snicker to myself as I grasp the base of my ever-hardening cock. "Yes, you will be. I saw how you licked your lips when my dick popped out for you. Since I can't touch you, sit up on the side of the bathtub. I need a clear view of that pretty pussy of yours." There is a slight hesitation before she complies as I become more demanding. "Now."

I am certain demanding "now" is what got her moving so quickly. She always liked to be the submissive one. I watch as she pulls her toy out of her and stands up, allowing me to watch the suds from her bath slowly slide down her perfectly shaped body. I want nothing else than to glide my callused hands down her body and kiss her feisty mouth. She leans against the back wall of the bath as I motion for her to put her legs up. I stroke my length while watching her prepare herself for me. If this woman knew what she did to me, how only she could do this to me, she wouldn't fight my desire to worship her body. The pressure I give myself is nothing like the pressure her cunt would give it. I know I have to play this game with her, if letting her feel as if she is in control one last time, the outcome will be explosive.

Before I knew it, the woman I love more than anything was leaning against the back ledge of the bathtub with both legs spread open on the front ledge of the bath, my hands resting next to both of her feet. It is physically painful to not reach for her, to tease her perfect clit.

"God, Mace. There you are, easily showing off your pink cunt for me, thinking I will be able to control myself. You are already dripping out for me. Taunting me with each drop." I can't help but lick my lips and squeeze my dick harder while I drag my hands up and down the length that is begging for her. "Fuck, baby. My tongue misses you."

"I said you can't touch me," she says, and when I look up at her, I see a naughty smirk across her plush, pink lips. "You just have to watch me, Luke." She grabs her purple toy and starts rotating it, making slow circles across her clit. "Maybe you will think twice before teasing me like you did last night." I clench the side of the tub with one hand, knuckles turning white under the pressure, while my other hand strokes my rod trying to ease any pressure building. "I didn't say you could touch yourself. Stop, now." Her demands shock me, but after last night, I deserve every ounce of her punishment. "And if you touch me, all of this ends for you." Out of fear that she would force me to leave, I reluctantly let go and grab the bathtub with my other hand. I take one deep breath at a time, trying not to lose control.

"What is the longer part for?" I ask, despite knowing the answer. It was more of an invitation for her to show me and show me she does as she glides the thrusting tip inside her pussy. Watching those lips part while she shows off to me is the most arousing thing I have ever seen. Her walls wrap around the rubber toy with a welcomed force. A small moan breaks across both of our lips while I watch the smaller tip circle at her clit. She can pretend it is a tongue on her, but we both know my tongue would bring her faster to the finish line. Her other hand reaches up and squeezes her pebbled nipple.

All I can do is take a deep breath, willing any self-control to kick in because I worry about how long I can stop myself from touching her... or myself. An idea jumps into my mind, an idea that will make sure I follow all of her rules but still allow me to participate in her game. I can't touch her, but that doesn't mean I can't make her scream my name. I reach for the belt I flung across the room and bring it to her. "Give me your hands, Mace."

Surprisingly, she doesn't hesitate or question me as I tie both hands together with my belt without ever touching her. Once they are as tight as I can make them, I hold them up and loop the belt around a towel holder I, luckily, installed a few years ago. Reaching down, I slide her toy out of her pussy and bring it to my lips to lick everything off of it. Macy's eyes widen even more while a small whimper escapes her. It is at that moment I know she is just as turned on as I am. "Fuck Mace. I need more of this."

I slide it back into her while I grab the remote to make the thrusts even deeper. Macy gasps and rocks her hips towards me.

"Sit still. I need to see all of you as you clench around this dick, the dick you secretly wish was mine. Imagine the damage I could do to your dripping cunt with my tongue right now." For good measure, I lick my lips again to remind her what she could be feeling right now. Her legs start to tremble, still propped up on the side of the bathtub. Right before I have her edging, I pull out the toy and lick every trace of her off the thrusting cock.

"Luke! Please! Let me finish." Her eyes are ablaze, begging me for her release and shifting this power struggle back to me being in charge.

"I don't know if it is worth it. My wife is splayed out for me, waiting for me to take her over the edge, despite my desire to see how far I can push her. What should I do, baby?" A sly smirk spreads across my face while I look into her heavy, lust-filled eyes. Her pupils dilated to a full as she rests her head against the tiled wall.

"Don't be an asshole, Luke. I could have kicked you out." Her words are laughable since we both know I wouldn't have followed her directions.

"You didn't, though, and I am going to make the most of it. Now, watch your mouth before I fill it with something to shut you up." I turn down the pulsated vibrations from the clit tip of her vibrator, lightly pressing it to her right nipple. Her back arches to me in order to chase the pleasure. I remove it from one nipple just to drag it to the other.

"More. I need more." Macy pants between swipes.

"More what?" I taunt, needing her to accept me as her dominator.

"Just more everything, babe." She speaks my nickname I haven't heard in years, causing me to snap any remaining control.

"Open your mouth." As she does, I slide the vibrating tip over her clit, collecting everything she has pouring out, before turning the thrusting cock to the highest setting and sliding it in her mouth. "Do you taste that? This is how I make you feel." I push it further into her mouth.

I hear a small gagging of her refluxes when my own hips thrust forward, hitting the side of the bathtub. "Damn it, Mace. I have needed to hear you gagging on me for years. I missed how good it sounded. Those lips wrapped around it with ease, taking every inch of me while you milk me." I push the toy the remaining amount I can down her throat. "You feel that? This is what I want to do to you. I want to tear your throat apart. I want to feel you gagging on me but begging for more. I want to watch tears fall down your cheeks from your arousal."

I look and see her eyes watering but slightly rolling back into her head from the pure lust and enjoyment she is also feeling. I then see she is rocking her cunt against the edge of the bathtub, and I know I have to stop her. She needs to rely on me for her pleasure and nothing else.

"Do you wish this was my cock in your mouth?" She erratically nods her head as I realize I am still thrusting my hips on the side of the bath to get my own pleasure. I grab the shower head and turn it on, allowing it time to get hot before placing it close to her swollen clit while her vibrator is still fucking her mouth. Her moans grow even louder to where it is drowning out the pop music she is listening to. "Let me fuck my hand, and I will let you come. Deal?"

She shakes her head no to me like a defiant slut, but I remind her I am the one in control right now and turn down the water flow in the shower head, halting all pleasure. Panic flashes across her features, and then, with a quick nod of her head, I pull out the toy from her mouth and listen to her try and catch her breath while I drop the shower head and get to my feet. Anger and despair fly across her face, which makes me laugh. Does she really think I would leave her like this two days in a row? Like hell, I would. I grab one of the towels sitting at the sink and quickly roll it the long way. "Lean your head up." She slowly shakes her head, but I use the towel and slap her still-shining pussy with it. This causes her to moan a barely audible curse at me and lean her head forward as I wrap the towel around her eyes and tie it behind her.

"Luke. Please. You promised." Her desperation fills me with my desire to pleasure her.

"And I don't break my promises. So, either stop asking questions, or I am going to cover your smart mouth, too." Her mouth clamps closed while she leans her head back to the wall behind her. I slide the vibrator back into her glistening hole while I reach into a drawer at the sink and pull out a handful of clothes pins I remembered seeing in there a few months ago. "Ok, Mace, you have two choices: you can either have pain or pleasure. What do you want from me while I am hand fucking myself?"

"Pain," Macy surprises me, making me shake my head out of admiration. She gives me a loud moan while her orgasm gets closer caused by the rubber dick is fucking her right now.

"Good. Now, just trust I am going to take care of you like you have never been taken care of before. Since I can't touch you, we have to get creative, but just know I wish it was my dick in you right now." I hum my hot breath against her thigh, making her aware of how close I am to her. "I wish I was getting to feel you around me. I wish it was my shower of cum that would be sprayed in you right now. But it can't be. So here is the best ride I can give you." Her gasp echoes between us, anticipation is eating her alive, wanting to know what each of my moves will be.

I slide the dense cock out of her cunt and loudly moan as I lick her all off again. "Macy. I have never seen a prettier sight than you tied up, legs apart, showing me how swollen you are for me, and able to watch your desperation flow out of you like it is." She may not have expressed to me he doesn't hate me as much as she did when she showed back in town, but knowing she allows me to have this control tells me we are getting closer.

"I could put my face under you and just let it fall into my mouth if I wanted. You love showing off to me, don't you?" I look up at her face and admire how truly beautiful she is under the candlelight. Yes, I want to fuck her so badly right now, but knowing she is blindly following my commands is the greatest gift she could give me. She is still partially mine and still trusts me.

Placing the first clothespin on her right nipple, a small yelp escapes her while I place another one on her bottom, pouty lip. I place a third one on her left nipple as I watch her arch to get closer to me. I set her vibrator on the tip of the clothespin to distract her from what I am about to do. "Sorry, baby," I say as I put the final clothespin on her clit. I put the shower head back on her and rotate it at a pulsating rate to send her souring in her orgasm. Her scream would deafen anyone if they weren't ready for it. I could have stopped, but I let the pulses sit there and follow through to the end.

"That's my good girl, always taking whatever I give to you. You always were a good, obedient girl for me. I guess you can't grow out of everything, huh?" I can't help but taunt her, completely owning my dominating role. "Now, are you ready for another one? Only a wife would be so damn greedy."

Macy nods her head while I remove the clothes pins from her nipples and lip. I take the vibrator, sliding it through her folds to gather as much lubrication as possible before ordering her to slide closer to the edge of the ledge. "Tell me what you want me to do now?" I demand. Granted, I don't need her to ask because I already know my next move. As she opens her mouth to tell me, I edge the thrusting dick to her back hole and start to slightly push it in. Macy jumps slightly but then relaxes back into it, making it clear this was not something she was expecting.

"Lucas. Fuck me. I need to feel you fuck me." Macy pleads with me, her desperation is a different level of arousal. Her words only encourage me to make her beg.

"I can't touch you, remember?" I mockingly say as I push the toy further into her and listen to a loud groan coming from her. I grab a hairbrush and quickly wet it. "Spread your legs wider for me, Macy." She spreads her legs even further apart while I slide my makeshift dick into her. You can tell she is shocked at first, but this isn't the first time we have been creative like this so I know she will relax into it. "You wanted every hole filled, remember? Now open your mouth because I am about to finish all over your face when you give me another orgasm. All three holes will be full for me."

I continue to stroke myself as her ass continues to get fucked, I thrust the brush in and out of her, and right when I can feel her clamp down on the brush, her head rolls back, her mouth still open, and screams my name. Her scream is what unleashes me as I spray across the tub onto her face and into her mouth. "Fuuck Mace. You took this so well." Seeing her like this is the sexiest thing I have ever seen. She wasn't expecting any of this, but I was determined to never let her forget it. "Fuck. I am sliding down your face like a trophy. That's what you do to me. Don't you ever think my dick doesn't want you." I grunt.

I pull out the comb and vibrator and then release her hands from the belt and remove the blindfold. She looks completely railed and exhausted from what we just did. Her deep breaths give weight to how well she did for me. I take my belt back while slowly still pumping out the last bit of myself. Her wide, brown eyes look up at me, pleasure tears spilling down her cheeks, while she collects my cum off her face and slides what she can into her mouth. This action alone could have made me start over again. "Don't do something you can't follow up with. I wouldn't be able to stop myself from touching you this time." I pump two more times as I watch her continue to collect all of me from her face and chest and smirk while she eats it all up.

I take a step back before I can't stop myself while putting my clothes back on. I put a clean towel next to her and turn to leave the bathroom. Before completely closing the bathroom door, I remind her to be ready for our date.

Chapter Twenty-Five

MACY

The last time I saw him dressed up like this was for our wedding. I may have had the perfect dress on and make-up done, but the moment we walked back down the aisle, we headed directly to one of the rooms the event center had for people to get ready in. We made work of each other as quiet as we could. Our friends and family assumed we were just sharing a quick, romantic moment together, but instead, we were ravaged for each other.

As he stands in my doorway now, in his nice slack pants and me in a black dress Abi dropped off for me early this morning, I realize I have fallen for this man all over again. He reaches for my hand and leads me out of the house, making sure I don't sink into the grass in my heels. His hand snakes around my waist as we walk up to the truck. "I am only going to give you a small kiss, I don't mess up your makeup, but know I want to wreak havoc on you right now."

A shy smile welcomes him as he wraps his hand on my jaw and pushes me up towards him. A chaste kiss covers me before he steps back and opens his truck door for me. He joins me a few minutes later, and we head down the dirt road. "Where are we going?"

"Headed to Dallas for the night."

I must give him a strange look since I was not expecting us to be staying out all night. Was I hoping we would end up in one of our beds? Without a doubt. I just wasn't expecting this much. "Should we go back and grab a change of clothes and stuff for me?"

"No need. Abi put a bag together for you, and I grabbed your toothbrush from my house." He throws a thumb backward, bringing my attention to the overnight bag sitting in his backseat. I am pleasantly surprised and can't find the emotions to express it to him. For the first time in many years, I feel so loved and taken care of. This man thought of everything I would need to make me feel comfortable, and he succeeded. I grabbed his hand and relaxed while watching the flat plains pass and listening to the 90's country music channel. He didn't let go of me until we pulled up to the hotel.

"This is where we are staying?" As I look in front of us, I see a five-story Art Deco masterpiece disguised as a hotel. It is beautiful, and each glass and metal detail take my breath away.

"Well, this is where I made reservations. If you don't like it, we can go somewhere else. Abi thought you would-" I cut him off by leaning over the armrest and shutting his mouth with a kiss. His hand vined through my curled hair as he pulled me closer. Kissing him has always been the best way to make him stop talking.

"It's perfect, Lucas. I was just shocked. It's so beautiful." We are both peering at it through his window when anxiety floods me. He thought so much about this date, and I want to make tonight everything he dreamed. Thoughts of my news, which I learned about right before he picked me up, causing my stomach to plummet and dread to envelop me.

As we reach the front desk, the receptionist reports he actually reserved two rooms. When I glance over at him, he becomes shy under my eyes. "When I made the reservations, I didn't know if you would want us to have one or two rooms, so I played it safe." He tries not to look me in the eyes as he is sure I was not expecting this, proving once again he always puts me first.

"One key will be fine," I report to the front desk clerk with a smile and a quick squeeze of Luke's hand. He clears his throat while he repeats the request to the clerk. "But make sure it is the bigger room reservation, please." The receptionist quietly nods her head while handing us the keys.

As we arrive at our room, I realize that Luke meant the suite when he referred to the bigger room. The room boasts tall ceilings, all decked out in art deco flourishes. Lush curtains fall down the far wall, while the granite bathroom floors lead me to a jacuzzi tub in the corner. Not only did Luke make us a reservation, but he also found the most beautiful room I had ever seen.

"What would you have done if I said two rooms?" I probe, just to push on his buttons one more time tonight.

"Give you this room, and I would have taken the other one, of course." He steps behind me and wraps his arms around me, leaning down to place a peck kiss on my cheek. "But I am so thankful you didn't make me do that." He chuckles as he leans back and spanks my ass. A yelp rings through the bathroom while he hurries away from me.

We make it to dinner in an upscale restaurant about a block away. It is one of those restaurants that, if you didn't know it was there, you would miss it. It requires you to ride up the sleek elevators to the top floor, where you are surrounded by the Dallas lights. I secretly regret not listening to Luke when he told me not to wear my heels for the walk, but I would never admit it to him. The way his eyes bulged out of his head when I stepped out of the bathroom was enough for me to commit to any sores I may have in the morning. Fire raced down me as he undressed me, completely unable to speak.

Over dinner, I realize I would be happy if I stayed in this bubble with him forever. This could be a beautiful life with us two, living back in Pigeon Lake, taking care of the ranch, and eventually having babies running around. I am not sure why I felt like my only option was to run from him when I now know he would have followed me anywhere. I guess I never had the nerve to ask him. That mistake is on me.

"Mace, why did you leave me? I know I was working a lot of hours, but I wanted to show you I could provide for you and our future family. I now realize I pushed myself too hard, which caused us to start living two separate lives." Lucas asks, pulling me out of my thoughts. As I look back at him, the fear and concern of what I was about to say was painted across his face like glowing neon paint.

"It all became fine too soon. I wanted electricity and passion between us, but instead, we found ourselves in the daily, mundane routine of everything. I wanted our lives to be on fire. But it was just... just fine." Over the years, I have given myself so many excuses and reassurances that leaving was my only option. I am not sure I was ever willing to give the full, unedited version of my decisions to not only my friends and family but myself."

"Being back here just proved to me it all wasn't enough. A piece of me knew you were working hard for me and our future, but the idea of telling you how I was feeling paralyzed me and made me shut down because you were doing what any responsible husband would do. I was terrified if I told you to stop or I still wasn't happy, you would take it as an attack like I was saying you weren't doing enough. You were just not what I wanted at that point in my life. I was being selfish before," tears start to fill my eyes, knowing the pain I am causing him. "But leaving like I did was even more selfish, I understand that now."

I was expecting him to get upset with me and push me to give any other answer, but instead, he gently reached across the table and squeezed my hand. This man was a lot of things, but the tender, loving man most didn't see was my favorite. "I will do everything in my power to never make you feel that way again, Mace." His rough hand reaches up to wipe away the single tear drop that has escaped my eyes before taking my hand in his again. "I'm not asking you to stay with me, that isn't fair. All I can do is show you what life could look like and hope you decide this is your home." A beat of silence halts everything around us. The world continues to move, but all I can picture is the life I am thinking I want to live right here. I give him a meek smile and nod, trying to stop any more tears from forming in my eyes from releasing. We continue our dinner as if we didn't have that moment, eating, drinking, and laughing until it was time to leave. His hand firmly wraps around mine as we make our way to the elevator.

The moment the elevator doors close, Luke moves in front of me, anchoring me to the wall. His hand traces my body and cups my ass as he leans in closer to me. "I am fucking you with those heels on when we get to our room, wife." His smooth demeanor envelopes me as he bites the ear he was just whispering in while he gives a small thrust into my stomach, proving how badly he wants me.

A small gasp escapes me as he pulls me even closer to him, squeezing my ass and giving me the need to drip my pleasure down my leg. Knowing everything he is going to do to me reassures me how tonight will be long, but oh so pleasurable. I reach for his belt the moment the elevator doors ding open, forcing us to stop what we are doing and forcing us to walk out into the cool night. We walk past an older couple staring at us, knowing exactly what we are doing.

Once we make it back to the hotel room, we mimic two furied teenagers, acting as if we will combust if we do not get to touch each other. The door clicks behind us as I feel Luke's rough hands reach for the zipper in my dress. He painstakingly drags it down slowly, allowing the cool air to send goosebumps across my body. As he allows the dress to puddle at my feet, leaving me only in my sky-high heels, I hear a visceral growl behind me. "Are you telling me you weren't wearing panties all night?" His mouth is next to my ear, fueling the heat pooling in my core.

"I thought any slut of yours wouldn't even consider it, sir," I whisper in a mischievous tone right before he slings me over his shoulder and walks us closer to the bed. A low chuckle escapes him, making a zing of scorching heat race through me.

He throws me on the bed while he spreads my legs apart, showing him the cunt that has been dripping for him all night. He drags his fingers desperately slowly through my folds before pushing a finger inside of me. "Have you been this wet for me all night long?" His long tongue glides up my upper thighs, licking off my pleasure that started sliding down my legs as we walked back from the restaurant. His eyes don't move away from watching his finger slowly pump in and out of me, making my folds wrap around him.

All words have escaped me, I am unable to give him any response as he slowly slides his finger in and out. "Tell me, Macy. Have you been this wet for me all night long?" He pulls out his finger and adds a second, not giving me a chance to respond. My body arches off the bed as he sits on his knees, staring at me lovingly.

"Yes," is all I manage to say as his fingers pick up speed. "If you would have paid attention to your wife, as any decent husband would, you would have seen it dripping down my legs on the way back to our room."

This unleashes all his restraints. His large hands grab my legs and pull me closer to the edge. His large, flat tongue slides through me while his fingers continue to destroy my tight hole. As small circles are traced on my clit, I hit my release, causing more cum to flood his tongue. As soon as I have come down from my high enough, I drag him up towards me by his hair and reach for his belt.

Chapter Twenty-Six

LUCAS

have somehow unleashed a monster in Macy as she pulls my belt off and tells me to lie down. She slowly removes the rest of my clothing while I catch small glimpses of her pussy still gleaming for me. Before I have a chance to stop it, Macy wraps my hands in my belt and ties me to the bed, replicating what I did to her earlier today.

"You aren't the only one who knows how to tie a knot, sweetheart." A wicked grin covers her face as she crawls down my body. She ever so slowly slides the condom down my shaft, licking her lips out of desperation. She sits on my dick slowly, allowing herself to stretch around me. The pressure grows within me, all desires to grab her are held back by my belt. Her rocking back and forth on me encourages me to thrust my hips once, egging her on to ride me. With the push, Macy lifts herself up over me and slams back down. Her glorious tits bounce up and down while she rides me. Her long, pink nails grate into my chest while she keeps her pace over me. I slide my tongue across her nipples, causing her to crumble around my cock. The tight squeezing around me does not allow me to pace myself as I explode. The heavy grunts echoing in the room are erotic, adding to our temptations.

Macy falls onto my chest, still not removing herself from around me. We are both sweaty as we fight to slow our pulses down. Eventually, she releases me from my restraints, and the moment she does, I pull her closer to me. My tongue slides into her mouth as her hands pull tighter on my hair. One orgasm was not enough for me tonight. Before I realize it, I am hard all over again for her. This time, though, I want the erratic nature to disappear, and I want to show her the love I have for her. I replace my used condom with a new one as I flip her over, wrapping her legs around me as I slide back into her.

"Lucas! Oh, God." Heavy pants draw me to her eyes. Her head leans back as I allow my tongue to trace the vein on her neck before landing back on her mouth. We make love right there, just looking into each other's eyes and lapping in every emotion we have towards each other. When I came up with this idea of having three dates, I never thought it would work. A large piece of me knows I may have won her back. Glee spreads through me as I allow my wife to milk me one more time while wrapped in her arms.

Eventually, I am forced to remove myself from her. Both of us are exhausted and don't have the energy to unwrap ourselves too much from each other. "Earlier, when I said this is your home, I didn't mean Pigeon Lake or Texas. I mean me. I want to be your home. I will go anywhere you want to be. I can make a home anywhere, I just want to be by your side."

I am not sure if the look she gives me is panic or not. It is as if she is trying to convince herself that sometimes the biggest risk of all is staying right where you are and loving it. We are taught at an early age that sometimes the best thing you can do is leave. I pull her even closer to me, wanting to project the love I have for her if she is panicking. I take in her warmth, her smell, her breathing. I don't want to forget any part of tonight.

"Luke, I need to tell you something." Macy shyly looks up at me as an immediate pit in my stomach emerges.

I lean up on my elbows, anticipating the need for space for what she is about to say.

"I got a job offer this afternoon. It is in New York."

"Okay. Um..." my throat immediately goes dry. So many thoughts run through my mind, but I know how I handle this will determine a lot of things for our relationship. "Are you going to take it?"

"Yes," Macy says while refusing to look at me. She changes her position so she can look anywhere, but at me.

"Do I have an option to go with you this time?" I hate to ask the question, but I can't stand to wait another moment. All Macy can give me is a shake of her head.

"So, you are just going to leave? Without me? Just going back to New York?" My anger is rising. I meant those words when I said I would go with her anywhere if she would let me. She has even said leaving like she did was a mistake, so why not give me the option to go?

"Lucas, I wasn't made to live here. I got a great job offer, and I would be a fool to let it pass by. I would tell you to go with me, but what about my dad? What about my parents? Asking you to leave makes me an even greater bitch than telling you you can't follow me. They need you. What do you want from me?"

Finding myself confused and hurt, I know my words will not help, but if I want her to be honest with me, I have to be honest with her. "I want you to quit lying to yourself about who you are. Your parents need you too, isn't that something you want to consider?"

"You don't get it. I know they need me, but I can always come back when my dad is worse." She grumbles, getting out of bed, finally slipping off her heels and reaching for the overnight bag Abi packed for her. Her dismissal may have been a sharper knife to my heart than hearing her telling me to stay in Texas.

"I guess I don't." While I have never been the runner in our relationship, I can't continue to lay here with her, waiting for her to walk away again. I gather my belongings and leave the hotel room. I guess it is a good thing I got two rooms after all.

Chapter Twenty-Seven

MACY

didn't get much sleep last night after Luke left the hotel room. The silence was like a knife to my heart. I knew he wouldn't take it well, knowing I shouldn't have allowed the moments we had together to escalate before telling him what our future held. I couldn't help it in the way a drug addict has to fight their next hit, needing him was my kryptonite.

I can't fight the feeling I may be making a mistake. If I take this job, I will be the assistant editor to a publisher. I won't immediately be working on big projects, but it is the right step into where I want to end up. Just like I have done many times before, I will put a small pause on the book I have been writing, reminding myself I can always come back to it. Plus, my recent inspiration left me alone in the bed last night. My heart tells me I shouldn't take the job, but my brain is screaming I am a fool if I don't.

When I woke up this morning, I had a text message from Lucas waiting on my phone. His direct, crass message let me know we would head back to Pigeon Lake at 9:00 a.m. The feeling of emptiness fills me as I start accepting how I have dug myself into this hole. I gather my belongings, having to find my dress, which was thrown across the room, before heading downstairs. This metaphor of my life does not escape me.

Luke is waiting for me in the lobby when I make it downstairs, looking just as tired as I am. I barely get more than a small glance my way as he reaches down to grab my bag from my shoulder. The drive back to my parents is just as tension-filled as our drive after our first date. Miserable. This time, he isn't even willing to fight and yell at me when we pull in front of the cottage. His finality told me everything I needed to know. I have drained him of the remaining fight in him and that is a feeling I wish I didn't have to experience.

Ever the gentleman, he still comes around to the passenger door, helps me out, grabs my bag, and walks me to the cottage door. As he leans down and gives me a peck on my cheek, I notice he still won't look at me. For once, I am grateful because I am not sure I can keep my emotions in check. Tears start stinging my eyes, and my hands start shaking as I watch him walk back to his truck. He serves a curt nod before backing away from me. The emptiness feels almost physically painful since my only sense of comfort over the last couple of months has been him. I no longer get to wrap my arms around him and take in all of his muscles and warm scent. I desperately want to run after him, beg him to stay, convincing him I was out of my mind and didn't mean any of it. Instead, I give in to my emotions and let the first sob release.

Once I finally make it into the cottage, I realize Abi has been repeatedly calling and texting me. Did Luke tell her? Surely not, right?

Abi

I just saw Luke driving through town. Want to grab drinks so you can tell me all about it?

Don't tell me he has placed you in orgasm overload, and

Mace! Where are you? I'm DYING for the details.

> I ran into your mom at the store. She said she hasn't seen you. I guess you are forcing me to bring wine and corner you in the house. See you soon.

Me

> Can we talk tomorrow?

It doesn't take long before I hear a car door shut outside. I am not ready to face Abi, but I also know asking her to wait would add to her curiosity and alarm. As any good friend would, she doesn't pause to knock on the front door, just walking right in. With one look on my face, she knows something went very, very wrong.

Before I can fight her off, she is sitting on the floor with me, wrapping me in a hug and petting my hair. Abi lets me sit there and cry without pushing. Once I am able to calm down, I give her the run-down of what happened, including the news that I got the job offer. Her face visibly falls, but she is able to quickly recover, showing me only joy at my news. I know she doesn't mean any of it. My parents are going to give me the same bit, which will make me feel worse.

Abi sends me to my room to change and wash my face. Decidedly, I am able to decompress and calm myself enough to look more presentable, removing the streaked mascara and smeared makeup I never got around to washing off last night. Without any warning, I hear her distressed voice echoing down the hall. Panic envelops me as I rush to her side. In her hand, she is holding a manilla envelope with a stack of familiar-looking papers - my divorce papers.

"Where did you get those?" I demand, attempting to stay calm. The copy I had in the cottage has been sitting on the top shelf of the closet for weeks now.

Her eyes go wide, and I can see the thick bob of her throat. "It was sitting on the doorstep. What are they?" Abi's confusion is clear on her face, but her panic may be overpowering before she slowly hands the packet to me.

"My divorce papers." I sputter out, flipping through the document and catching my eye on his signature floating on the bottom. "I guess he finally decided to sign them." A new wave of emotion floods me, causing me to throw the papers across the room, watching them float down around me like confetti. I broke him. I pushed him too hard this time, and he finally gave me what I wanted. Was it really something I still wanted? I was starting to believe it wasn't, even after our fight last night, but telling him to stay in Texas was his breaking point. This unbreakable man is now breakable. I reach for the wine Abi brought and drink straight from the bottle, hoping my gulp will soften the blow.

Puzzlement shines on her face. "Wait! You weren't already divorced?" I'm not surprised she, or anyone else, didn't realize we were still legally bound together. Why would they assume anything other than that?

"Nope! He never would sign them. This is how he got me to agree to the dates." I take another long swig of the wine, realizing we may need something much stronger than this. "He promised me if we went on the dates and I still didn't want him, he would sign them. Looks like he kept his promise." Emotion chokes in my throat while I try to finish my thought to my friend. I don't want to think the thought, let alone say it out loud.

"We need something significantly stronger than this cheap wine, Mace. Do you have anything here?" Her frantic eyes start doing laps around the small cottage, coming up empty of any liquor. I make a mental note to thank her later. Not only did she comfort me first thing this morning, had to hear I was leaving again, but then found out neither Luke nor I ever admitted we were still married. Why would she still take my side? I have been a disgrace of a friend and she is more worried about me right now.

"I agree," I say while shaking my head. Before I barely finish, Abi is on her phone, calling someone to ask for them to drop off alcohol at the cottage. One potent difference between this breakup, if you would call it that, and the one from James is the support and love I have surrounding me. I dealt with that breakup completely alone, and this time, I have a friend who is ready to support and love me through the heartbreak, even if she doesn't agree with how I am handling the job offer. She is there no matter what, and proving she is the true beauty of lifelong, ride-or-die friendships. They have your back, even when you are wrong.

Abi opens the door, talking to a man dropping off Abi's "order" and when she turns around, I also see a large pizza box. If anything can cure a broken heart, it is pizza and alcohol. We stay up the rest of the night eating, drinking, crying, and laughing. Abi helps me pack up my few belongings and helps me tell my parents I am moving away again. Both are disappointed, but when my dad makes a joke, I know it would all be ok.

Chapter Twenty-Eight

LUCAS, SIX MONTHS LATER

My life has finally gotten back to what it was before Macy rolled back into town. I never expected to have her back in my arms, so I've spent my days trying to convince myself this second chance at love is something I should be grateful for. Deep down, I know it's a lie, and the pain of losing her all over again is eating away at me. Maybe I forgot what it was like the first time she left, but this time feels significantly worse. How did I live through this once before? Everything in my world feels off, not aligned in the way it should be, leaving me feeling empty. I have been trying to distract myself when I can, spending time with friends and working, but it has made seeing Tessa and Loch more difficult. I know they are just as devastated as I am, so going around them makes me feel like I am reminding them of our wounds.

Her parents are struggling with her departure, although they try to hide it behind forced optimism. We all hoped her dad's cancer diagnosis, Abi being back in her life, and our building relationship would keep her grounded in Texas, but once again, Macy turned into a runner when faced with fear. This time is no different. My heart breaks every time I see Tessa's face each morning, remembering how it felt when Macy left without a word. Like we did before, we've fallen back into our roles with each other; giving space and avoiding uncomfortable conversations. I think they know I am not the naive young man I was in the past and now a man who has built a life for himself. A life I can fall back into at a drop of the hat.

The hardest part is seeing the ghost of her in every aspect of my life. I see her at the pond where we recently spent time, dancing around each other and flirting with each other. We pushed the limits with each other there, and those memories demand to reappear any chance I see the pond. I see her curled up in corners, typing away on her laptop and flipping me off in the middle of the street. Her scent no longer lingers in my sheets, and even the Redbird Cafe has moved on from their summer menu, taking with them the memory of the lemon cake she used to love. Yet, despite all of this, I can still feel her presence - her touch when she hugged me from behind as I made us a lazy breakfast and the way she laughed at my jokes - these memories still surround me and live rent-free in my mind.

Eventually, I will let go of them all again, burying them deep down until they become distant echoes of a past love. As much as it hurts, I don't regret a single thing I did to try to win her back. I will love that woman for the rest of my life, and no running will stop me. My friend Chase has tried to set me up on a couple of dates, but my heart just isn't ready. I know the logical thing would be to move on and date other women, but I can't bring myself to do it just yet.

Thankfully, I have found solace in working at the ranch and helping Tessa with her booths at the farmers markets and events. These distractions have helped me stop reminiscing and find some semblance of peace. I will always be grateful for Tessa and Loch's unwavering support.

Abi stopped by a few times as well right after Macy left. As time passes, her visits have become less frequent and for that, I am thankful. We both see a piece of Macy in each other, seeking comfort in the familiar. She was both of our friends growing up, but in the last several years, we have become much closer. I think we both realized that seeing each other made our hearts hurt a little bit more.

The most daunting aspect of all of this is having to face the town of Pigeon Lake. It's a small community where everyone knows your business, and I can't hide at my house forever. I know the town was all rooting for Macy and me to end up together, understanding her leaving again would not be easy for me. I still have to make appearances at Meryl's, grab groceries from the local market, and visit the hardware store. Their pity looks have lessoned, and Abi has even convinced me to continue loaning books from the library. I haven't continued my lessons on how to write a book like I was for Macy, but I have picked up other hobby books I may branch out with later.

Despite it all, I know I will be okay and will eventually heal. My rage-filled music choices have mellowed down to my '90s country hits, a reflection on my current state of mind. My days are now filled with things I love, and for the time being, that is exactly what I need.

Like most nights, when I come home from Tessa and Loch's for dinner, I head out to my shop to continue working on my woodworking projects. The peace I have found out here has fueled a lot of my inspiration. Tonight's music of choice is 2000's emo.

I usually choose this genre when I know I need to bang on wood or material to get the design I am looking for. This may feel like an odd choice, but to me, it hypes me up. My Spotify playlist is eclectic at best, but it hits perfectly tonight, even making me drop my tools to do a little air guitar. Nobody is as good at playing the guitar as those who are using the air guitar. I am no exception.

A high-pitched laugh breaks my concentration as I quickly abandon my guitar solo and quickly look around for a weapon if I need one. It isn't until I look up, my gaze settling on Macy standing there with a smile on her face and confusion in her eyes, that my body relaxes and anger takes over instead.

"Damn Mace! What are you doing here?" I sternly say as I can feel my jaw clenching and my hands balling into fists. How does this woman always show up when I am least expecting her? It isn't like nobody is allowed in my shop, but it is my safe place. Not even my employees come in here unless I ask them to. I don't like people to see what I am working on until I deem it completed. Not only do I not let people in here, but I never shared this piece of me when Macy was home. I didn't get a chance to, she ran too quickly. Now, I have no choice but to let her in on the last piece of me.

As I glance down, I see a crumpled manilla envelope in her hand while her chest heaves in beat to her deep breaths. *Fuck.*

Chapter Twenty-Nine

MACY

As soon as I got back into town, I borrowed my dad's truck and drove like a bat out of hell to Luke's house. I hadn't taken time to draft a speech to give Luke when I saw him, I just knew I had to get to him as soon as possible. My parents were rattled by my abrupt request to come home, just as much as I was. As my dad handed me the keys to his truck, he asked if I was headed to see Luke, but I didn't have the courage to speak, I just gave him a nod and hoped he didn't push for more.

Once I arrive at Luke's house, I jump out of the truck and run to the front door. The truck barely stopped before my feet hit the ground. I first knock on his door and wait. Nothing. I knock again. Nothing. I decide to just walk in, and as I walk through the house, I hear no sign of him. I can't help but take my time and look at my surroundings, wanting to take in every way it has changed since the last time I was here. Uncertain about how this conversation was going to go, I want to make sure I allow myself time to appreciate the beauty he has built for himself.

After I don't find him on the first floor, I head upstairs. Heat flushes my cheeks as I walk into the master bedroom and then the bathroom. The things this man did to me in this room sends a spike of heat through my veins. "Concentrate Mace!" I mumble to myself.

It is not until I am walking out of the master bathroom, past his bed, that a shimmer catches my eye. Curiosity gets the best of me as I find myself walking towards his bedside table. As I get closer, I realize it is a round object that has been built inside of the table. Almost like it was hammered into it, but it doesn't appear to have any real purpose. Like a moth to a flame, I am unable to walk away nor able to understand why I am so drawn to this circle. I rub my fingers over the indention with puzzlement. Just as I choose to continue my hunt for Luke, it dawns on me what it is. It is his wedding ring. The ring I gave him so many years ago. The ring I thought I would never see again. But there it is, built into this table as if to keep it safe. How did I not notice it when I was staying in his house? There is no way he could have hidden it. Instinct tells me to try and pry it out of the wood, but I remind myself to come back to it later after I find Lucas. Was I really not paying that much attention to my surroundings? What else have I missed?

I head back downstairs, my feet falling on the steps, causing an echo throughout the house. My heart begins to race with each step I take. I didn't think I could be any more anxious than I was when I got here, but here I am, standing in Luke's house, wondering if I am having a heart attack or just not managing my anxiety well. As I step onto the back porch, I hear loud music coming from around the corner. My feet automatically lead me to follow the noise, but when I round the corner of the house, I see the giant metal doors to his barn are open, and I can hear the source of the music intertwined with the sound of his saws going on and off. "What in the hell is he doing?" I say to myself as I head towards the noise.

As I take a step right inside the doorway, I am stunned at what surrounds me. Different types of tools are everywhere, on multiple shelves, hanging from the walls, and even lying on his worktable. Accompanying all of the tools are wooden chairs, benches, tables, and anything you can think of stacked up around the barn. My brain stops as I try to make sense of what I am seeing. I had no idea this was what was in his barn, just assuming it was his lawn mower, a tractor, or minor tools, but seeing all of this, I realize he is doing much more in this barn than keeping his equipment safe.

It isn't until my eyes finally land on Lucas that I notice how much concentration he is giving the piece he is working on. He hasn't even noticed I have walked in. I see his bicep muscles taut against his t-shirt and then relax as he works his tool back and forth on his piece. I can see his back muscles flex with each stroke and my lower core clenches with admiration. This man is beautiful. He has always been attractive, but to see how much his body has changed from his skinny, gym-made muscles to the kind of muscles you can only get doing hard, manual labor for hours every day is breathtaking. He should have women lined up down the road for just a glimpse of this show he is unknowingly giving me. If I watched this too long, that heat building up in my core could quickly turn into a desire much stronger than just finding him attractive.

When Lucas quickly places his tool onto his table and lifts his arms to play an air guitar to his early 2000s emo music, the spell I was under is broken, and I start laughing. The stark difference between the muscular man who is tan from his long days working on the farm to my memory of him at senior prom, barely able to fill out his suit completely takes me by surprise. You may live your whole life not seeing someone for who they are. With a startle, Lucas quickly looks up at me, shock evident all over his face. "Damn, Mace! What are you doing here?"

"Can we talk?" Lucas doesn't move from where he stands, almost in a daze. His music is still loudly pumping out of the speakers, so with a quick turn of the wrist, he turns it down, making the pounding sound manageable. "Please, Luke. Can we talk?" I see his eyes shift to my hands, holding a crumpled-up envelope, causing his jaws to clench at the sight. I know he wasn't expecting to see me today, nor did my parents give him a heads up, but I was hoping he wouldn't be as angry as it appears he is right now.

"What is there to talk about? I signed your papers. I have gone back into my normal routine, almost like you were never here." A low, sarcastic chuckle burns my ears. He is hurt, and this time, he isn't going to be nice about it. His words sting me, just like he intended, but I can't hold it against him. The sting of words taunts me, causing me to force down the emotions threatening to take over me.

"Yeah, I got them." I fiddle with the papers in my hand, my sweaty hands making them damp feeling. It is the same stack Abi gave me that horrible night after Luke and I's third date. When I returned to New York, I made an appointment with my lawyer, but when I got there, I couldn't let go of the envelope. This stiff old man was not amused with my antics, but I wasn't trying to waste his time, I just wanted to do what I should have done almost a decade ago.

"Then why are you here? I did my part, now do yours." His jaw tightens as he reaches back down to his tools, swindling away at a piece that looks like it may become a chair. His jaw is still strained as he clamps down, making it known he fears opening his mouth since anything he has to say to me will only make the situation worse.

I walk up to him, reaching my hand to place it on his. The shock of my touch did not go unnoticed as his entire body becomes rigid. "Luke. Please just take five minutes to talk to me. I moved back." His head whips to face me, confusion lacing all of his features as his eyes bounce between mine, attempting to read my mind. "Yeah, my dad picked me up a couple of hours ago. I'm coming home, and this time, I'm not leaving. Everything I need is right here." I feel my tears wanting to escape, but instead, I consciously take deep breaths, keeping myself calm in case he refuses to speak to me.

Neither of us says anything or moves a muscle. Our deep breaths surround us as we both try to read the other one. "I don't know if I can do this again, Mace." He breaks the silence. His hard hands reach up and rub down his face while it bobs backward, allowing him to look at the ceiling. I can see his mind working over everything I just said. I wouldn't blame him if he refused to take me back. I don't deserve him, and while I am aware of that, I hope he doesn't care. "I never thought you leaving a second time would hurt worse than the first time." When he looks back at me, his eyes and jaw have softened towards me.

I fight hard to keep my emotions in check, not wanting to make this situation worse. "What are you making? When did you learn how to do this?" I ask, trying to deflect from any negative thoughts he may have. When push comes to shove, I always deflect.

"There's a lot you don't know about me anymore, baby. Some people change..." he looks down at me and into my eyes, "but then again, some don't."

"Will you please just hear me out? I know I messed up - again - but I have so much I need to say to you." I plead, my face heating with embarrassment I allowed myself to be in this position. I catch myself biting my lip hard enough to taste blood, using this as a way to ground myself as my mind starts racing. My brain is screaming at me to run from Luke, but running is what I have always done and the pattern I'm trying to stop.

Luke sits his tools back on his table before grasping the edge of it and dropping his head between his arms. As he begins taking counted, long breaths, I begin to understand he is trying to calm himself down, not allowing himself to react in the way he initially wanted to. A low growl escapes him as he slowly lifts his head to face me. "No. There is nothing you will say I need to hear. I'm sure your parents are glad you are home, but I need you to leave me alone. I can't do this with you again."

My lips start to tremble as each of his words slam into me. I deserve everything he is saying to me, if not more, but that doesn't mean I want to hear it. "Please?" My words are soft, barely audible, as I find myself still standing in front of him. I want to beg, plead, and throw myself in front of his tools if that means he will hear me out one more time. I will do anything I need to get that chance. It isn't until I see the stiff shake of his head that I slowly start backing out of his barn.

Over the next few days, Lucas stays away from my parents' house or the cottage. If he sees the truck I am driving in the driveway, he refuses to stop, opting to call or text my parents to communicate with them. Neither of my parents has said much about it, and every time I have seen Abi, she hasn't asked about Lucas. These are all signs that he has spoken to all of them, and they are respecting his decision not to engage with me.

I have created my own habits in his absence and everyone else's silence. Each morning, I use my time to finish up my novel, and once I become restless, I take a walk down to the pond or through the field to take in my surroundings and get out of the cottage. I even went into town to Meryl's one night, but the only townsfolk who acknowledged me was Abi, and she was visibly uncomfortable about the situation. After that, I decided I needed to stay home and out of everyone's life for a little longer.

After being home for almost two weeks, I began to wonder if I truly did burn every bridge I rebuilt all those months ago. I keep catching myself thinking back to when Lucas kept trying to talk to me, and I refused to listen. His shutting me out is similar to what I did to him. During one of my long walks to the pond, it hits me. I am going to start showing up to see him every night like he did with me every morning. It may not break him, but if anything, I may break him enough to at least have a conversation with me to get me to leave him alone.

Starting tonight, that is what I am going to do. I do this for a full week, but instead of taking him coffee, I take him a cold beer. Each night, I find him in his barn working away. After the first couple of nights, he starts wearing headphones so he can't hear me. Nevertheless, I proceed in my mission and start bringing a lawn chair to sit in while I watch in the shadows as he ignores me. If I show up at his house and he isn't there, I sit on his front porch and wait until he gets home. Even if it is after midnight, I sit there and wait for him to dismiss me before I leave. One night, he even came home to me sleeping in my chair on his porch. When I realized he didn't just walk around me and leave me out there all night, I started to believe that maybe I was wearing him down.

Tonight would be considered my eighth night in a row as I pull into his driveway. I make my way into his barn, carrying my lawn chair and his beer, but as soon as I walk in, anger explodes throughout his features. "Macy, please. Please just stop. I understand you feel like you have changed, but I can't do this again."

I walk over and slide his beer bottle across his table before taking a step away from it, giving him space in case he feels the need to throw something at me. "I'm not going to stop fighting for you, Luke. I won't do it. Up until recently, you never gave up on me, so I won't give up on you." My voice shakes as I recite the speech I have been tirelessly working on and perfecting for when I had this opportunity. I run my hands through my long, black hair, unsure if he will dismiss me again tonight. Until he does, I continue. When he realizes this, he turns his back towards me, leaning against his table with his face in his hands. My desire to run my hands up his back does nothing to help slow my heart rate.

"I have loved you my entire life, and while you don't see it because I am horrible at showing it, I do. I still do. The first time I left -"

"Macy, please. Please just go." His voice is rough as exhaustion fills it, but he still refuses to turn and look at me.

"No." I walk around the table to stand in front of him. He may turn his back on me, but I will continue putting myself on the line for him. "No, I'm not leaving until you hear what I have to say." Taking a deep breath, I nervously continue. "The first time I left, I did it in the most cowardly way. It is disgusting how I chose to do that. I didn't deserve any of you to take me back when I returned, but everyone did. Why? Why would anyone continue to give me chances when all I did was disappoint you?"

"I refuse to let you go again without a fight." I continue to stare, looking directly at him until he gives in to looking back at me. "I love you, and I love us. I love how we fit perfectly together, even when I run away." This causes him to finally shoot his glance at me, a look that almost stops me in my tracks. "I went to get the papers finalized, but as I sat there, I couldn't do it. I won't do it. I was wrong to leave you both times, but especially the last time. When I got back to New York, I saw you everywhere I went, and it was physically painful for me to not be able to pick up my phone to call and tell you about my day. Then it just hit me, I didn't belong there. I choose you. I choose you every single day. I don't deserve you, but I'm hoping you can give me one more chance to prove how much I love you."

Luke pushes himself off the table he was leaning on and stands to attention as I proceed, "I was so angry about those three stupid dates when you brought them up, but you broke down my walls and made me fall so deeply in love with you again that the thought of not being with you is much scarier than any other obstacle I will ever face." Tears fill my eyes, emotion clogging my throat, threatening to boil past the point of return. "I can write anywhere in the world, but more importantly, I can write wherever you are. You were right, you are my home."

I realize just how close he is standing next to me, and I stand up fully and face him, all of the space between us is gone. I can feel his rigged chest push up against my breasts. A surge of electricity fires through my body. "If you really want me to leave you alone and sign these papers, I will. Just like your three dates, I continued to keep showing up for you until you did what I requested and listened."

I am unable to read what he is thinking, unable to read his thoughts as I see them spinning through his mind. I refuse to get my hopes up, but I almost believe his features have softened a little since standing this close to me. "Don't look at me like that, Luke. Talk to me." I request as I watch his eyes darken, and his breathing become more ragged.

"Look at you, how Mace?" His unrelenting stance causes a multitude of emotions to fight within me.

"Like you might forgive me. Like you still feel the same way about me as I do you. Like you want to kiss me." I whisper so quietly that if you didn't see my lips move, you wouldn't think I said anything at all. I'm too afraid to say them much louder, fearing my heart is about to be shattered into a million little pieces. Pieces so small that he will be finding little shards of it in his barn until the day he dies.

"I do want to kiss you. I've wanted to kiss you since I was 14 years old following you around everywhere you went like a puppy. No tantrum and moving across the country will change that for me.

Not even when you do it twice." The smallest smirk rises as he peers down at my lips. "But I'm not going to lie to you. I am scared shitless, and every ounce of my mind is telling me to never give you another chance. But my heart? My heart is telling me never to let you go. I don't know if I can live through watching you leave again, and by letting you in again, I am risking myself once again."

All I can do is nod, understanding I don't deserve anything this man gives me. We continue to stand there as if in a faceoff, and I can watch his brain work faster than it ever has before. I know what he is thinking, and it is that he wants to throw all his care into the wind and kiss me. I want him to kiss me. His love is potent and admirable when I deserve neither of those things.

Before I'm able to make those secret thoughts come true for him, he turns around to walk away, but before he can, I grab ahold of his wrist and stop his path to leave. Chest to chest, right there in the middle of his barn. I slide one arm across his arms, linking around his neck to pull him even closer to me, pulling his head down and allowing his lips to join mine, leaving a moan floating between us.

I have not felt at home since the day I woke up and left my side of the bed cold for him but touching him and kissing him right now makes my world feel like it finally makes sense. My sun and moon revolve around this handsome, loving man who has melted into my kiss. I walked away from him once - well, twice now - but it isn't a mistake I'm willing to make again. I am going down swinging in this relationship, and the quicker he realizes I have no plans to turn in those divorce papers, the easier this will be.

In my shock, he doesn't pull away automatically and I take that as my sign I can keep going. I will never stop reassuring him he is where I belong. His hands slide to my hips, and my tongue between his lips. I want him to devour me and take everything he will let me take. I want this man to own me, stake his claim over me. He spreads his lips to welcome me to take our kiss deeper, more passionate. I can feel him shift his hips closer to me, and there is no denying I can feel just how hard he is for me. His small whimpers and groans feed my flames of heat, spreading everywhere with each touch, squeeze, and stolen breath. He wraps my hair in his hands and pulls my head back so he can kiss and taste all down my neck with ease. I have forgotten how he smells like warm oak and campfire. I forgot how rough his skin is over my smooth body. "Fuck, baby. I need you." I moan, arching into his touches.

We stand chest-to-chest for a long moment. Deep breaths and puffy lips encapsulate us while he is trying to decide if he can trust me or not. I'm not sure if my words hold any weight to him, but like a light switch, his demeanor changes, thrusting his lips to mine.

He slides his hands up my tan legs and underneath my dress. Grabbing onto my thighs, he pulls me up and even closer. I wrap my legs around his waist as he pushes me back against his worktable. None of this is graceful, but more like an elephant running a marathon. More importantly, he can feel just how wet I am as his hands slide back down my thighs, pushing his thumb against my soaking clit. A stark moan rings through his chest as he pulls back just enough to let me drag his shirt above his head and watch me throw it to the other side of his table.

"Mace, I'm not going to be able to hold back if we continue. There is no going back to not being us. There is no escape clause or changing your mind. Do you understand that?" He barely grunts out while he continues to lick and nibble my throat.

"Don't you dare stop," I warn through my moans as he rubs my pebbled nipple through two fingers, and my back arches even further because my body doesn't know how to not chase his heat.

"Get ready, baby. I will die if I don't get to slide my fingers between your slick folds. They are begging me to feel you." The shift I witnessed after he realized I really meant it when I said I was staying gave him the approval to let loose on me, taking me as his.

"How do you know I even want you?" I taunt back, keeping the atmosphere lighthearted.

"Because you are 30 seconds from creating a pool of your juices on my table, just like you did in my kitchen. You are just as wet as I am hard. Can I please test my theory now?" He teases while not losing eye contact and still rubbing my nipple that's begging for his mouth. A blush spreads across my cheeks under his watchful eye.

"O—" I gasp, him not giving me time to finish my approval before he places his lips on mine, and he runs his hands up my legs before meeting my soaked panties.

"I thought I told you I never wanted to see your pussy covered again. Was there a misunderstanding?" He slides his fingers through both sides of my panties and tears them into pieces, leaving me in shock as I lay spread out in his barn.

"Fuck, Mace. I have never felt you so wet. Have you been keeping all of this for me all these months? There is no way some snotty New Yorker could make you scream their name as loud as I can," he hisses as he thrusts a finger into me. My gasps and moans fill the night air. "Would any of those boys lick you clean over and over until you covered their face with your orgasms?" He grunts as he pulls out one finger just enough to push a second in with it. Luke pumps and twists inside of me as if it is second nature between us. Luke still knows my body like the back of his hand. He knows how to get me off in record time, proving during the brief time I was home, but nailing it home now. No New Yorker can compete against that.

I am rushing towards my climax and shaking under Lucas' touch, taking in him thrusting the air, chasing his own release. "Shit, Mace, I can't let you finish laying on my dirty table with sawdust and tools everywhere. A pretty lady can't ruin her overly priced dress on my watch." Before I cum all over his fingers, he quickly pulls both fingers out and picks me up with one arm while he reaches for his disposed shirt.

"No. No, Luke. Don't stop —" I plead.

"Patience is a virtue, sweetheart." He barely gets out. His dick is about to pop the button of his pants if he isn't careful.

He places me back down on top of his shirt and shoves everything behind me away. "Now, lay back and let me get you there."

Without hesitation, I lay back while he reaches up to pop my boob out of my bra and dress and squeeze until I am panting his name. "Still like the pain I see." He taunts me with a chuckle. Along with a third one, he returns his fingers to its rightful owner, my glistening pussy. He slides in with such ease I wonder how I lived without him. He pumps in and out, and when he can feel me edging, he leans down and starts circling my clit with his tongue. "Give it to me, baby. Get my fingers even wetter." With those words, he places his lips back on me and sucks just enough to send me to ecstasy. He pumps and twists until I come down from my high. The way he looks at me with hunger tells me he is barely holding himself together for me.

Lucas grabs my legs to yank me closer to the edge, gets on his knees, and places both legs over his shoulders. "You ready for this baby? Your cunt is taunting me like it didn't just have the best orgasms of its life."

"Luke..." I moan as I grab his hair as if I am preparing to mount him for the ride of my life.

He returns his long, thick fingers back in me and returns to feast on my beauty. I am no fool, though, and I know he is upset with me. Upset with me leaving again, and upset I walked back into his life without any warning... again. His roughness right now is his way of lashing out and showing me those emotions. To be honest, I deserve every ounce of roughness he wants to display to me, letting him throw me around like a rag doll, he also looks at me like he did so many years ago. He still loves me the way I love him. As part of his payback, he pumps his fingers until I am ringed so tight around his fingers that right when I was about to explode, he removes his fingers and his touch, throwing my legs off his shoulders.

I am faced with shock while he stands over my limp body and stares at me. "Luke, please."

Before I can stop him, he drags me off his table, throws me over his shoulder, and stalks toward his house. "Lucas!" We both laugh at each other, securing that feeling of being at home again. This is the moment I know he is going to take me back into his life.

Chapter Thirty

LUCAS

take two stairs at a time, climbing my stairs with a buzzing anticipation of seeing her in my bed again. I throw her down, and the sight of her hair flared out around her takes my breath away. "You aren't leaving again?" I question, needing validation before my heart gets too carried away. All I get in response is a serious shake of her head, while the look in her eyes tells me this isn't a motion to placate me. I refuse to let this woman leave without me again. "Then I'm going to fuck you first to place my claim on you for the rest of your life, and then I will make love to you to show you how much I truly worship you. Is that ok?"

If I blinked, I may miss the small tears welling up in the corner of her eyes. A shy nod of her head gives me the approval to continue stalking toward her. I flip her over to unbutton her dress before pulling it over her head. I use it as a rope to tie her hands together so I can fuck her cunt without her fights.

I pop her ass in the air, landing a sharp spank on it. I feel guilty seeing a small hand-shaped red mark popping up on her delicate skin, the sharp intake of her breath causing me to pause, but the moment she wiggled her ass for me, it tells me I was on the right track. "Can I take you bare? I want to feel you without anything between us?" Just the thought causes my dick to twitch in my hand. If she wasn't ready for that, I wouldn't push her, but in my own way, this is the only way I can fully stake claim over her.

"That would be the husband-y thing to do, don't you think?" Macy states while looking over her shoulder at me, a wide smile on her face. The stormy twinkle in her eyes gives me everything I need.

With a small smirk, I growl, "That's right, Macy. Say it again. Who is your husband?" I wrap her long, black hair around my hand, making sure I hold her exactly where I want her.

"You are, Lucas. You are my husband," she pants. "Who is your wife?"

"You are baby girl. You are my wife. Now let me feel all of you. I want you to milk me dry with your cunt. Can you do that?" His voice growls against my skin before he gives me a small bite, reminding me who is in charge right now. "Any wife of mine would be able to do that." I land another slap on her opposite ass cheek, reveling in the red outline popping up.

"Fill me, husband." She breathlessly speaks, her words burn me from the inside out, every touch flaming my desire.

Inch by inch, I slide into her folds. Gripping her hips gives me the only willpower to not give her my release instantly. I have forgotten how perfect she feels around me. The way I fill her to her hilt gives me the satisfaction I will never forget. Once I am able to take a second to pause and calm myself, I continue to drag myself slowly in and out of her. Once she is stretched for me again, I release the pounding into her. My balls slap her cunt with each powerful thrust. It doesn't take long for her to tighten around me and hit her orgasm. I follow right behind her as we both scream each other's names.

We fall to the bed as I untie her hands, both attempting to catch our breath. Once our hearts slow, Macy leans on her elbows and looks at me with the type of love that mirrors the love she had when we were teenagers. "Can I ask you a question?"

"Anything." I run my fingers through her hair, pushing a loose strand behind her ear before twirling the end around my finger.

"Is that your ring in the side table?" Out of all the things I thought she might say, this was not one of them.

"Yes. Yes, it is." I try to sound confident, but letting her in still brings me fear. I could have put my ring in the box with the rest of the things she left behind, but I couldn't bring myself to do it. I wanted it to sit next to me every day and night, reminding me how buried in my heart she was, unable to be removed.

"Did you make those tables?" Macy continues, as questions still dance across her face and her eyebrows crease.

"Yes," unsure if this will cause unwanted fear or if she will happily accept it.

"It's beautiful. Is that what you were working on when I came into your shop?" Her smile is genuine as my nerves slow, realizing she isn't upset or spooked by my work.

"Yeah, it is kind of a business I started a few years ago." Nervous energy surrounds me as I scratch at my beard, hoping she isn't upset by this revelation.

"Wait, are all of the tables and chairs around town I have been talking about, are those yours?"

"Yes, ma'am." This causes her to share a smile with me. I clock this as a good thing and pull her closer to me.

"They are beautiful, Lucas. I wish you would have told me every time I complained about random circles indented in the tables that it was actually a replica of your ring from your own side table." She finally gets it. Those circles are my way of stamping my work, an everyday reminder that you can have it all, just for it to leave.

"Well, now you are the only one who knows that connection." I pull her in to give me a soft kiss. My tongue teases her seam until she lets me in.

"Do you think there is a way to get it out so you can wear it again?" A meek look spreads over her features. "You know, in case you still want me and to be married."

"I bet I can figure it out." These simple words tell me she has no plans of leaving again. She is home and I finally get my sunshine.

Epilogue

MACY, SIX MONTHS LATER

"Hey baby! You ready to head to Meryl's?" Luke sing songs while walking up the porch steps, giving me the smallest, teasing kiss, knowing I will want much more from him. I lean into him, wrapping my arms around his torso, hoping to hold him in place. It's not that I don't want to go to Meryl's tonight, I would just prefer his lips all over my body instead.

"Don't you need to take a shower first?" I shoot him an overly dramatic wink.

"I suppose. You want to join me?" He bites my shoulder, causing a small hiss from me. His tongue quickly runs over it, soothing the pain.

"Only because I want to supervise. You don't always get clean enough when I'm not there to watch over you." I barely finish my sentence before Luke throws me over his shoulder and places a brisk spank on my ass. This man can still turn me on faster than what should be normal. I would let this man carry me anywhere.

It has been six months since the day I returned to Lucas. I have been working diligently on finishing my novel, but the time has come I need to return, temporarily, to New York to beg for meetings with the same agencies I used to work with daily when I lived here in hopes my book gets picked up. I have been dreading this return for months now, but this time, it feels different. I am no longer running from anyone or anything but instead counting the minutes until I can return to Lucas.

When I returned to New York for the new job after being home for so long, I diligently worked on convincing myself I really was doing the right thing, chasing my dreams and all of that. It wasn't until I walked the streets of New York that the only thing I wanted to do was show Luke each nook and cranny of the town I tried so hard to love. Every time I would stop by my favorite coffee shop, I wished I could share a pastry with Luke or share a sandwich in Central Park while we people-watched. Then, I found myself despising the crowds, endless noise, and the busy lifestyle.

Like the first time, my pride initially took over and I wanted to prove I could stay here, living this life. Despite my pride, I struggled to find my place there again. It isn't like I had friends I could call and meet up with, nor did I have co-workers I could pawn myself onto until I made new friends. I was lonely, and the feeling shined bright each moment of each day. Instead of the busy streets fueling my motivation, it only drained me. I missed my connection to those who cared about me longer than to advance in their career, but those who have known me my entire life loved me during my best and worst times. As much as I didn't want to admit it, I also missed not having the ability to reach out for Lucas, and he would be there to love me without hesitation.

It wasn't until I ran into James, my ex, at a networking lunch I knew my future was not here. Not because I was heartbroken seeing him with a new girl on his arm, it was how I noticed I didn't fit in with these people, the upper crust, snotty part of society that would never allow you to get too close to them. The next day, I gave my notice to my boss; two weeks later, I was flying home, and after fighting for him for a couple of weeks, I was with Luke. It all happened so fast, but nothing we have ever done has been conventional. Most men wouldn't give a woman another chance if they kept leaving him spontaneously. But Lucas isn't just any man; he is the strong, loving, hot-ass man who comes home to me every night. I don't deserve him, but he would never age.

After being back in his - our - home for a few days, I found a spark of inspiration I couldn't find in New York and was able to finish a book fairly quickly. As fate would have it, the same publishing company I left picked it up for print. It has all been a whirlwind, and looking back now, I know it all happened for the right reason. Lucas and I both understand that while I can do a majority of my work from Pigeon Lake, traveling may be part of it, but this time, he knows I will be home as soon as I can.

Abi has been a huge rock in my return as well. She was hard on me when I came back the second time, but once she realized it was for good this time, she really opened up more about what was going on in her life. She told me how she has been struggling with feeling lonely, sad, or down on herself for not having a husband or even a boyfriend. I am making it my mission to find this girl a man because if anyone deserves it, it is her. She rolls her eyes every time this comes up, but I am too stubborn to let this go. It is my new pet project while I wait for my book to be released.

Abi convinced me to host the first romance book release party at the library where she works. I am not sure the other patrons who use the library in Pigeon

Lake are ready for my type of romance, but I guess we will find out. I can't wait to watch the old ladies turn red and start sweating as they turn each page. Maybe one day I will write a book with less spice, but since being back here and waking up next to my husband each morning, it is difficult to think of anything but spice. I am forever grateful this community continuously welcomes me back, ensuring I feel their love and support, no matter what.

My day-dreaming halts as Luke continues to walk us up the stairs, walking into the master bathroom before sitting me down on his shoulder as he expertly starts to undress me in front of the bathroom counter. He places quick bites and sweet kisses down my body as he works my clothes down. When he kisses my stomach, I freeze. He catches it, but when he looks up at me, I slide my fingers through his hair and push his head down, moving past my flat stomach and closer to my core. Luke lifts me and sits me on the counter, widening my legs so he is at eye-level with my pussy, his eyes glistening as he takes me in. His long tongue meets my bud and starts running quick circles over me before inserting two of his fingers into me. He hits his perfect tempo, sending me over the edge quicker than I would like. When I look down at him once I have come down from my high, his beautiful eyes meet mine as he wipes his mouth, cleaning himself of me.

Before I can stop them, tears prick my eyes. My emotions have been sporadic lately, making it difficult for me to maintain my mood from moment to moment. Lucas rises to his feet immediately, fear quickly lacing his eyes as they bounce across my face, looking for the answers to his questions. Embarrassed, heat rises up my chest and to my cheeks.

"Sweetheart, what's wrong? There is no reason to cry." His rough fingers trace over my cheek, wiping away each tear that falls. His lips land on my forehead as I try to calm myself, taking in his smell and grounding myself in his touch.

"Lucas -" I try to break my eyes from his gaze, but his hands shift my head back to him, forcing our gazes to meet again. "I'm pregnant." My tears become steady, raising my hands to cover my face, unsure of what I will find when I look back at my husband.

"What?" Luke asks fear is deeply laced in his voice, but he releases his grip on my cheeks to pry my hands from covering my face.

"I know. I know we have talked about it, but we are still settling into our life together again. When I stopped taking my birth control, I believed it would take a few weeks to be out of my system. Obviously, that isn't true." I'm still crying, but through my tears, his face becomes brighter, his smile shining bright right back at me. "Did I mess everything up?"

"Mace, don't you ever think any child of ours is 'messing something up.' I'm just -" he turns away, but I know it is because he is trying to manage his own emotions. "I love you. I love this baby." His hands roam down my body before landing back on my stomach, cradling it like precious cargo. So much is being said between us without using any words. "I, um, ok..."

Before I can stop him, Luke walks away from me, headed to his dresser across the master bedroom. When he returns, his own tears are streaming down his face. "I wasn't going to do this until tomorrow, but now is as good of a time as any." I look down between us and see his large, shaking hands holding a ring.

"I know we are already married, but I want to do it over again. I want us to commit to each other all over again, both older and wiser. I even asked Loch, which he thought was odd but went along with it anyway." His chuckle sends my arms around his neck, pulling him closer to me and kissing his lips all over again.

Sometimes, if something is fine too soon, it just means it became perfect before you expected.

Sometimes, if something is fine too soon, it just means it became perfect before you expected.

About the Author

Kayla is a contemporary romance author who loves to love. Her books will make you giggle, blush, cry, and build multi-layered characters that will sweep you off your feet.

When she isn't creating your next book boyfriend, Kayla enjoys reading as much as she can, being a single dog mom, and watching the University of Oklahoma football games.

Follow me at @thebookishkayla on Instagram

Acknowledegmts

Firstly, I want to thank each of my friends and family who didn't laugh in my face when I told you I wrote a book. This was a project I put so much time and energy into, but when it was time to tell people, I was scared to death and found it such a vulnerable thing to do. Each of you could have told me I was wasting my time, and maybe I am, but you never once said that to me. For this, I am endlessly grateful.

Thank you to my friend, Adam. You never stopped listening to my ranting and ideas, always willing to tell me when something did or didn't make sense. You also read this story before everyone else knew it existed. Thank you for that. You encouraged me from day one, and I am eternally grateful for that. You also offered your last name for my pen name, which in my opinion, is above and beyond. But for the record, I am trying to find a way to include my favorite Adam story in one of my books. AKA, when you broke up with me and didn't tell me.... Good thing I know how to forgive because that was such a dick move. But look at us now! The best of friends, and I couldn't imagine my life without you. Love you so much!

I reached out to many, many friends and family to read my (very) rough draft. But nobody rose to the occasion like my friend Courtney. She read every word of this book before I sent it on to additional beta readers. She provided vital feedback for this story that I believe made it better than I could have ever imagined. She also encouraged me from the moment I told her about it and continued to remind me how just writing this story is an achievement and is "enough." For someone who has always struggled to view myself as "enough," these motivational speeches truly pushed me to keep going and to give it my all. But for the record, Courtney, yes, I know the difference between waist and waste, my fingers don't. I'm also really sorry you had to change breathe and breath so many times. I'm comfortable in saying I still have to look that one up just about every time. Prepare to continue having to fix this one. ☺

To my therapist, Pam, thank you for putting up with my shit. I have met with you for almost two decades, and while many don't understand why I continue seeing you, I know it is because you are the first one to call me out on my delusional thinking and hold my hand to the fire when I am irrationally irrational. I find it annoying but effective. When I told you about this project of mine, you essentially said, "You have always had some sort of creative outlet, but this is the creative thing that makes the most sense for you." Damn, were you right, but those words also gave me the last push I needed.

To him, fuck you.

For those of you in my inner circle, I hope you caught some of those little tidbits I threw in there as a nod to my own personal life. Most people wouldn't think twice about it, but I put so much thought and care into these pieces it makes me giggle to myself, knowing most won't get it. One of my favorites is the old peach-shaped cookie jar that Tess and Loch have in their house. My Mema, Pawpaw, and Uncle Mike all had a peach orchard when I was growing up. My mema also stayed up with me late into the night on many occasions to bake cookies with me. Here is my way of building each of these personal moments within these pages. My second favorite is an NSFW one that very few friends know about. Sorry, family, for that one. Don't ask, I will not clarify which scene I am referring to. 😊 I won't list all of my personal nods out (because that is no fun), but I encourage everyone to try and find them. Also, know that I have already written a nod to my college alma mater and our disgustingly ugly rival school. It will appear in the second book of this series, and I seriously can't wait. Let this dig be cemented into eternity in writing and in my heart. At the end of the day, I had no idea how much building these tidbits throughout my stories would give me the peace and joy that it did. I can't wait to continue the tradition in my future books.

I believe the true MVPs in this process are Vacca and All About Cha, the two coffee shops where I wrote 90% of this book. Your endless cups of coffee and snacks kept this going, and without knowing it, you allowed me to fulfill this dream of mine.

My greatest acknowledgment and accomplishment will always be being the niece of my Uncle Mike. He passed over 20 years ago, and I still think about him every day of my life. He provided me with pillars of success, and he would be thrilled I wrote a book. Granted, I never would have allowed him to read any book I wrote which is this spicy, but that isn't the point. I have hit many of the goals we talked about as I was growing up, and I am proud of myself for meeting those. I hope you are proud of me, too. The level at which I miss you cannot be measured or put into words. You have been with me during every single one of my highs and lows throughout my life, but I still find it complete bull shit you aren't physically here to see it all. You Should Be Here by Cole Swindell is forever dedicated to you. It was important to me to make you the beginning and end pillars of this book: my first dedication and my last thank you. Saying I love you doesn't feel sufficient, but it's all I can offer.

Coming Next

I hope each of you loved Abi as much as I did when writing her. She is snarky, leaves her shit at the door type of friend, and I love that for her. Throughout this book, her lack of luck in her own love life often comes up, so giving Abi her own love story only seems fitting. While I made her in Fine Too Soon as a more bubbly, fun character, she has her own demons, and she will quickly become a complex individual that (hopefully) you continue to love. The biggest question is, who will she fall for? Hmmmm...

Chase is rarely seen throughout this book, but I wanted to build him enough so the reader would know he is a grumpy single dad. While he doesn't always go along with the "fun" plans his friends come up with, he will still show up for them. Chase is going to be a much darker character than Lucas, Macy, and Abigail, and I can't wait to build this man throughout the book. Picture him as a tattooed, backward hat-wearing, grey sweatpants, and pierced 😏 man who is just trying to raise his daughter the best way he can.

Their worlds have been weaving together for a while, but it isn't until they both meet each other where they are that love will finally take off. Not all love stories are rainbows and unicorns, and this story will prove this. The question is, were they both Found Too Late?

When I first started writing Fine Too Soon, I very quickly knew who I wanted the second and third books to be about and how their stories would come to life. I can't wait for you to love them as much as I do.

For those wondering and impatient like me, yes, you have met the characters for the series already. I am way too sneaky to not give you hints of them from the beginning.